The KnowHow Book of
Paper Fun

Usborne Publishing Ltd
Usborne House
83-85 Saffron Hill, London EC1N 8RT

©Usborne Publishing Ltd 1989, 1975

This abridged edition contains the best projects from the original 48-page version

Printed in Italy

About This Book

This is a book about all kinds of things to do and make with paper, from tricks with newspaper to paper flowers and paper sculpture. There are lots of big projects and some quick ones to do as soon as you take the book home. The projects at the beginning are easier to make than those at the end of the book.

For many of the projects all you need are paper, scissors, ruler and glue. Remember that the right kind of glue is important – use Bostik 1 or UHU. Page 32 tells you where to find special materials.

Boxes with this sign give you special tips for making the projects work.

The KnowHow Book of Paper Fun

Annabelle Curtis and Judy Hindley

Illustrated by Colin King
Designed by John Jamieson

Educational Advisor: Frank Blackwell

Contents

Paper Tricks

1 Magic Ladder

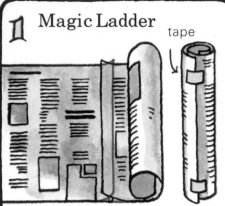

tape

Lay out two sheets of newspaper, like this, and roll them up. Fasten the ends with sticky tape.

2

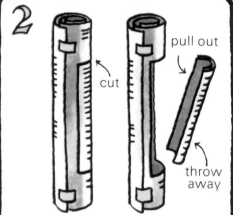

cut

pull out

throw away

Cut out the piece shown here. Throw this piece away.

3

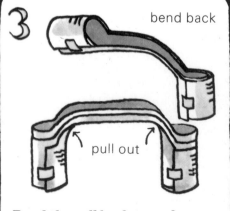

bend back

pull out

Bend the roll back to make a bridge shape. Gently pull out the insides from each side. Here comes the ladder!

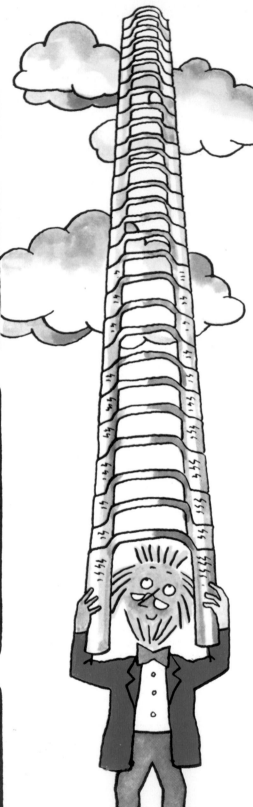

The more sheets of paper you use, the higher your ladder will go. Paper ladders can go as high as a two-storey house! (But you need strong hands to cut or tear through so much newspaper.)

Surprise Tricks

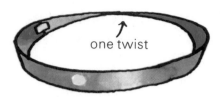

one twist

Twist a strip of paper and tape it into a loop. Put a red spot on the paper. Run your finger round and round the loop. Which is the inside of the loop?

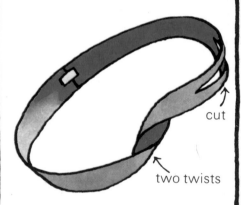

cut

two twists

Now make a loop with two twists. Cut as shown to make two loops. Surprised?

Q: If you got lost in a blizzard with the Sunday papers, what would you do?

A: Cover your head and stuff your clothes with newspaper. Layers of newspaper trap thin sandwiches of air warmed by your body. (This is a real survival trick.)

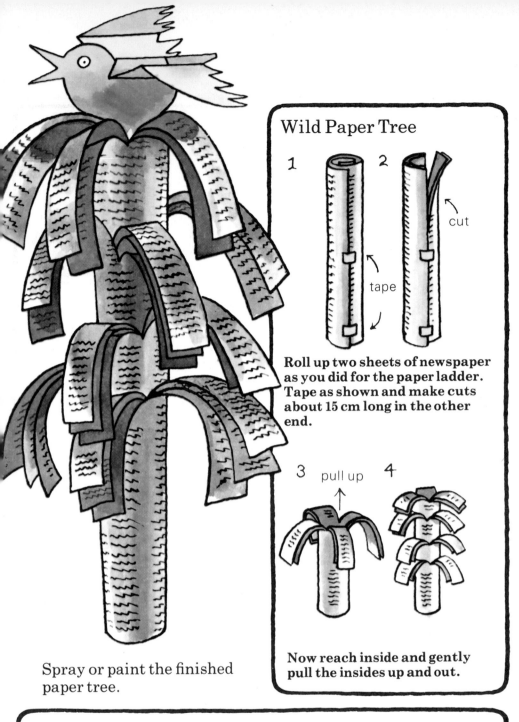

Spray or paint the finished paper tree.

Wild Paper Tree

1   *2*

cut

tape

Roll up two sheets of newspaper as you did for the paper ladder. Tape as shown and make cuts about 15 cm long in the other end.

3 pull up   *4*

Now reach inside and gently pull the insides up and out.

Sitting Bird

1

same size

Draw a long-legged bird on stiff paper and cut it out. Fold some paper and make a wing to fit the bird's back.

2   score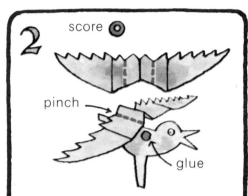

pinch

glue

Unfold the wing and score as shown. Fold each side towards the centre. Put glue on each side of the back, pinch on the wing and poke the leg into the top of the tree.

Walk Through a Postcard

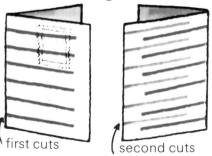

first cuts   second cuts

unfold

Fold the card. Make cuts from the fold almost to the edges. Now make another set of cuts from the edges almost to the fold. Don't cut through!

Open the card out and cut along the fold. But don't cut through the outside edges! Tug and see what happens.

How to Score

To score a straight line run the tip of your scissors along the paper against a ruler. Score curved lines without a ruler. Fold the paper firmly.

5

Pop-Up Cards

You will need
scissors and ruler
paints or crayons
pencil and glue
stiff paper

Fold carefully and crease hard
to make a pop-up card that really
pops. If you use very stiff paper,
it is a good idea to score the folds.
Remember – How to Score, p.5.

1 Ghost Pop-Up

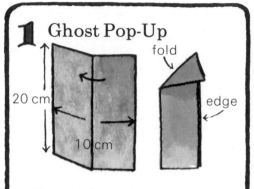

Use a piece of paper twice as
long as it is wide. Fold in half
as shown. Then fold the top
corner from the centre fold to
the edge. Crease by folding
back and forth.

2

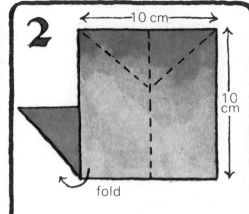

Open the card. Now fold
the bottom edge to the top
as shown.

3

pull
out

close

Now close the card, pulling out
the middle piece.

4

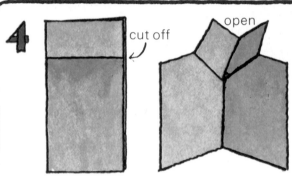

cut off

open

draw and
cut out
shape

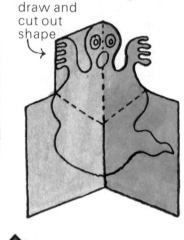

Cut off the top edge of the card.
When you open it again the
inside will pop up. Cut out and
decorate the pop-up.

**How to Mark a
Straight Line**

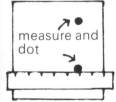
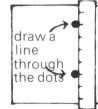

measure and
dot

draw a
line
through
the dots

To cut paper the right size,
measure from the edge and
make a dot at the right number
of centimetres. Do this twice.
Draw a line through the dots
and cut this line.

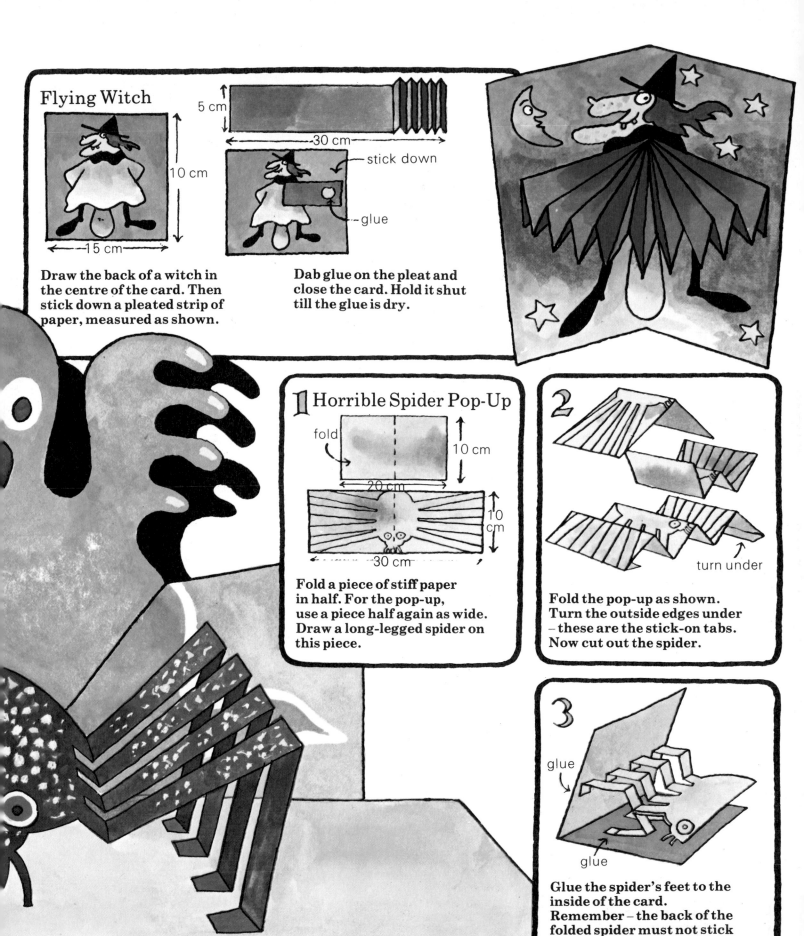

Flying Witch

5 cm

30 cm

10 cm

15 cm

stick down

glue

Draw the back of a witch in the centre of the card. Then stick down a pleated strip of paper, measured as shown.

Dab glue on the pleat and close the card. Hold it shut till the glue is dry.

1 Horrible Spider Pop-Up

fold

10 cm

20 cm

10 cm

30 cm

Fold a piece of stiff paper in half. For the pop-up, use a piece half again as wide. Draw a long-legged spider on this piece.

2

turn under

Fold the pop-up as shown. Turn the outside edges under – these are the stick-on tabs. Now cut out the spider.

3

glue

glue

Glue the spider's feet to the inside of the card. Remember – the back of the folded spider must not stick out over the card edge.

Haunted House Peep-Show

Because of the way your eye works, paper figures can look mysteriously large and real when you squint at them through a peep-hole. Attach some of the figures to threads and pull-tabs and you can make a tiny theatre inside the box.

You will need
shoe box
tissue paper
stiff paper
ruler and scissors
needle and thread
glue and paints

How to Cut Panels

To start, turn the box so that the side you want to cut lies flat against something hard. Jab with the tip of the scissors. Pick it up again to finish.

Fix the Lid

cut

cover

dab glue

Cut panels in the lid. Dab glue around the panels on the inside and cover with tissue paper. Make small bats and spiders. Take a

needle and knotted thread, push through a bat, through the lid, and then through a paper stopper, to keep the bat dangling.

1 Fix the Box

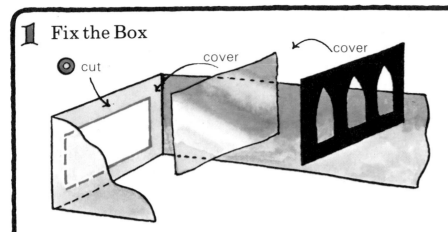

Cut a panel from the back of the box. Turn it into a special window by covering first with tissue paper, then with cut-out paper. Now paint walls and floor.

2

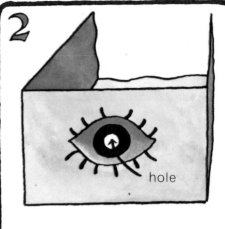

Make a small hole in the front and paint a scarey eye around it.

3

Make stand-out figures and scenery with tabs on one side. Glue tabs to the side of the box. Make figures with tabs at the base to stand up in the middle of the box. They must all face forwards, tabs towards the back.

Action Figure – Rising Spirit

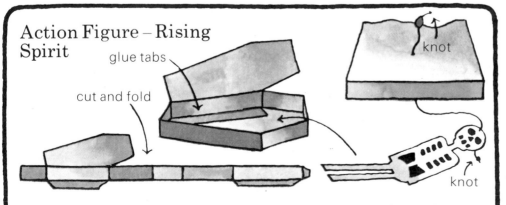

To make the coffin, bend a strip of paper and stick down with tabs. Glue together at the ends. Then make a ghostly figure. Use needle and thread to make a cord that goes through the lid as shown. Pull and the spirit rises– let go and the spirit drops.

Action Figure – Prowling Monster

Cut slots in the box and make a long slide of stiff paper. Glue the figure to it. Glue paper stops at the ends. Push back and forth.

Mobiles

Blow on the mobile very gently to make it move. The balance is so delicate that it will move with currents of air that you don't even notice. Each hanging piece has a balance point and the arms of each move from side to side as well as up and down. Once you see how the balance works, you can invent new moving patterns.

You will need
wire or thin sticks
button thread (strong thread)
stiff paper and glue
scissors and needle

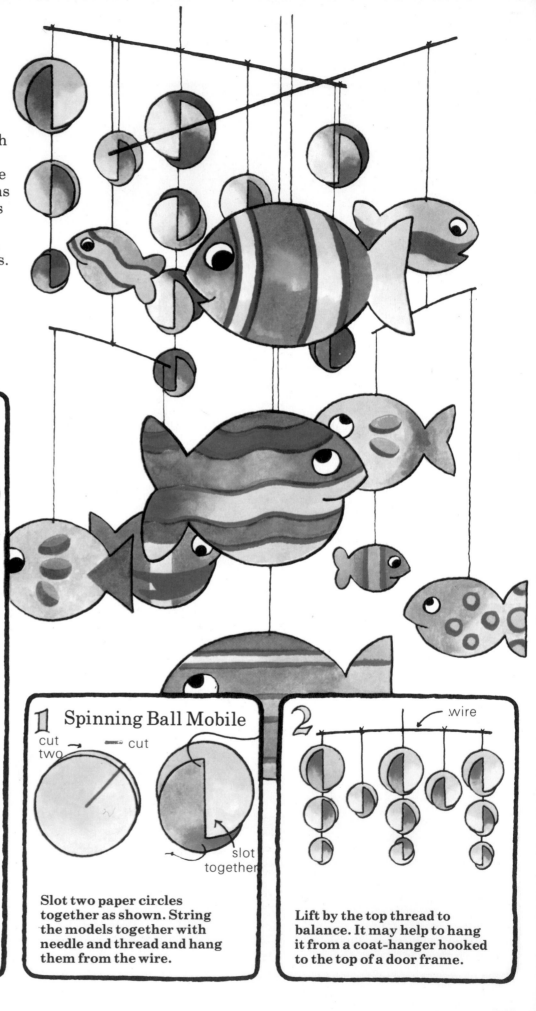

Balancing a Mobile

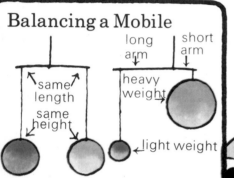

long arm   short arm

heavy weight

same length

same height

light weight

If both arms of a mobile are the same length, they balance equal weights. A short arm balances a heavier weight against a long arm.

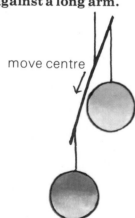

move centre

When a mobile doesn't balance, move the centre thread very gradually towards the down end. Do this for each hanging piece.

1 Spinning Ball Mobile

cut two   cut

slot together

Slot two paper circles together as shown. String the models together with needle and thread and hang them from the wire.

2

wire

Lift by the top thread to balance. It may help to hang it from a coat-hanger hooked to the top of a door frame.

Lacy Lanterns

Folded paper is hard to cut through, so use the thinnest paper you can find. Make the cuts very deep and as close together as possible. When you first make the lantern it will be shaped like a flying saucer. As it hangs, it will gradually open up.

You will need
thin paper and scissors
string and glue
stiff paper for the base and top

1 Lacy Lantern

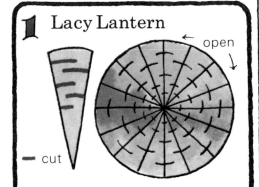

Cut two paper circles, using a big plate. Fold each in half four times. Then make very deep cuts from the sides as shown. Open flat.

2

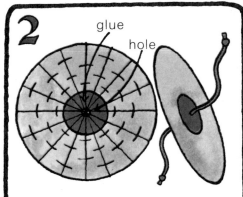

Glue small circles of stiff paper to the centre of each. When dry, make a hole in one of these and thread with string. Knot both ends.

Flying Fish Mobile

This pattern uses three balancing pieces. Make all the models first and lay the whole pattern flat on a table to fit together.

3

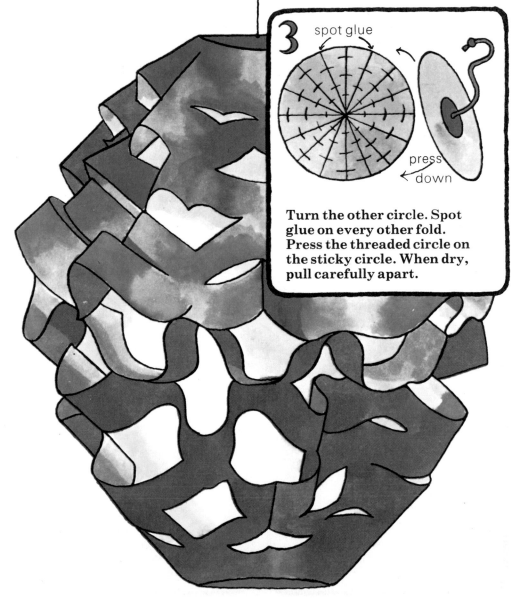

Turn the other circle. Spot glue on every other fold. Press the threaded circle on the sticky circle. When dry, pull carefully apart.

11

Paper Soldiers

You will need
stiff paper
ruler and scissors
pencil and paints
glue

Remember – use strong glue with a nozzle, so that you can dab spots of glue to add cut-out eyes, moustache, etc. Use a pencil end when your fingertips get sticky.

1 Paper Soldier

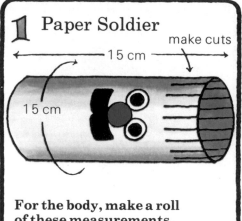

make cuts

15 cm

15 cm

For the body, make a roll of these measurements. Make cuts at the top. Paint the face and glue on eyes, moustache, etc.

2

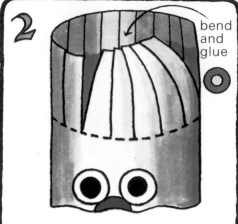

bend and glue

Dab glue on the top strips. Bend one on top of another to make a dome shape.

How to Curl

pull

Hold an end of the paper in one hand. With the other, hold it tightly between thumb and closed scissors and pull away with a quick, sharp movement.

5

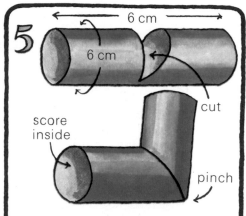

6 cm

6 cm

cut

score inside

pinch

Make two rolls for the arms and glue one to the body. Cut the other as shown. Score it at the bend.

6

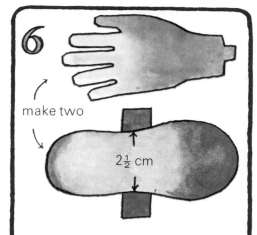

make two

$2\frac{1}{2}$ cm

Make hands and feet with tabs, from these patterns. Curl the hands.

Gluing Paper Sculpture

press with pencil

To glue a roll, press the join with a pencil held inside as shown. Use a pencil whenever you can't reach inside.

8

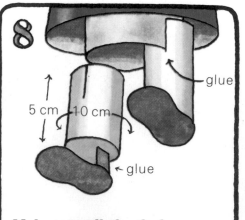

5 cm

10 cm

glue

glue

Make two rolls for the legs. Glue on the feet. Then make cuts as shown to slot the legs to the body.

9

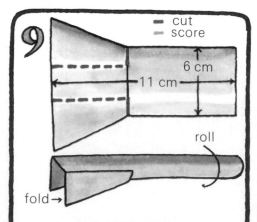

cut
score

6 cm

11 cm

roll

fold

For the gun, cut a shape with these measurements. Cut and score. Then fold and roll as shown.

3

mark and draw

cut

Hold a piece of paper around the body to make a cone shape and draw the jacket as shown. Then cut out the jacket.

4

— score

push down

Cut and score the jacket neck as shown. Bend at the scored line to glue to the body. Join at back. Glue on a collar.

For the hat, glue a long strip of curled fringe round the head. Push down an extra bit of fringe.

7

glue

Glue the bending elbow to the body and glue both hands to the arms.

13

Paper People

KnowHow Circle-Maker

Measure and punch holes in a strip of cardboard. Stick pencils through two holes. Hold one pencil firm and swing the other around.

Hats with Brims

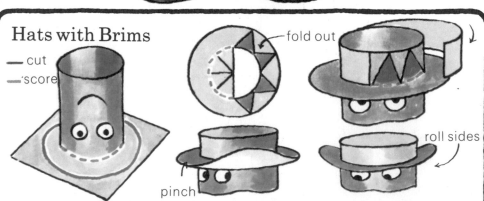

— cut
— score

fold out

roll sides

pinch

Trace around the head and score this mark. Then draw a larger circle and cut it out. Make cuts from the centre to the scored line.

Push the head through the centre. Glue a strip around the top. Pinch front or roll sides to make different brims.

Faces

Glue on a cone nose, or cut and fold the shape shown. Glue big circles for eyes,

or roll a tiny strip and glue before sticking on. Add eyelashes and moustache.

Cone Hats

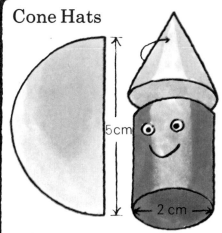

Make a semi-circle at least 2½ times as big across as the head. Use the KnowHow Circle-Maker. Roll into a cone and glue.

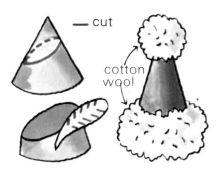

For a Santa Claus hat, glue on cotton wool. For a Robin Hood hat, slice off the top. Make cuts in a feather shape and glue it on.

Hair

cover

bald head

Cut and score a strip of paper as shown. Curl the bottom strips. Bend and glue

the top strips to the head. Cover with a circle, or stick paper curls all over.

For finger puppets, make tubes that fit your fingers.

15

Paperville

Make a small house first, to see how the pattern works. It's easy to make if you start at the edge of the paper and first measure all the lines across, then the lines going down. Remember – How to Mark a Straight Line, p.6.

You will need
large sheets of stiff paper
scissors, ruler
pencil, glue and paints

Chimney

1

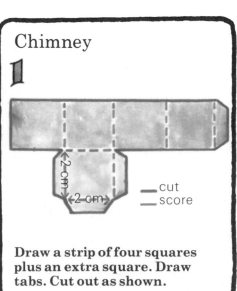

← 2 cm →
← 2 cm →

— cut
— score

Draw a strip of four squares plus an extra square. Draw tabs. Cut out as shown.

2

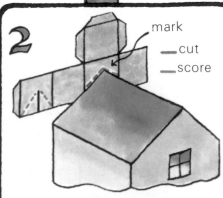

mark
— cut
— score

Hold next to the roof and mark the shape on every other square. Cut and score both as shown and fold in the triangles.

House

1

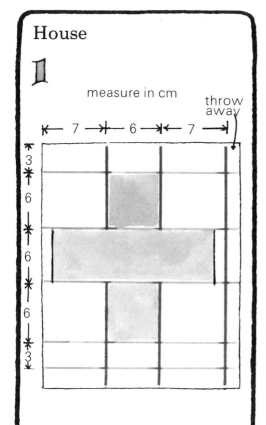

measure in cm

throw away

7 6 7

3
6
6
6
3

Measure three lines from the side of the paper, like the red lines. Then start from the top and measure down to make five lines, like the blue lines.

2

— cut
— score

centre   throw away

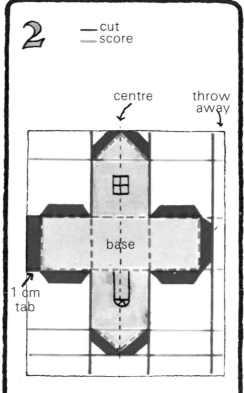

base

1 cm tab

Draw lines from a centre point to the sides as shown. Draw tabs. Make doors and windows. Then score all round the base and along the tabs. Cut out.

3

6 cm

9 cm

Fold the tabs, fold up the house and glue. For a roof that just fits, fold paper measured as shown. Make it bigger to stick out.

3

Dab glue on the roof and fold the chimney round, using the folded triangles as tabs. Glue into a box.

4

— cut
— score

For a chimney pot, make a small tube. Cut and score one end to bend inwards and glue it to the chimney.

Making Boxes

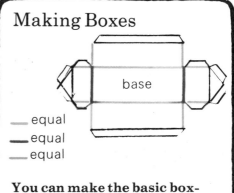

base

— equal
— equal
— equal

You can make the basic box-shape as long or as tall as you like. But remember –
1. **Make all the sides equal.**
2. **Make opposite sides of the base equal.**

17

Paper Zoo

To make a stand-up animal, just cut the shape with its back along a fold. Then you can curl, glue and fold to make bending necks, curling tails and 3-D ears and wings. You will find patterns for all the animals on the next pages.

You will need
stiff paper
scissors and glue
paints or crayons to decorate
Remember – How to Score, p.5.
and How to Curl, p.12.

Stand-Up Deer — cut

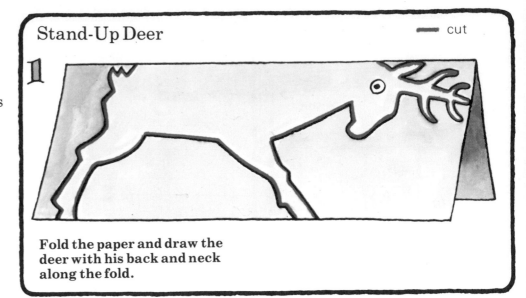

1

Fold the paper and draw the deer with his back and neck along the fold.

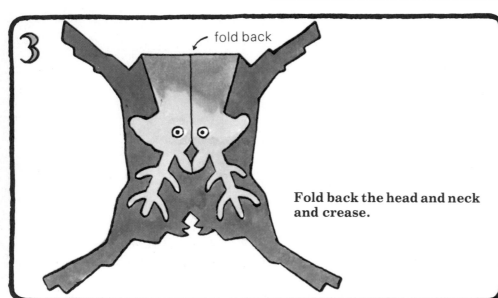

3

fold back

Fold back the head and neck and crease.

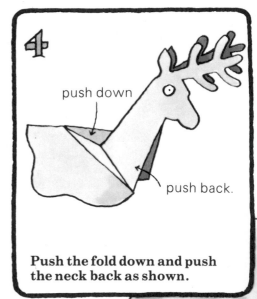

4

push down

push back.

Push the fold down and push the neck back as shown.

2

score

Open flat and score as shown.

19

Paper Zoo Patterns

Piglet

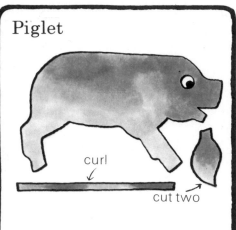

curl

cut two

Cut ear shapes with a tab. Curl the ears and tail before gluing them on.

Mouse

push down

fold back

score

Fold and score as shown. Push down and back so that the mouse's head is tucked between its shoulders. Add a long curling tail. Hang by the tail.

Lion and Tiger

curl

cut two

For the lion's mane, cut a deep fringe in a strip of paper. Curl the fringe. Fold and glue on the neck.

Flapping Duck

score

Score and fold the wing and glue it to the duck. If the duck is nose-heavy, put a very tiny bit of plasticine behind its tail.

Seal

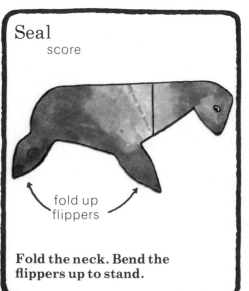

score

fold up flippers

Fold the neck. Bend the flippers up to stand.

Snake

Curl a short way, then turn to curl another bit. Keep on like this to make a ripply body for the snake.

Giraffe

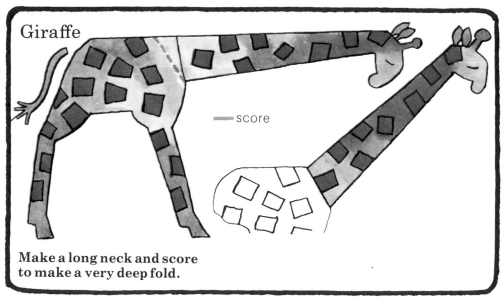

score

Make a long neck and score to make a very deep fold.

Duck and Chicken

score

Cow and Elephant

cut two

curl

Curl tusks before gluing on.

Pony

cut
score

glue mane

Make a neck fold as for the deer. Then slit along the neck and glue a fringed mane between the neck halves.

Add a tail the same way. To lower the head, just push down the neck and crease again.

Zebra

cut
score

The zebra is like the pony.

Castles and Things (1)

You will need

a large cardboard box
stiff paper
straws
glue and sticky tape
a paper fastener
silver foil
a cereal packet
a small pencil
a small strong cardboard box
cardboard
scissors
felt pens and paints

About Castles

On the right is a bird's eye view of the castle above. A soldier enters over the drawbridge and past the outer gatehouse or barbican. The land between the curtain wall and the keep is called the bailey. All the windows in the keep are very narrow. This makes it more difficult for an enemy's arrow to shoot in. On the next three pages you will find out how to make the keep and some of the things that go with it.

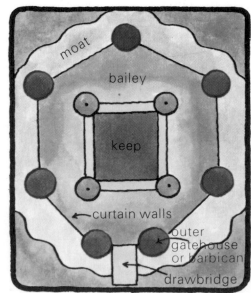

Battlements

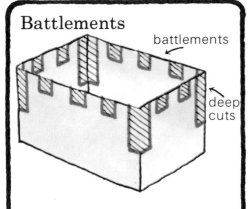

Use a large cardboard box to make a keep. Cut battlements along the top. At each corner make a deeper cut.

1 To Make a Turret

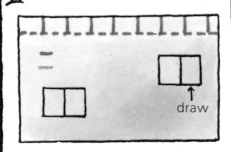

Score and cut a tall sheet of stiff paper as shown. Decide how many turrets you want and do the same to each sheet. Draw some windows.

2

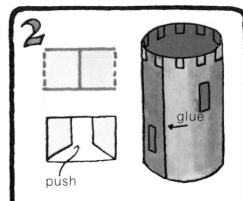

Cut the windows across the top, bottom and down the centre. Score the sides and push them in. Roll the turret up and glue.

3

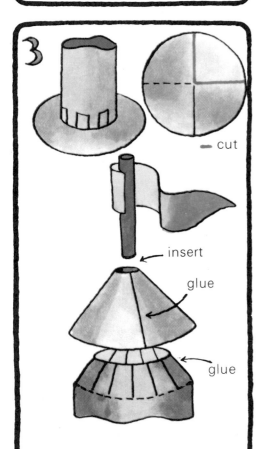

Cut a circle twice as wide as the tower and cut a piece out of it. Glue the rest into a cone. Glue a paper flag to a straw, snip off the top of the cone and push the straw in. Bend the cuts on the turret top inwards, dab on some glue and press the cone onto the turret.

Finishing the Keep

Hold a turret over a corner battlement and make two marks where it touches the keep. Cut two long slots from the two marks on the turret and push the turret onto the corner.

Curtain Walls

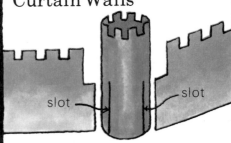

Cut battlements along the top of stiff paper with deeper cuts at each end. Cut two slots in each turret as shown and push the walls in. Make a line of walls.

1,500 Miles of Battlements

The Great Wall of China is so long that it is the only man-made building that can be seen from outer space.

Castles and Things (2)

The Drawbridge

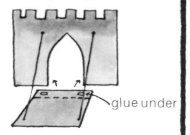

glue under

Cut a door out of the wall. Glue card under the door, bend it up against the wall and make two holes above the door as shown. Thread string through the holes and knot.

1 The Rampart Walk

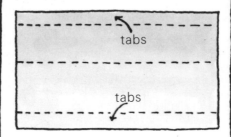

tabs

tabs

Cut out a piece of stiff paper wider than the box. Put the box on top and draw lines at both sides. Score and cut as shown.

2

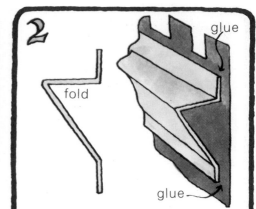

glue

fold

glue

Fold the paper like this. Glue the tabs to the keep just under the battlements. This is a rampart walk.

1 The Seige Tower

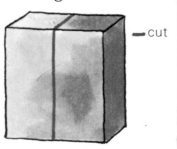

cut

Siege towers are pushed up to the castle walls. The top door opens and out come the soldiers. First cut a cereal packet as shown.

2 For the Floors

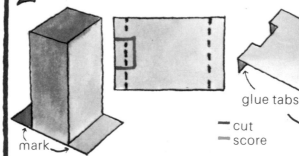

mark

glue tabs

▬ cut
▬ score

Cut out a piece of stiff paper the same length as the keep wall. Score it as shown. The outer folds are the tabs.

Fold over the tabs and glue them into the box. Draw a ladder running up the inside. Make as many floors as you think it needs.

3 For the Door

paper fastener

Cut a door opening at the top of the tower. Use a paper fastener as a catch.

4 For the Wheels

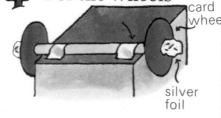

card wheel

silver foil

Cut out two cardboard circles. Make holes in the centres. Tape a round pencil under the front end of the tower. Slot the wheels on. Crunch silver foil over the pencil ends.

5 Handles and Legs

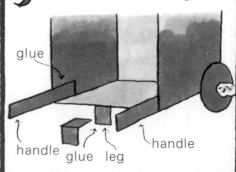

glue

handle   glue leg   handle

Cut out two card handles and a card leg. Glue them onto the tower.

1 Making a Catapult

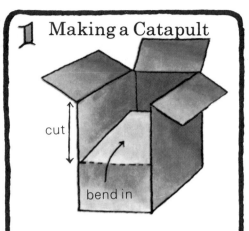

Cut half way down one side of a small strong cardboard box. Bend the flap inwards.

2

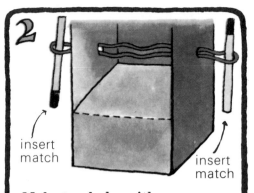

Make two holes with your scissors 2½ cm above the flap. Push the ends of a strong rubber band through the holes. Keep the band in there with matches.

3

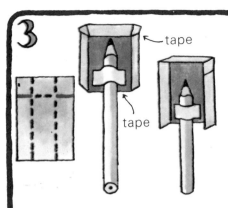

Score and cut a small piece of card as shown. Tape the sides up and tape it to the end of a small pencil.

Push the catapult arm back. Put your ammunition in the ammunition holder, let the catapult arm go and fire.

4

Twist the rubber band round and round until you can't twist it any more. Push the catapult arm into its middle.

5

Let the catapult arm spring up until it is pointing straight up. Fold back the top front flap and tape.

Paper Flowers

The stretchiness of crêpe paper is very useful. You can pull it into petal shapes or ruffled edges. With tissue paper you can show the vein of a leaf by making a lengthwise crease.

You will need
crêpe paper
tissue paper
sticky tape and scissors
strong glue with a nozzle
thin sticks or light wire (such as florist's wire or medium fuse wire) for the stems

Daisies

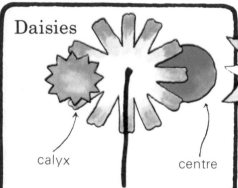

calyx

centre

Cut petals round a circle. Sandwich petals and stem between a centre circle and calyx shape and glue together.

Crêpe Paper Poppies

1

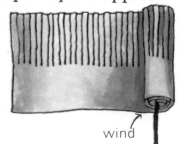

wind

For the centre, make cuts in a strip of paper as shown. Fasten it to the stem with thread, or glue the edge and wind it round and round.

2

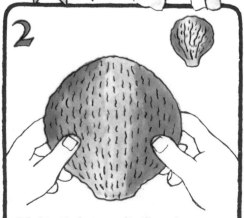

Make eight petals. Cut them with the grain of the paper running up and down. Shape them by stretching sideways.

3

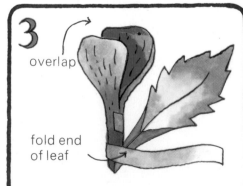

overlap

fold end of leaf

Glue the petals one by one around the stem. Then glue a long strip of paper under the flower and wind it down the stem, gluing in leaf shapes as you do so.

Tissue Paper Roses

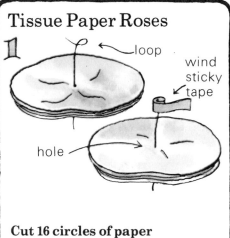

1 loop / wind sticky tape / hole

Cut 16 circles of paper about 16 cm across. Make a wire stem as shown.

2 Turn upside-down and pinch the flower tightly round the stem as shown. Bind into shape with sticky tape.

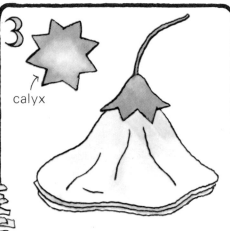

3 calyx

Cut out a calyx. Slide it down the stem and glue it to the flower.

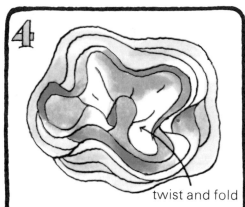

4 twist and fold

Turn the flower up again and shape it by pulling the petals out as shown. Twist and fold to make a centre. Cover the stem as before.

Carnations

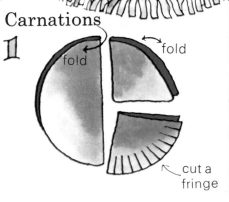

1 fold / fold / cut a fringe

Cut 13 circles of thin paper, about 9 cm across. Fold each into a quarter-circle. Make cuts as shown.

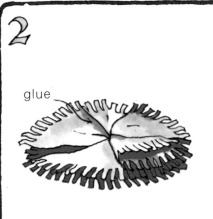

2 glue

Open one circle flat. Glue the quarter-circles onto it in layers as shown.

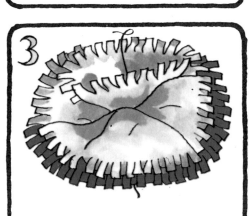

3 Loop the end of some wire and push it through to make a stem. Glue a strip of green paper round the stem.

Crocodile Marionette

1

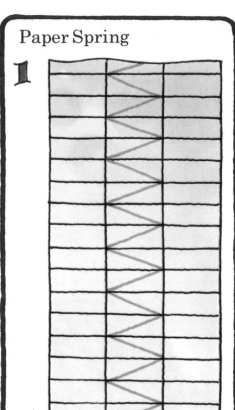

$1\frac{1}{2}$ cm

←4 cm→←4 cm→←4 cm→

Use paper 12 cm wide and
as long as possible. If you
glue strips together, let
the glue dry before you do
the next step. Rule lines
as shown and make a coloured
zig-zag down the centre.

The body of this crocodile
marionette is made from a strip
of paper folded into a special
spring. This makes a shape that
can bend and twist and wriggle
when you move the hanging
strings. The fold is tricky until
you get the knack, so follow the
instructions carefully.

Remember – How to Mark a
Straight Line, p.6.

You will need
coloured paper
ruler and scissors
glue and string
coloured pencil or felt pen
2 small sticks or rods

Turn the page to see how to
make the head of the crocodile
and how to work the strings.

2

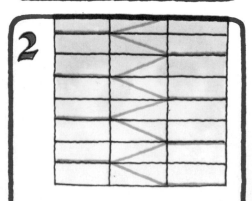

Now make coloured lines
joining the points of the
zig-zag to the edges. Score
all the coloured lines and
crease them firmly.

3

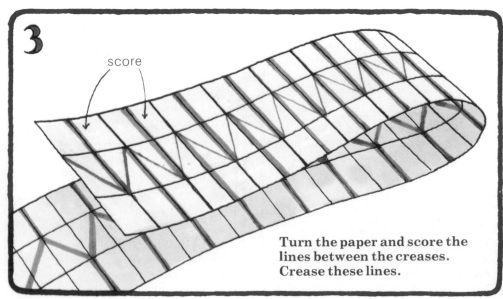

score

Turn the paper and score the
lines between the creases.
Crease these lines.

4 Hold the paper as shown. Walk your thumbs along the sides to push the creases inwards and pinch the folds between your fingers.

5 Continue until all the folds can be pinched between your fingers to make a shape like this.

Crocodile Marionette (2)

Make the Croc

1

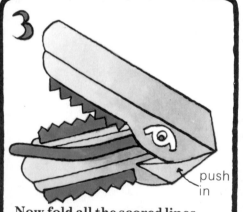

— cut

Take some paper about 40 cm long and 10 cm wide and fold in half. Draw and cut out the head shape.

2

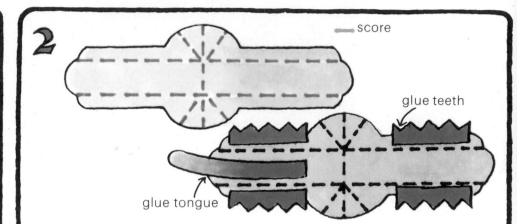

— score

glue teeth

glue tongue

Open and score as shown. Turn the head and glue strips of paper teeth inside the jaw.

Glue the end of a long tongue to the back of the top jaw.

3

push in

Now fold all the scored lines inward. Push in the crease between the V-shaped score at each side of the jaw.

4

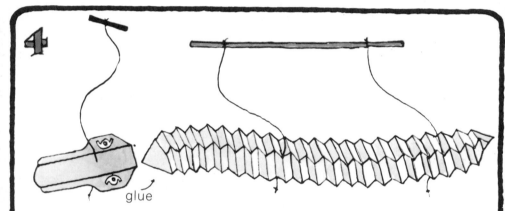

glue

Glue the paper spring to the back of the head. String up the crocodile with a needle and knotted thread as shown.

Tie the head string to a small stick. Tie the two back strings to another stick.

Work the Croc

Raise the head string to make the crocodile rear up and jerk the string to make its jaws open and close.

Rock the stick back and forth to make the crocodile hump its back as it moves along.

Hold your arms like this to make the crocodile turn and chase its tail.

Jack-in-the-Box

You will need
thin card for the box
coloured paper
ruler and pencil
scissors and glue

As you open the box, give it a shake to make the Jack jump out. If the Jack loses its spring after a while, stretch it out and fold it up again.
Remember — Making Boxes, page 17.

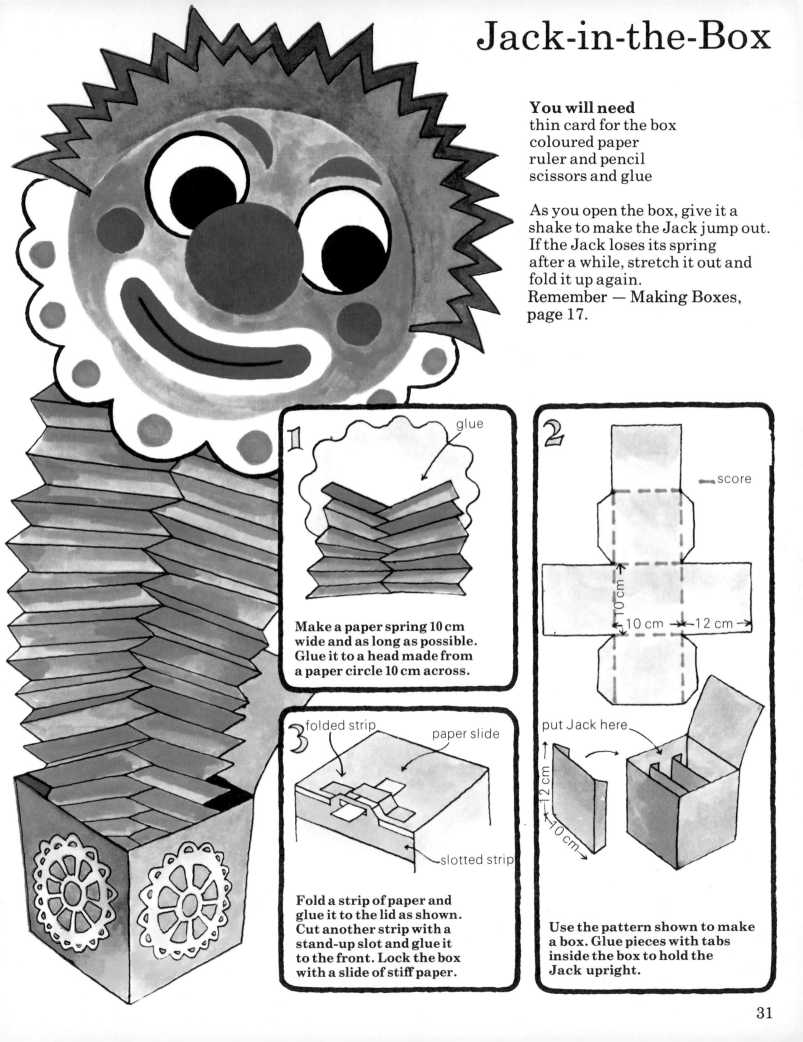

1 glue

Make a paper spring 10 cm wide and as long as possible. Glue it to a head made from a paper circle 10 cm across.

2 score

put Jack here

Use the pattern shown to make a box. Glue pieces with tabs inside the box to hold the Jack upright.

3 folded strip

paper slide

slotted strip

Fold a strip of paper and glue it to the lid as shown. Cut another strip with a stand-up slot and glue it to the front. Lock the box with a slide of stiff paper.

Tips on What to Use

Here are some suggestions to help you find the right materials for the projects.

Canes and Florists' wire — Buy at a gardening shop or at a florist's.

Cold-water paste — Buy Rex Cold-water Paste at an art supply shop or buy wallpaper paste at a hardware shop. Wallpaper paste is not a good thing to get in your mouth, so be sure to wash your hands when you have used it.

Glue — Use strong glue with a nozzle, like Bostik 1 or UHU.

Fuse wire — Buy at Woolworth's.

Medium galvanized wire — Buy at Woolworth's.

Sticky tape — Use Scotch Tape, if you can find it. It's very strong and doesn't split.

Stiff coloured paper — You can buy it in sheets at an art supply shop. Ask for cartridge paper. It can be light or heavy, so be sure to say what you want it for.

Thin paper — Buy at an art supply shop. Ask for a layout pad or for sheets of detail paper.

Cartridge paper and detail paper are sold in packets at many stationery shops, but the sheets are too small for several of the projects.

Did You Know?

You can buy paper that is strong enough to bear the weight of a car.

Did you Know?

Up to 20 miles of paper can be produced every hour by a large papermaking machine.

The KnowHow Book of Print and Paint

Heather Amery and Anne Civardi

Illustrated by Malcolm English
Designed by Sally Burrough

Consultant: Jim Corless
Additional projects and prints: Jim Corless

Contents

About This Book

This book shows you how to print patterns and pictures in all kinds of different ways on paper, card and cloth. You will need poster paints, coloured inks and fabric dyes. There is a list on page 2 to tell you what to ask for and where to buy it. You can probably find sheets of paper, card and brushes at home.

At the end of the book there are ideas for framing and showing your pictures.

The patterns and pictures in this book show you just a few of the marvellous things you can do with prints and paint. Try inventing your own, using as many colours as you like.

First published in 1975 by Usborne Publishing Ltd
Usborne House, 83-85 Saffron Hill,
London EC1N 8RT.

©Usborne Publishing Ltd 1989, 1975

Printed in Belgium.

Before You Start

These are the things you need to make the prints in this book:

Paint – powder or poster paints are good for printing.

Paper – use drawing paper for the best prints. Practise printing on rough paper. Try using rolls of white shelf paper, wall lining paper or the back of a roll of old wallpaper. Some art shops sell sheets of thick, cheap paper called sugar paper.

Coloured card – for picture frames. Stationery and art shops sell sheets of brightly coloured card.

Waterproof inks – these are made by Reeves and Windsor & Newton. They are sold in stationery and art shops.

Fabric Dyes – ask in art or craft shops for water-based dyes, such as Reeves Craft Dye. You have to buy a fixer for this dye. Read the instructions on the bottles carefully.

Glitter — you can buy tubes of different colours at toy or stationery shops.

Expanded polystyrene – this white, light plastic stuff is often used for packing breakable things. Try asking for some in a shop or store. Use thick pieces for printing blocks.

Sheet sponge – this artificial sponge is usually sold in Woolworth's and furniture stores. Use it to dab on paint and to make sponge rollers.

Paste – for paint and paste prints, use any good paste.

Glue –use any good glue to stick cardboard and sponge rollers.

Black Indian ink – this is sold by stationery and art shops.

Water-based block printing colours – these are made by Reeves and are good for monoprints.

Getting Ready

Printing and painting can be a messy business, so it is a good idea to get everything ready before you start. Cover a table or bench with lots of newspaper and put it over any furniture which could be splashed with paint. If you are making very long prints on rolls of paper, put newspaper on the floor and use it as a working surface. Wear old clothes or something over your clothes. An old shirt makes a good painting smock.

Collect all the things you will need for one kind of printing and have them ready to use. Rags are useful for wiping paint off your hands and mopping up spilled paint or ink. When you have made a print, hang it up or lay it down flat to dry. Remember to clear up when you have finished printing. Put the tops on bottles and tubes of paint and wash the brushes.

1 Making a Dabber

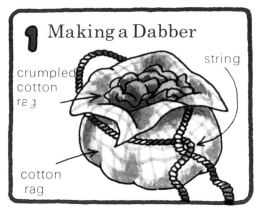

crumpled cotton rag

string

cotton rag

Crumple up a small piece of cotton rag into a ball. Put it in the middle of a small square of rag and tie with string, like this.

2

Dip the dabber in some paint and use it to cover printing blocks evenly with paint or to spread the paint on a tray for monoprints.

Brushes

wipe with rag

When you have finished with a brush, wash it in clean water and dry the bristles with a rag, wiping from the handles to the tip. Store brushes standing on the handles.

Printing Base

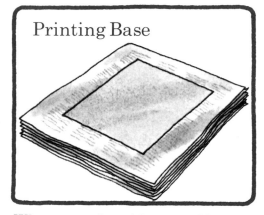

When you print with vegetables, leaves or with blocks, put a thick wad of newspaper under the printing paper. This will help you to make good, clear prints.

1 Making a Print Pad

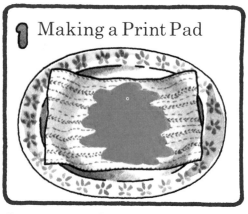

Cut a square of old, thick cotton or wool cloth. Put it on a flat plate and pour on some paint. Press printing blocks and vegetables on the pad to cover them with paint.

2

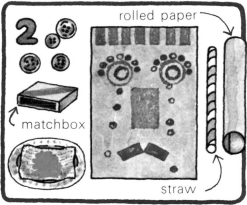

rolled paper

matchbox

straw

Try using the pad for putting paint on such things as matchboxes, straws, buttons, erasers, rolled-up paper and printing with them. Make up a pattern or a picture.

Paper Stretching

When paper gets very wet with water or paint, it sometimes dries in wrinkles. Try this way of stretching paper before you use it for printing, for Paint and Paste Pictures and for Wash-off Pictures. The paper will then dry flat.

1

board

paper

wet sponge

Put a sheet of paper down on a board or old table top. Rub it gently all over with a clean sponge dipped in clean water.

2

wet paper

strips

Wet four strips of gummed paper, a little longer than the paper. Press them down on the edges of the paper, sticking it to the board or table. Leave to dry. Pull off strips.

Finger, Thumb and Hand Prints

The secret of making good fingerprints is to use paint that is not too wet, just sticky. Spread some poster paint on an old tray or plate, or use a paint pad (see page 3). Dab your fingers in the paint and press them gently on to a clean sheet of paper. If the paint stickiness is just right, it will show up the swirls of tiny lines on your fingertips.

To print bigger shapes, spread paint on a tray or plate. Press down your fists, palms or the sides of your hands and roll backwards and forwards to cover them with paint. When the prints are dry, draw or paint in details to make pictures.

With a magnifying glass you can see that the lines on your fingertips are really grooves and ridges.

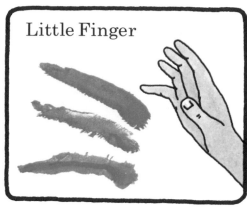

Little Finger

Curl your little finger and rock it towards the tip as you press it down.

leaves
(little finger)

trunk
(side of hand)

cavemen
(rolling forefingers)

cavemen
(forefingers)

legs
(rolling fist)

4

Rolling Thumb

Press down your thumb, and rock it slightly towards the knuckle.

Rolling Fist

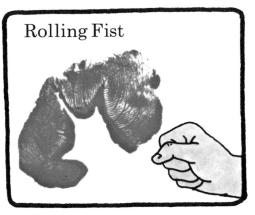

Make a fist and press it down with a rolling movement.

Side of Hand

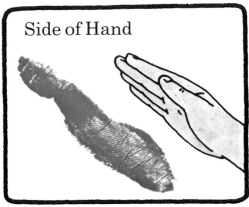

Press down the side of your hand and rock it from side to side.

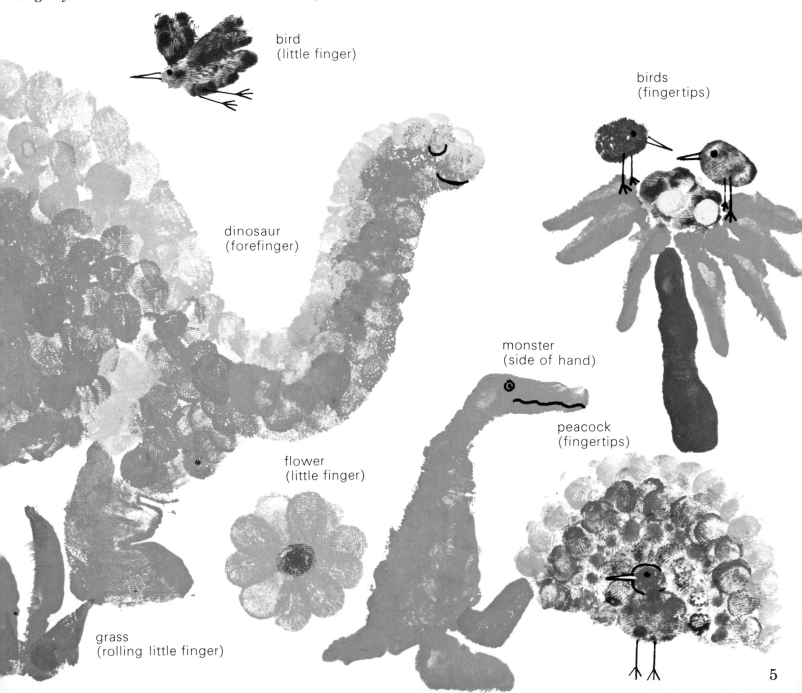

bird
(little finger)

birds
(fingertips)

dinosaur
(forefinger)

monster
(side of hand)

peacock
(fingertips)

flower
(little finger)

grass
(rolling little finger)

5

Mirror Prints

These prints are called mirror prints because the two shapes on either side of the folded paper are exactly the same, like the reflection in a mirror. They are quick and easy to make and every one is different.

You will need
thick poster paint
sheets of paper
pieces of string for string
   prints
a paint brush
an old plate
newspaper

1 Mystery Blob Prints

newspaper

Fold a piece of paper in half. Open it and drop or flick big blobs of wet poster paint on to one side, near the fold. Use lots of different colours, like this.

Mystery Blob

2

fold paper over

press and rub

Fold over the paper so that the clean half touches the paint. Rub the paper hard all over with your hand.

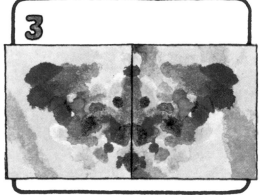

3

Try making lots of blob prints, in different shapes, using lots of colours, like this.

Painted Print

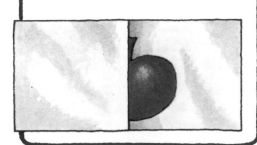

1 Painted Prints

Fold a piece of paper in half. Open it and paint a shape or pattern on one side of the paper, near the fold. Use paint that is not too wet.

2

paint in leaves

Fold the paper over and rub all over it with the side of your hand. Open the paper and draw or paint in details to make a picture.

String Pull Prints

1 Put some thick poster paint on an old plate. Dip a piece of thin string in the paint and brush the paint over it to cover it with paint.

2 *drop on string*

Fold a sheet of paper in half. Open it out and drop the painted string on to one side of the paper, leaving one end of the string hanging over the edge of the paper.

3 *press* — *pull out string*

Fold over the paper and hold it down with one hand. Pull out the string hanging over the edge of the paper with the other hand. Now open out the paper.

4 Try dropping lots of pieces of string, each dipped in a different coloured paint, on to the paper. Hold down the folded paper and pull out all the strings at the same time.

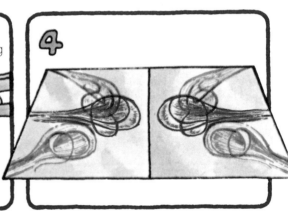

String Drop Prints

1 *drop string on paper*

Dip a piece of string in some paint, making sure it is well covered. Drop the string on one side of a folded sheet of paper. Fold over the paper and press hard on it.

2 Open up the paper and pick up the string. Let the print dry. Do the same again using a different colour paint. Do it lots of times until you have a really colourful print.

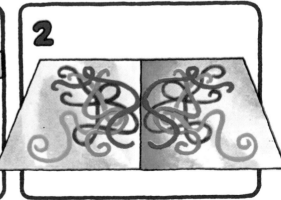

Glue and Glitter Prints

You will need
tubes of different coloured
  glitter
glue or paste
scissors
sheets of paper
a paint brush
thin card
old newspaper
leaves and ferns

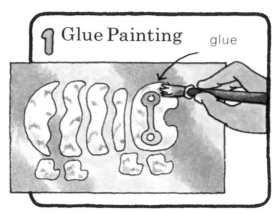

1 Glue Painting

glue

Draw a shape, perhaps an elephant
or a monster, on a piece of paper.
Paint glue over the parts you want
coloured, either all over or in
stripes or dots.

2 glitter

Sprinkle one colour of glitter over the
glue shape, making sure that it is
well covered. Leave it to stick for a
few seconds.

Fern and Glue
Print

1 Glue Print Pictures

glue

press

Cut a shape out of cardboard. Paint
one side with glue and press it,
glue side down, on to some paper.
Lift the shape up quickly so that it
does not have time to stick.

2

glitter

Sprinkle some glitter on to the paper
and then shake it off gently. Do this
lots of times until you have a row of
glue prints, like this.

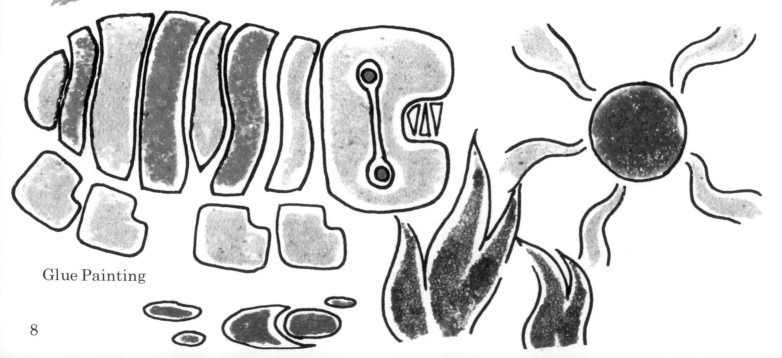

Glue Painting

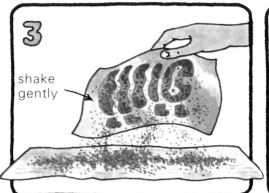

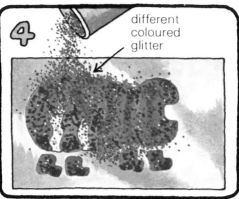

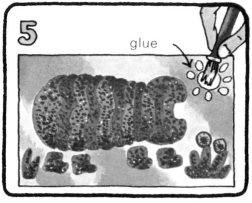

Pick up the paper and shake it gently over some newspaper. A lot of the glitter will stick to the glue and leave a coloured shape.

If you want to put another colour on the glue shape, paint the uncoloured parts with glue and sprinkle on a different coloured glitter. Shake it off gently.

Decorate the picture by painting more shapes with glue and sprinkle on more colours, one at a time. You can use the glitter left on the newspaper again.

Leaf and Glue Print

Leaf and Glue Prints

Use leaves or ferns to make prints. Cover one side of the leaf with glue, press it down on paper, lift it off and sprinkle glitter over the glue print.

Home-made Colours

Try using kitchen powders like cocoa, instant coffee, paprika and mustard powder instead of glitter. Mix them with sugar, sand or sawdust.

Roller Prints

You will need
a cardboard tube about 7 cm
    long
a small piece of cardboard
two pencils
a sheet of foam sponge (see
    page 2)
strong glue
a knitting needle
an empty cotton reel
some plasticine
poster paint
an old baking tray
sheets of paper
scissors

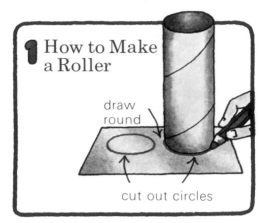

1 How to Make a Roller

draw round

cut out circles

Draw two circles on some cardboard, using the end of the cardboard tube as a guide, like this. Cut out the circles with scissors.

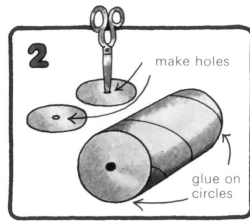

2

make holes

glue on circles

Make a hole in the centre of each cardboard circle with scissors, like this. Glue the circles to the two ends of the tube with strong glue and leave the glue to dry.

3

draw line

Cut a piece of sheet sponge the same length as the tube. Put the tube on the sponge and roll it up, like this. Draw a line along the edge and cut along the line.

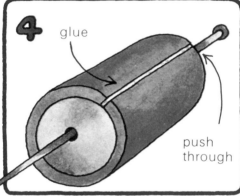

4

glue

push through

Roll the sponge round the tube and glue the edges together. Do not glue the sponge to the roller. Leave it to dry. Push a knitting needle through the tube, like this.

5

roll

Spread paint on an old baking tray. Roll the paint out with the sponge roller until the roller is evenly coated with paint.

6

roll across paper

Put a piece of paper on top of some newspaper and push the roller across the paper, like this. You can use the roller to colour in part of a picture like the sky, sea or grass.

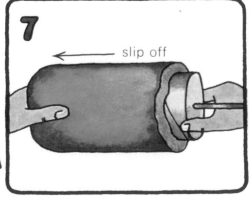

7

slip off

To clean the sponge, slip it off the cardboard tube and wash the paint off with soap and water. Leave it to dry and then slide it back on to the tube.

Sponge Cut-Outs

cut out shapes

You can print lots of different patterns by cutting shapes out of the sponge on the roller with a pair of scissors, like this.

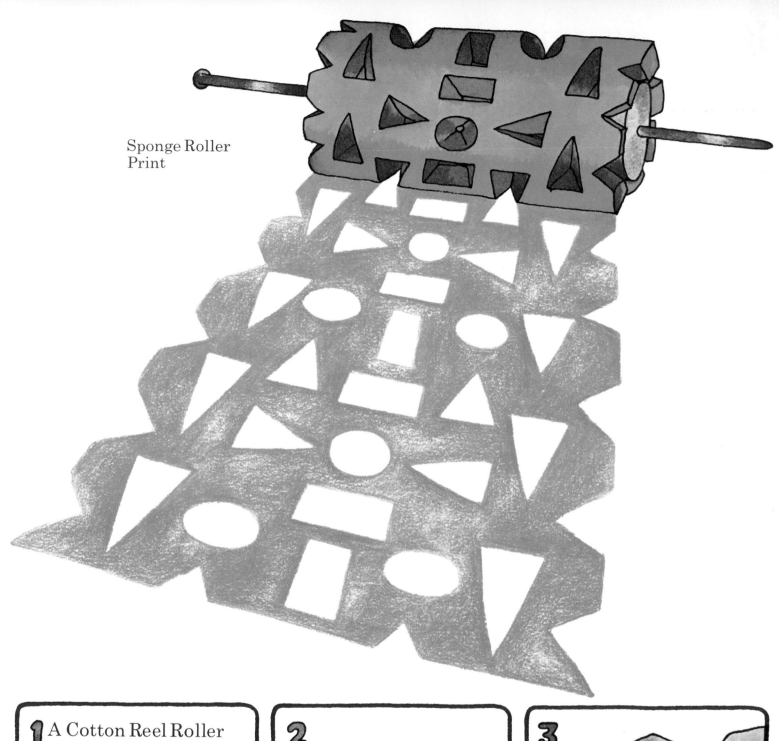

Sponge Roller
Print

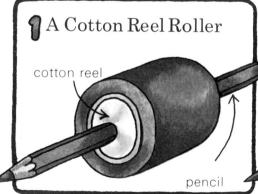

1 A Cotton Reel Roller

cotton reel

pencil

Cover an empty cotton reel with a thick layer of plasticine. Push a pencil through the holes in the cotton reel.

2

make shapes

Press different shapes into the plasticine, using either end of a pencil. Press hard on the pencil to make deep marks in the plasticine.

3

Roll the cotton reel in paint and push it across the paper. Before using another colour, wash the paint off the plasticine with some soap and water.

11

Printing with Blocks

Make a printing block and use it as many times as you like. Try printing a border or rows of shapes to make a pattern. When you have printed one colour, wipe the block with a damp rag and use it again for another colour. Remember, when you print a shape, it will be the other way round from the one you cut out.

You will need
small blocks of wood
poster paint
strong glue
an old plate or a baking tray
sheets of paper to print on
string for string block prints
thick cardboard for card blocks
corrugated cardboard for
    stripey block prints
old newspaper
scissors

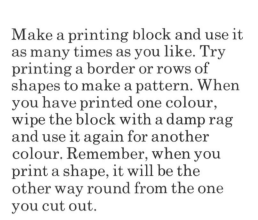

Card Block Fish

Stripey Block Tigers

1 Card Block Prints

Draw a shape, smaller than the block of wood, on a piece of thick cardboard. Cut out the shape in one piece or cut it into lots of different pieces, like this.

2 stick on shapes

Spread glue over the block of wood. Arrange the shapes on the wood and press them down on the glue. Let the glue dry before starting to print with the block.

3 press

Pour some thick paint on to a tray or plate and spread it out evenly. Dip the block on to the paint, making sure the card shapes are well covered with paint.

12

String Block Snails

String Block Prints

1 draw shape on block

Instead of card shapes, try using a piece of string. Draw a shape or pattern on a small block of wood, like this.

2 glue   string

Cover the block with glue. Put the string on the shape or pattern you have drawn. Leave it to dry and then dip it in some paint to print with it.

4 press hard

Put a sheet of paper on top of some layers of newspaper. Press the block on to the paper. Press hard and evenly on the block, like this to get a good print.

Stripey Block Prints

1 thick cardboard

Cut a shape out of thick cardboard and glue it to a block of wood. Dip the shape in thick, bright paint and make a print with it on a sheet of drawing paper.

2 corrugated cardboard

Cut the same shape out of some corrugated cardboard and glue the flat side to another block of wood. Dip it in a dark paint and press it over the first print.

13

Printing a Cartoon

Cut out this cardboard cartoon man and you can print a whole story with one block. You will need a piece of thick expanded polystyrene (see page 2). This is often used as packing for office equipment and cameras so try asking in a shop or store for some. When you have made one printing block, you can add more pieces of cardboard. You could give the man a stick or an umbrella to carry.

Mix up lots of thick but runny paint on a plate. If the card pieces of the cartoon stick to the paint, stir more water into the paint with a brush.

You will need
a piece of expanded polystyrene, about 3 cm thick
thick cardboard, or two pieces of thin cardboard stuck together
some pins
thick poster paint
a plate or old baking tray
sheets of paper
old newspaper
a paint brush
scissors

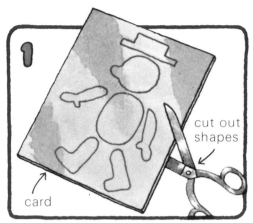

Draw the shape of a cartoon man on a piece of thick cardboard. Cut out the shape in pieces so the arms, legs, head, body and hat are separate bits.

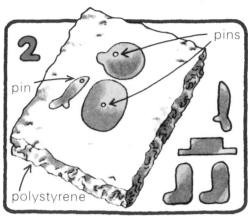

Push a pin through the body and into the polystyrene block. Pin on the arms, legs and head close to the body. Pin the hat near the top of the head.

Put some thick poster paint on the plate or tray and spread it out with a brush. Dip the cardboard shape in the paint, making sure it is well covered with paint.

Press the polystyrene block, paint side down, on a piece of scrap paper. When you can make a good print, put a sheet of paper on newspaper and print the shape.

When you have printed the man standing, try moving his legs apart to make him walk or step forward. Then make a print.

To make him run, move his legs farther apart and tilt his body forward. Then print him again.

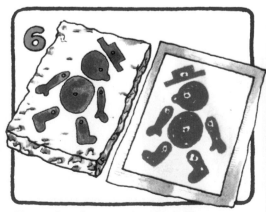

To make the man go the other way, take his legs and head off the block. Pull out the pins, turn the shapes over and pin them to the block again.

Charlie Card

When you have made a cartoon block, you can print as many pictures as you like, changing the man a little for each print. Try printing a dog by cutting out a body, four legs, a head and a tail. Pin them on to a separate block. When you have made lots of prints, draw or paint in a path, trees, houses and other things. Make up a story to go with the pictures. We have started a story about Charlie Card and his dog, Mr. McGreedy, and have left it for you to write an end.

One day Charlie Card takes his dog, Mr. McGreedy, for a walk. Mr. McGreedy lags along behind and thinks the walk is very dull.

Suddenly a great gust of wind blows Charlie Card's hat off. Mr. McGreedy watches it whirl away down the road.

Mr. McGreedy thinks this is more fun and chases after the hat. Charlie Card runs after Mr. McGreedy.

Charlie Card watches the hat and does not see a stone in the road. He trips over it and falls flat on his face.

Slowly Charlie Card gets up. He is wet and muddy and his toe hurts. He wishes he had stayed at home.

He brushes himself down and starts to run after his hat and Mr. McGreedy who is a long way away. Now it begins to rain.

Charlie Card has almost caught up with Mr. McGreedy when they come to the bank of a river.

Mr. McGreedy is watching the hat. He does not see the river and over he goes. Charlie Card just manages to grab his tail. Now write the end of the story.

Printing Letters

Make these stencil, block and string alphabets to print letters and numbers. Or make up your own letters in any shape and size you like.

You will need
thick paper for the stencil
   alphabet
thick cardboard for the block
   and string alphabets
scissors and some string
a pencil and a ruler
sheets of paper
glue
an old baking tray

Marking Up

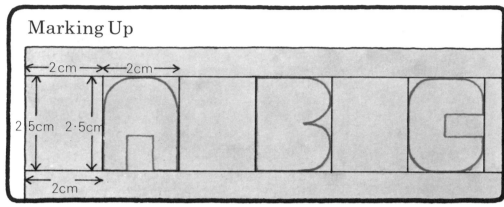

For the stencil letters, use thick paper. For the string and block letters, use thick cardboard. First rule a line on the paper or cardboard.

Rule another line 2·5 cm below it. Put a ruler on the top line, mark off 2 cm spaces and rule lines as shown. Draw the letters of the alphabet in every other space.

Stencil Letters

cut out letters

Draw the letters on a sheet of thick paper and cut out each letter. Be careful not to tear the edges of the letters. Use the stencil to print names and words.

String Letters

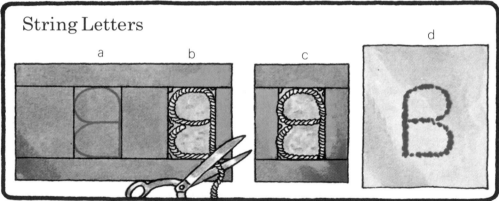

Rule lines and draw a letter (a). Spread on glue and press down the string in the shape of a letter. Cut off the extra string (b).

Cut round the letter to make a small square of cardboard, like this (c). Dip the letter in poster paint and print with it (d).

Block Letters

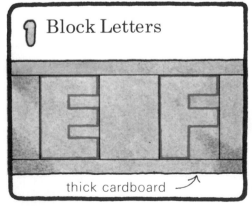

thick cardboard

Mark up the alphabet on some thick cardboard and cut out the letters. Put the cut-out letter on another piece of cardboard, draw round it and cut out a second letter.

glue together

Glue the two letters together, like this, to make a very thick cardboard letter which will print clearly.

Cut out a piece of cardboard a little bigger than the letter. Glue the letter, back to front, on to it. Press the cardboard block in some paint and print with it.

Stencil and Block Alphabet

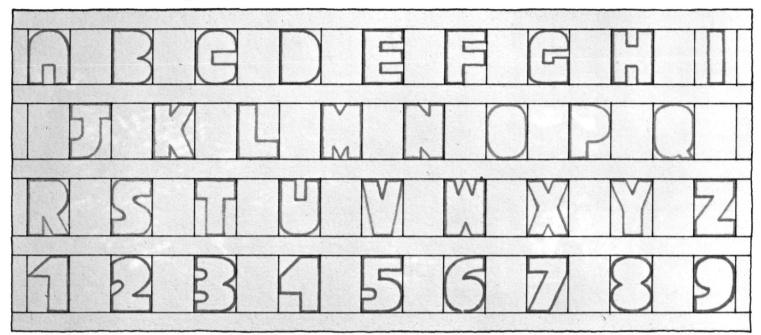

Printed Stencil and Block Alphabet

String Alphabet

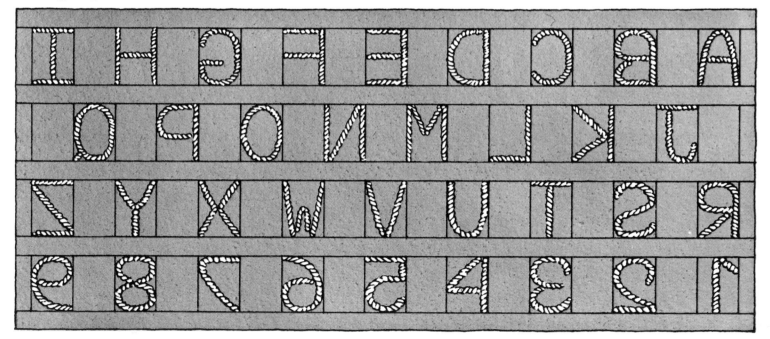

Printed String Alphabet

A B C D E F G H I

Monoprints

These prints are called monoprints because you can never make two prints exactly the same. Before you start, cut out a window mount. It holds the paper just above the paint and makes prints with tidy edges. The paint for monoprints must be sticky and not too wet. If a print has splodges on it, leave the paint on the tray to dry a little before trying again. If there is too little paint on a print, add a few drops of water to the paint and mix it with a brush.

You will need
poster paint or block printing
    paint (see page 2)
an old baking tray or old mirror
a sponge roller (see page 10)
thin cardboard for a window
    mount
a ruler and a pencil
sheets of paper
a paint brush
scissors

One-Colour Monoprints

Cut some card to fit on the tray or mirror. Put a ruler on one edge of the card and rule a line, like this. Rule lines along the other sides. Cut along the lines.

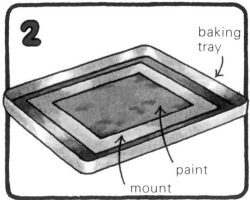

Spread sticky paint with a roller over the tray or mirror. Put the card mount on the paint. The paint should fill the inside of the mount.

Put a sheet of paper over the mount. Hold the paper down very gently at one corner, like this. Draw a shape or pattern on the paper.

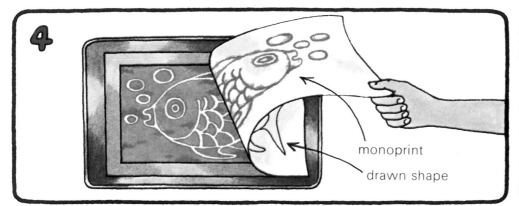

monoprint

drawn shape

negative print

Lift up one corner of the paper and peel it off the paint. You now have a monoprint on the other side of the piece of paper.

When you are drawing a picture, remember that the monoprint will be the other way round.

Before the paint dries on the tray or mirror, put a new sheet of paper on it and rub it all over with your hand. The print you make like this is called a negative print.

Three-Colour Prints

first colour

second colour

third colour

Shading

Make a monoprint using one colour and let it dry. Wash the paint off the tray or mirror and spread on a different colour. Put the mount over the paint again.

Put the print down on the second colour, paint side down. Draw in more parts of the picture or pattern. Lift up the paper and let it dry. Do the same with a third colour.

Put a sheet of paper on the paint and press it lightly with your fingers to get shading or patches of colour. Or drag a comb across the paper to make wriggly lines.

Stencil Monoprints

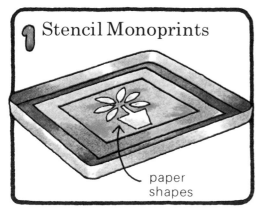

paper shapes

lift off shapes

Scrape Prints

scrape lines

Cut or tear different shapes out of paper and arrange them on the paint. Put a sheet of paper over the shapes and press down on the paper.

Lift up the paper. Pick the paper shapes off the paint very carefully, like this. Put a new piece of paper on the paint and rub over it to make a negative print.

Scrape a shape or pattern in the paint with the handle of a paint brush. Put a piece of paper over the paint and rub all over it to make a print.

Scratch Pictures

Use lots of brightly coloured wax crayons to make these scratch prints. Dark colours will not show up on the black paint or ink. Try scratching animal or monster faces and cut them out to make masks.

You will need
coloured wax crayons
black poster paint or black
   drawing ink
a white candle
sheets of white paper
a paint brush

1 Paint on Wax Prints

Draw thick lines with different coloured wax crayons on a sheet of paper. Press down hard on the crayons so that you make bands of thick colour.

2

black paint or ink

Paint all over the lines with black poster paint or drawing ink. If the wax colours are difficult to cover, brush on two or three coats of black paint or ink.

3

When the paint or ink is dry, scratch it off in a shape or pattern with the handle of a paint brush to show the wax colours underneath.

Black and White Prints

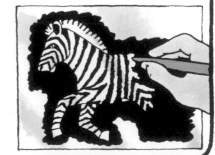

Rub white candle wax on a piece of paper. Cover the wax with lots of coats of black poster paint. Let it dry and then scratch off the black paint in patterns.

Paint on Wax Snake

20

Wax on Paint
Monster

1 Wax on Paint Prints

black
paint
or ink

Paint a shape on a sheet of white
paper using black poster paint
or black drawing ink.

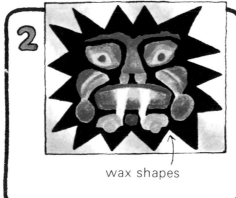

2

wax shapes

When it is dry, draw patterns all
over the black shape with coloured
wax crayons. Press hard on the
crayons to make thick bands of
colour, like this.

3

scratch out
patterns

Use the handle of a paint brush
to scratch black patterns and
shapes in the coloured crayon.

21

Paste and Paint Pictures

Try making these bright paste and paint patterns and pictures. Take a print of each one to make another picture. They will all be rough and bumpy.

You will need
white or coloured cardboard
   or thick paper
thick paste
poster paint
sheets of paper
a paint brush

1 Paste and Paint Patterns

Brush three or four stripes of thick paste on to a piece of white or coloured cardboard or some thick paper. Brush thick poster paint over the paste.

2

Slide your fingertips or the end of a paint brush through the paint to make different patterns. If you make a mistake, brush over the pattern and start again.

1 Paste and Paint Prints

Spread paste on some cardboard in the shape of an animal or flower. Brush paint over the paste. Add details by sliding your fingers and brush handle through the paint.

2

To take a print of the picture, lay a sheet of paper on the cardboard, being careful not to smudge the paint.

Rub all over the paper very gently with the side of your hand. Pick up a corner of the paper and peel it off the cardboard.

Wash-Off Pictures

When you have made a wash-off picture, the paper will be very wet. To stop the paper from drying in wrinkles stretch it before you start (see page 3)

You will need
white poster paint
black Indian ink or coloured
   waterproof ink
thick paper
a pencil and a paint brush
a fine sponge

Draw a picture or a pattern on a sheet of thick paper. Brush white poster paint on the parts of the picture you want to be the colour of the paper.

Try dabbing white poster paint on the picture with a fine sponge to make light splodges. Leave the poster paint to dry completely.

Cover the paper and the white poster paint with a layer of black Indian ink or coloured waterproof ink. Leave the ink to dry.

When the ink is dry, hold the picture under a running water tap and gently rub the picture with your hand, like this. Lay the paper down flat to dry.

Mixing Colours

Red, blue and yellow, black and white paints can be mixed together to make all the colours of the rainbow. Try mixing your own colours, adding a little black or white, to make new colours.

You will need
poster paint
light coloured tissue paper
glue
white paper
a string block (see page 13)
a paint brush
an old plate for mixing colours

Primary and Secondary Colours

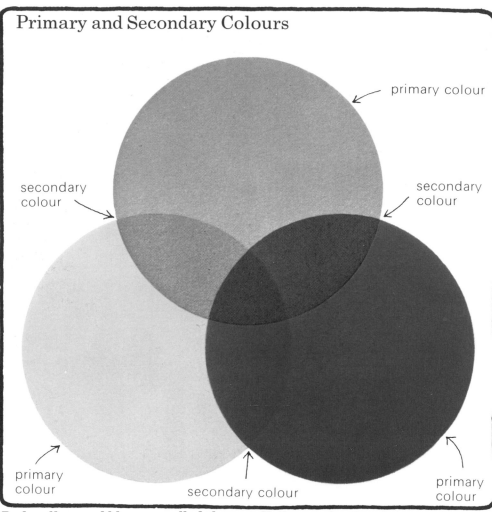

primary colour

secondary colour

secondary colour

secondary colour

primary colour

primary colour

Black and White

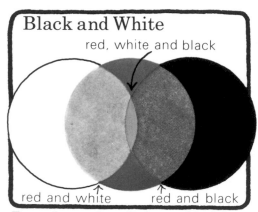

red, white and black

red and white   red and black

To make a colour lighter add white. White mixed with red makes pink. To make colours darker, add a little black. Red mixed with black makes dark red.

Red, yellow and blue are called the primary colours. If you mix two primary colours together you get a secondary colour. Red and blue make purple. Blue and yellow make green.

Yellow and red make orange. Purple, green and orange are secondary colours. When you mix two colours, mix the lighter colour first and then add the darker colour.

1 Tissue Pictures

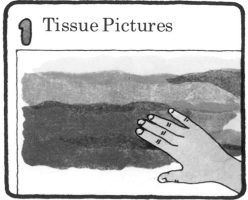

Tear sheets of light coloured tissue paper into strips. Glue the strips on to some white card, overlapping the edges to make new colours, like this.

2

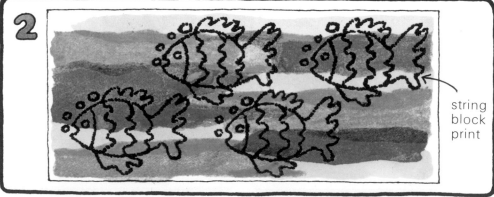

string block print

When the glue on the tissue paper is dry, use a string block and black paint to print shapes or patterns on it, like this.

Instead of using a string block, try printing over the tissue paper with a card block (see page 12) or a plasticine block (see page 26).

Overprints

Instead of mixing colours before you use them, try printing one colour on top of another to make a new colour. To make neat pictures, the cardboard shapes must be printed exactly on top of each other.

You will need
pieces of thick cardboard
poster paint or waterproof inks
scissors and a pencil
sheets of paper
sticky tape loops (see page 31)

Draw a shape on thick cardboard and cut it out. Put the cut-out shape back on the cardboard, draw round it and cut out a second shape. Do this once again.

Stick one shape to a cardboard block with sticky tape loops. Brush ink or paint on the shape and make a print. Before you lift the block off the paper, draw round it.

Draw round the shape on the cardboard. Pull the shape off. Cut pieces out of the second cardboard shape and stick it to the block so that it fits inside the pencil marks.

Put a second colour on the shape. Fit the block inside the marks on the paper and print over the first colour. Cut bits out of the third shape and print in a new colour.

Printing on Cloth

Use fabric dye or waterproof inks to print bright patterns and letters on all sorts of materials, clothes and canvas shoes. Buy water-based fabric dyes which are used with a fixer and follow the instructions on the bottles very carefully. These dyes are quite expensive so get just two or three colours and try mixing them together to make other colours.

Put down lots of newspaper before you start. If you get dye or ink on any furniture or the floor, wipe it off at once with a rag and lots of water, or it will stain. Practise on a scrap piece of cloth before printing on clothes or material. Make sure they are dry and clean before making a print. Remember to print dark colours on light-coloured cloth. Light-coloured dyes and inks will not show up on dark material. You can try printing on almost any kind of material but you will get the best results on cotton cloth.

You will need
water-based fabric dyes and
  fixer (see page 2)
waterproof inks
pieces of cloth and clothes for
  printing on
plasticine for plasticine blocks
biscuits for biscuit prints
a white candle for wax and dye
  patterns
expanded polystyrene,
  cardboard and pins for
  printing blocks
a long stick or bamboo for wall
  hangings
string
needle and thread
a paint brush and a pencil
an old baking tray or plate for
  mixing colours
lots of newspaper

1 Plasticine Blocks

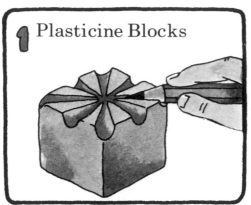

Shape some plasticine into a square block. Make patterns or shapes in one side by pressing the end of a pencil into the plasticine.

2

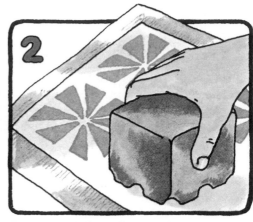

Put some ink or dye on the tray or plate. Press the block, pattern side down, on to it and print the pattern on a piece of clean cloth or on old clothes.

Biscuit Prints

Use a hard biscuit with a pattern on it as a printing block. Brush ink or dye on to one side and then make a print on some material.

Wax and Dye

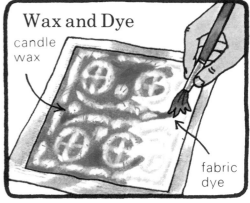

candle wax

fabric dye

Draw a pattern on a piece of white cloth with a white candle, pressing down very hard. Brush ink or dye over the cloth. It will stay white where the candle lines are.

1 Card Blocks

pin

cardboard shapes

Cut a flower shape out of thick cardboard. Push a pin through the middle and then into the block of thick expanded polystyrene.

2

card block print

Stuff white canvas shoes with newspaper. Brush ink or dye over the cardboard flower and print the shape on the shoes.

T-Shirts

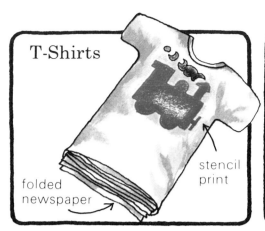

folded newspaper

stencil print

Put folded newspaper inside a T-shirt to stop the dye going through to the other side. Use a stencil to print a pattern or your name in bright ink or dye.

1 Wall Hangings

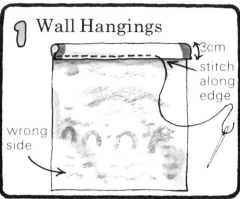

3cm
stitch along edge

wrong side

Print a picture in dye or ink on a large white cloth. A piece of old sheet is good for this. Fold over about 3 cm at the top and stitch the edge down, like this.

2

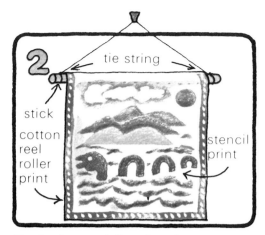

tie string

stick
cotton reel roller print

stencil print

Push a long stick or bamboo through the stitched pocket. Tie the ends of a piece of string to the stick or bamboo and hang the picture up.

Blue Jeans

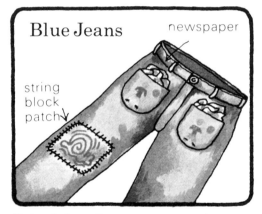

newspaper

string block patch

Print ink or dye patterns on the pockets of light blue jeans or print patches and sew them on. Remember to put newspaper in the pockets before you begin.

Scarves and Handkerchiefs

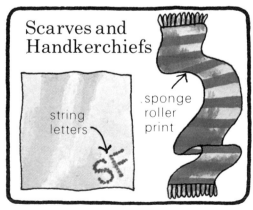

string letters

sponge roller print

SF

Try printing stencilled names or initials on handkerchiefs to make presents. Or use a sponge roller to print stripes on a scarf.

Poster Factory

clothes pegs

clean paper

newspaper

baking tray

rag for wiping hands

Several people working together can set up a production line and produce lots of good posters quickly. Each person should have a particular job to do. Lay out everything carefully so that they have the tools they need. Stack newspaper on the work tables. Hang the posters up to dry after each step.

First make the poster borders using a light colour. Then print patterns on top of the border in a darker or brighter colour. Use the stencil, block or string alphabets on page 16 for the lettering on the posters.

You will need
paper and poster paint
a sponge roller (see page 10)
   or a fine sponge
thick paper for stencils
a cotton roller (see page 11)
a plasticine block (see page 26)
a string block (see page 13)
thick cardboard and some string
a baking tray and some scissors
strong glue
lots of newspaper and rags for
   keeping clean

Poster Borders

sponge roller

weight

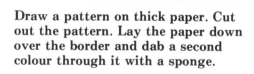

Lay a neat rectangle of thick paper in the middle of the poster. Roll or dab paint round the edges, like this. Lift up the rectangle and let the paint dry.

Stencil Borders

Draw a pattern on thick paper. Cut out the pattern. Lay the paper down over the border and dab a second colour through it with a sponge.

One-Block Posters

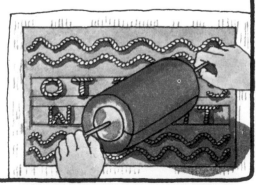

Instead of using lots of different prints on a poster, try making a one-block poster. Cut a piece of cardboard the same size as the poster paper.

Mark up the cardboard (see page 16) and glue string letters on to it. Glue a string pattern round the edges. Roll paint over the string letters and print with it.

String Block Borders

Try making an oblong poster, like this, and printing patterns round the poster border with a string block or a card block.

plasticine block

plate for paint

stencil letters

baking tray

sponge

delivery van

Cotton Reel Borders

Make a pattern on a cotton reel roller to go with what the poster is advertising. This poster could be advertising a play or a puppet show.

Plasticine Block Borders

A plasticine block is easy to make (see page 26) and you can print patterns quickly with it. Use lots of different colours and try overlapping the pattern, like this.

KNOW HOW PRINT SHOW

When you are making posters remember to use thick paper which will not crumple or wrinkle. Print them with large, simple patterns in bright colours.

Instead of printing poster borders, try gluing on strips of coloured paper. If you hang the posters out of doors, put them in large plastic bags to keep them dry.

Putting on an Exhibition

When you have printed lots of pictures and patterns, try putting on an exhibition. Frame or mount your pictures on coloured card first. Here are some ideas on how and where to hang your pictures if you have an outdoor show. For an indoor show, tie string to points in a room and hang the pictures from the string. Send printed invitation cards telling everyone where to come, at what time and whether it will cost them anything. Make posters to advertise the exhibition.

You will need
printed pictures
sheets of coloured card for the
    frames
a ruler
a pencil
sticky tape
string
an old sheet
scissors
clothes pegs, paper clips or pins
posters (see page 28-29)
invitation cards

Coloured Card Mounts

glue on

Dab a little glue on the four corners of the back of a picture. Put the picture down on a sheet of coloured card, like this, and rub all over it with your hand.

rule lines

Put a ruler on the edge of one of the sides of the picture and rule a line like this. Do the same with the other three sides of the picture.

cut along lines

Cut along the four ruled lines with scissors. Put sticky tape loops on the four corners of the back of the card to hang the picture up.

Sticky Tape Loops

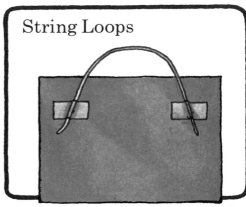

Curl a small piece of tape, the sticky side outside, into a loop and stick the ends together. Put a loop in each corner of a picture to hang it up.

String Loops

Tape a piece of string to the card on the back of a picture, like this. Hang the picture from the middle of the string.

How to Hang Pictures

Think how tall the people you are inviting to your exhibition are and hang your pictures so that they are on a level with the people's eyes.

Ask a friend to hold the picture while you stand back to see if it is in the right position. With two rows of pictures, hang one just above eye level and one just below.

1 Card Window Frames

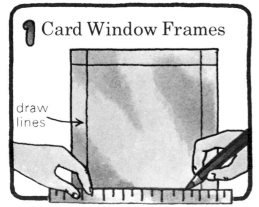

draw lines

To make a window frame, cut a piece of coloured card the same size as the picture. Put a ruler on the edges of the card and draw four pencil lines, like this.

2

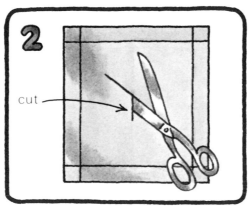

cut

Cut out the centre of the card by pushing one blade of the scissors through the middle of the card. Cut to one corner and then along the lines you have drawn.

3

picture in centre

glue on frame

Put a little glue on the four corners of the back of the frame. Place the frame on top of the picture and press down.

Party Prints

Before you have a party, you can make lots of things for it. Start the day before so that the paint and ink have time to dry.

You will need

white paper cups, plates and napkins
sheets of paper, about 40 cm long and 30 cm wide
waterproof inks
poster paint
a cotton reel roller (see page 11)
string or stencil letters (see pages 16-17)
a pencil and scissors
a sponge and glue

Paper Plates

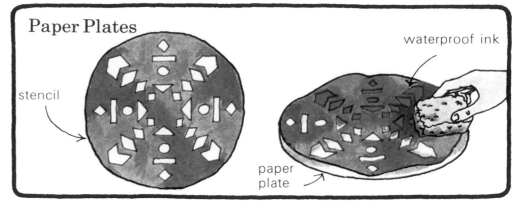

Put a paper plate down on a piece of stencil paper and draw around it. Cut out the circle and fold it up several times. Cut bits out of the folds to make a stencil.

Unfold the stencil and put it down on a paper plate. Use waterproof inks and a sponge to print the stencil in **different colours** on the plate, like this.

Paper Hats

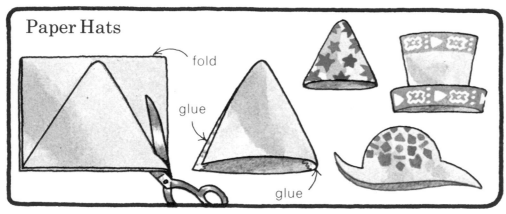

Make a hat by folding a big sheet of paper in half. Cut out a hat shape and glue the two pieces together along the top edges. Try cutting out different shapes.

When the glue is dry, decorate both sides of the hats with plasticine roller prints or stencil prints in several different colours of poster paint, like this.

Paper Cups

Cut a small pattern in a stencil. Wrap it round the outside of a paper cup and use waterproof inks and a sponge to print a pattern.

Paper Napkins

Fold napkins into small squares or triangles. Dip corners or edges in waterproof inks. Press the napkins between newspaper. Unfold and hang up to dry.

Paper Mats

Fold the large sheets of paper in half and cut along the folds. Decorate the edges with plasticine roller prints.

Use string or stencil letters to print on the mats the name of each friend coming to the party. Put the mats on the table so that they will know where to sit.

Flying Models

Mary Jean McNeil

Illustrated by Colin King
Designed by John Jamieson

Models designed by Derek Beck
Educational Adviser: Frank Blackwell

Contents

About Flying Models

The aeroplanes in this book are all made from paper and card. If you want to colour them, use Magic Marker, not paints. For the planes which need gluing, use quick-drying, powerful glue such as UHU or Bostik 1.

Boxes with this sign give you special tips for making the models.

Boxes with this sign give you special tips for flying the models.

We have used the words 'paper' and 'card' and 'thick card' in this book.

Paper means any normal writing paper, not newspaper.

Card means any thin card about the thickness of a postcard, although actual postcards will be too small. You may use old card folders. If you have to buy them, ask at a stationer for a document folder or square cut folder.

Thick card means really stiff strong card such as the card you find on the back of some writing pads and calendars.

First published in 1975
by Usborne Publishing Ltd
Usborne House
83-85 Saffron Hill, London EC1N 8RT

©Usborne Publishing Ltd 1989, 1975

The name Usborne and the device are Trade Marks of Usborne Publishing Ltd.

This abridged edition contains the best projects from the original 48-page version.

KH01 Prototype

The KH01 Prototype is a very easy plane to make. You can make it from a sheet of paper 21cm × 29cm. Ask for A4 paper. If you cannot make it fly properly, look at the Flying Boxes in the middle of this page. You can find out how to launch it on the next page.

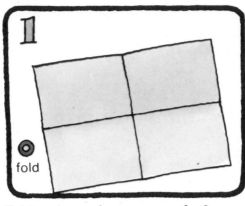

Fold a piece of paper exactly down the middle. Unfold it. Fold it exactly down the middle in the other direction. These folds are your guide lines.

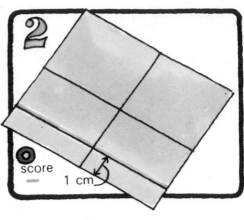

Score a line 1 cm from the long edge of the paper. Then fold the paper up along this line as shown.

The KH01 Prototype

⚑ If it Stalls

paper clip

Planes can fly badly in lots of different ways. Sometimes they stall. A stalling plane goes up and down and up and down like this. It stalls because its nose is not heavy enough. Put a paper clip on its front like this. Launch it. If it still stalls put on another one. Or try putting a bit of tape along the folded edge.

2

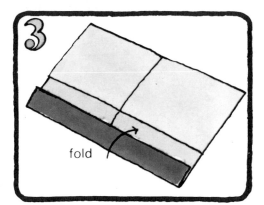

Fold the paper again and again until your folded edge reaches the middle guide line.

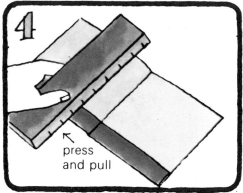

The last fold has to be really tight, so press your ruler down hard on the paper and run it along the edge.

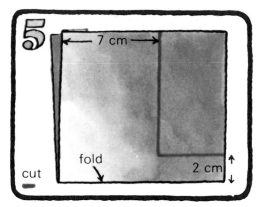

Fold the paper in half with the folded paper on the inside. Draw and cut out the aeroplane shape as shown.

If it Dives

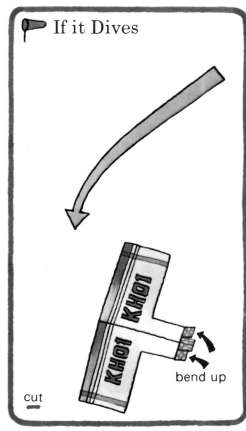

Your plane may dive nose first to the ground. This may mean that the nose is too heavy. Or it may mean that the tail is not working properly. Make a small cut each side of the tail and bend the paper up as shown. Launch it again. If it still dives, bend the paper up a bit more. Keep doing this until the plane glides smoothly.

Aeroplanes

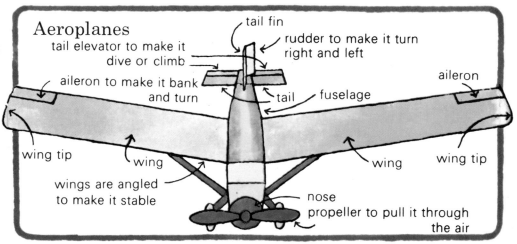

Aeroplanes have lots of different parts. Each part has its own special job.

Look at the aeroplane here and see where the parts are and what they do.

Folding Paper in Half

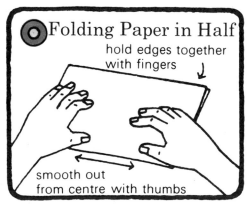

For paper aeroplanes, paper folds must be really accurate. The best way is to hold the edges together with your fingers while you smooth the fold down with your thumbs.

Scoring

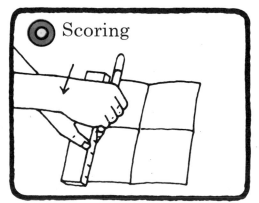

Lay the paper on something hard and flat. Put your ruler along the line you want to score. Rule a line with a ball point pen. Press the pen down hard all the time.

The Free Flyer

The Free Flyer flies through the air in a very smooth, slow glide. You can make it from a sheet of paper 21cm × 29cm (A4 paper). On this page you will find out how to launch it properly and how to make it turn left and right. All flattish planes like the Free Flyer are launched in this way.

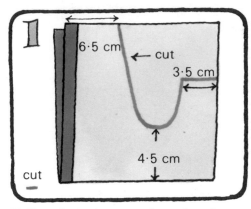

Follow boxes one to four for the KH01 Prototype. Then fold the paper in half with the folded edge on the outside. Draw and cut out the Free Flyer shape as shown.

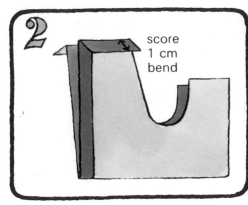

Score a line 1 cm from the tips of the wings. Bend the top wing edge over the score line and bend the bottom one over in the opposite direction as shown.

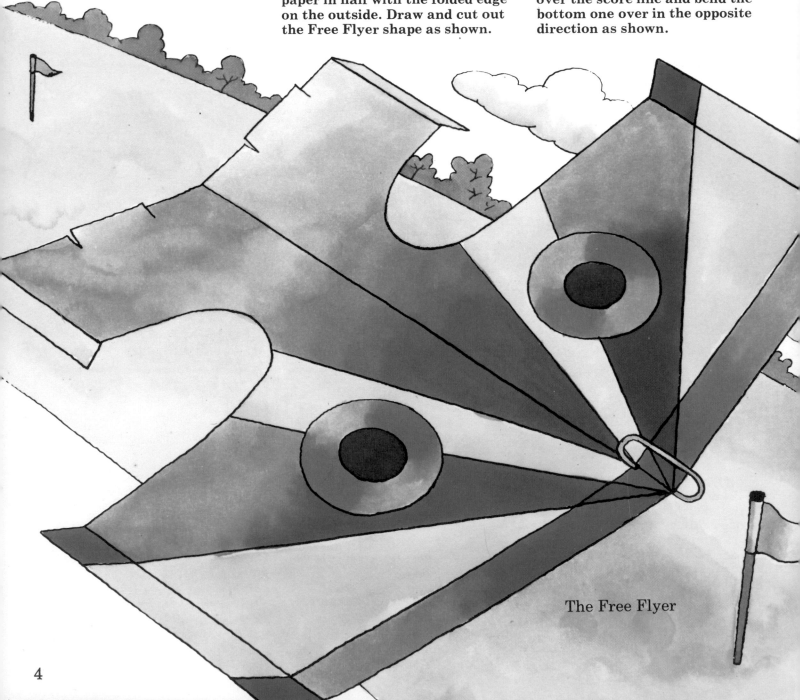

The Free Flyer

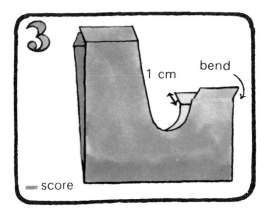

3 1 cm

bend

score

Fold the plane the other way. Score a line 1 cm from the tip of the tail as shown. Bend the tail tips over the score line in opposite directions to each other.

4 bend down

Bend the back wing edges down by running them between your thumb and fingers. This will curve the wing edge and the plane will fly better. It is called cambering.

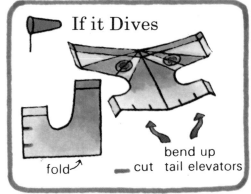

If it Dives

fold

cut

bend up tail elevators

Fold the plane and make two snips in the tail as shown. Unfold the plane. Bend them up until the plane flies smoothly. These are called tail elevators.

Launching a Free Flyer

Put your fore-finger on top of the plane like this with your thumb and other fingers underneath. Point the plane in the direction you want it to go.

Move your hand forward at the speed you think it will fly at and just let it go. Do not jerk or push it forward. Just let it glide from your hand.

Making it Stable

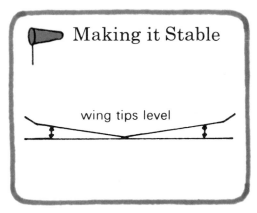

wing tips level

An unstable plane will spin and somersault to the ground. Hold it up like this. Make sure that the wing tips are level. Push them up or down to make them level.

Making it turn Left and right

bend up aileron

bend down aileron

bend up aileron

If you want to, you can make the Free Flyer fly in different directions. Make two little cuts in the back of the wings as shown, to make ailerons.

To make it go left, bend the left aileron up and the right aileron down. To make it go right, bend the right aileron up and the left one down.

A Flying Tip

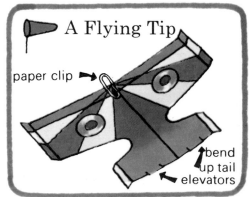

paper clip

bend up tail elevators

The Free Flyer will fly very well if you put a paper clip on its nose and bend the tail elevators up a bit.

Buffalo Mark 1 and 2

Buffalo Mk 1 and 2, with their big, heavy folded noses are very good at flying tricks. You can make them from a sheet of paper 21cm × 29cm. Ask for A4 paper. As they do not have keels you will have to launch them in the same way that you launched the Free Flyer.
See page 5

See page 5

Buffalo Mark 1

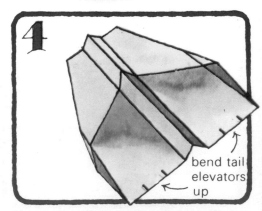

1 Buffalo Mk 1

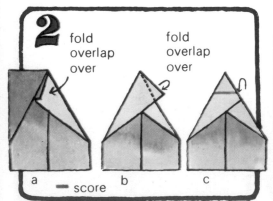

mark on both edges

— score

Fold the paper in half and put it along the line at the top of this page like this. Mark A on both edges of the paper and score a line as shown.

2

fold overlap over

fold overlap over

a — score b c

Open the paper. Fold one corner along the score line (a), fold the other corner over and fold back any paper that overlaps (b). Score across the top and fold it back (c).

3

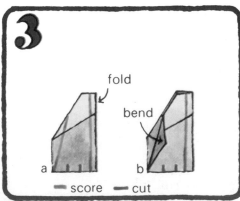

fold

bend

a b

— score — cut

Fold the paper in half like this. Score two more lines as shown (a). Bend the paper over both score lines and cut two snips in the bottom as shown (b).

4

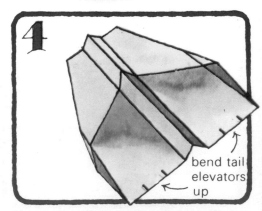

bend tail elevators up

Open the paper out again so that it looks like this. You launch it this way up. Bend the tail elevators up if it dives or glides too steeply.

Buffalo Mark 2

1 Buffalo Mk 2

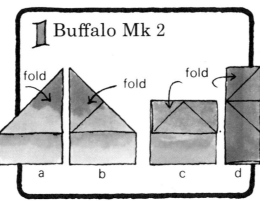

a b c d

To make guide lines you will have to fold the paper four times, a, b, c, d, and unfold it four times. You unfold it after you have made each fold before you make the next.

2

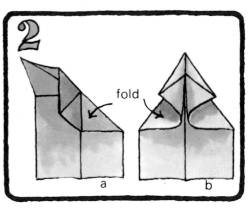

fold

a b

Open the paper out flat. Fold one side down like this (a). Then fold the other side down in the same way (b).

3

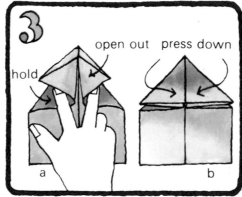

hold open out press down

a b

Hold the folds you have just made down with one hand. Open the top of the paper out with the other (a). Press the paper down as shown (b).

4

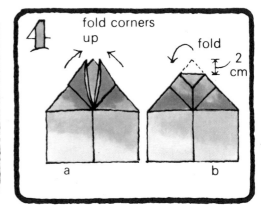

fold corners up fold 2 cm

a b

Fold the two corners up to the point (a). Press them down. Fold 2 cm of the pointed nose down on to the dart as shown (b).

5

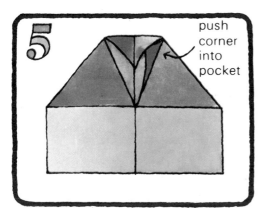

push corner into pocket

You will have made two pockets at the top of the paper. Push the remaining two corners into the pockets as shown.

6

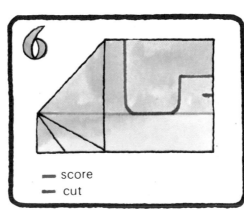

— score
— cut

Fold the paper in half and score a line as shown. Draw and cut out the aeroplane shape. Cut two tail elevator snips in the back.

7

Bend the paper over at the score line so that the plane looks like this. The middle should point downwards as shown. The dart is quite open. It has no keel.

The Air Scorpion

The Air Scorpion is a racing plane. It has swept-back wings and it flies very fast and straight.

You will need
THE PATTERN FOR ITS TAIL
   FIN ON PAGE 28
a sheet of paper 21cm × 29cm
a ball point pen for scoring
scissors
a ruler
sticky tape

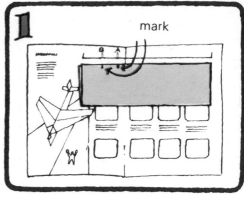

1

Fold the paper in half like this. Put it along the line at the top of this page. Mark A and B on both edges of the paper.

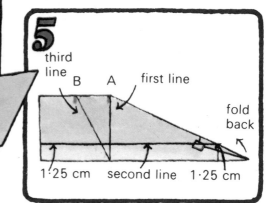

5

third line   B   A   first line

fold back

1·25 cm   second line   1·25 cm

Fold the paper down the middle and fold the nose in. Draw three lines, one from A down to the fold, another across the bottom of the paper and the last from B as shown.

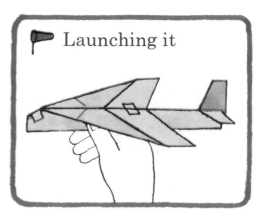

Launching it

Hold the plane by its keel. Point it down a bit and let it go gently.

The Air Scorpion

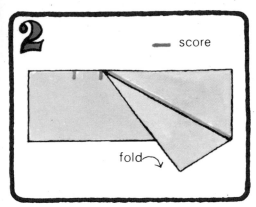

2 — score

Score a line from A to the top of the fold. Fold one of the corners over along this line as shown. Then fold the other corner back the other way.

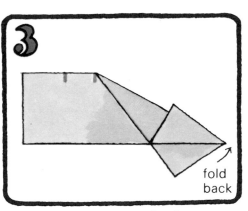

3

Fold both the corners back as shown.

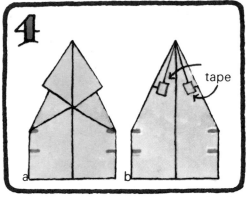

4 tape

Open the paper out. It should look like this from the front (a). Turn it over and fold both the corners over tightly. Tape them down (b).

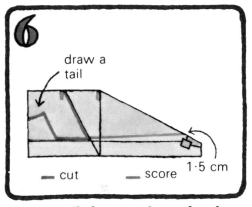

6 draw a tail — cut — score 1·5 cm

Draw a tail shape and cut the plane out as shown. Score a line across the wings as shown. Score another across the tail.

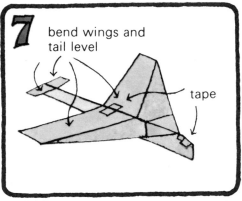

7 bend wings and tail level tape

Bend the tail and wings along the score line so that they are level. Keep the wings in place with tape and tape the front of the nose.

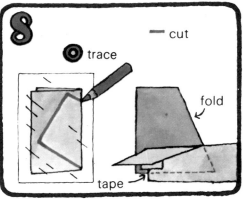

8 — cut trace fold tape

Trace the tail fin pattern on to a folded piece of paper. Cut it out. Tape it inside the body of the plane, fold first, so that it sticks out a bit like this.

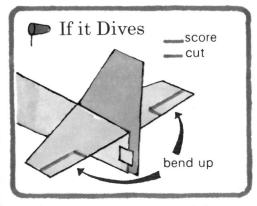

If it Dives — score — cut bend up

You can stop it diving by giving it tail elevators. Make a cut each side of the tail fin as shown. Bend the tail elevators up a little. (see page 5).

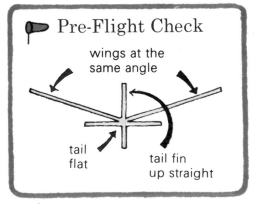

Pre-Flight Check wings at the same angle tail flat tail fin up straight

Hold your plane up and see if it looks like this. The wings must be at the same angle. The tail should be flat and the tail fin should point straight up.

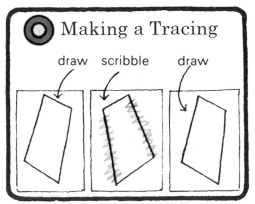

Making a Tracing draw scribble draw

Draw the outline on tracing paper. Turn it over and scribble over the outline with a pencil. Put the tracing, right side up, on paper and draw round the outline again.

The Range Moth

You will need
THE PATTERN FROM
   PAGE 28
a big sheet of paper at least
   30cm × 44cm
tracing paper and a pencil
a ball point pen cap, bits of
   card or plasticine
scissors, sticky tape and glue
see page 9 on making a tracing

If you want to, you can make a
parachute as well.
You will need
some polythene 20cm × 20cm
a big paper clip
scissors and thread

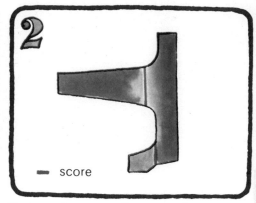

Trace the pattern on to a folded
piece of paper. Remember to trace
the score line as well. Cut the
plane out, but do not cut along
the fold.

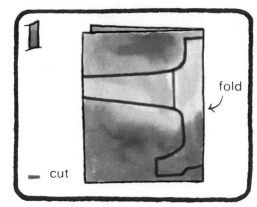

Put a ruler exactly on to the score
lines. Score one line across the
wing, score another line across the
tail as shown.

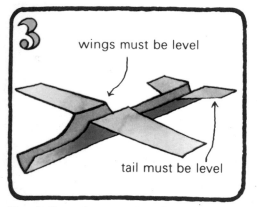

Bend the wings and tail down along
the score lines as shown.

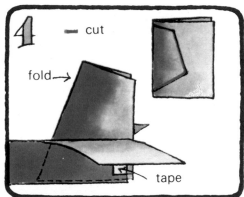

Trace the tail fin on to a folded
piece of paper. Cut it out, but not
along the fold. Tape the tail fin,
fold first into the inside back of the
plane as shown.

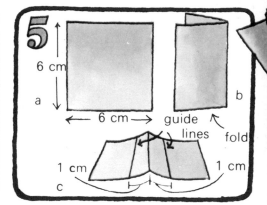

Cut out a piece of paper 6 cm ×
6 cm (a). Fold it in half (b). Open it
out and draw two guide lines 1 cm
from the fold as shown (c).

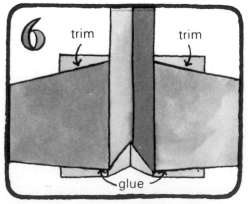

Glue the plane down on to this
piece of paper as shown. The wings
are following the guide lines you
drew on the piece of paper. Trim
any paper that overlaps.

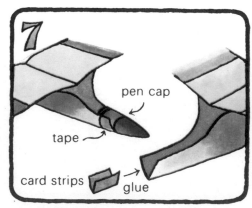

Tape the plastic cap of a felt or
ball point pen into the nose. If
you want to, you can cut out small
strips of card and glue them into
the nose instead.

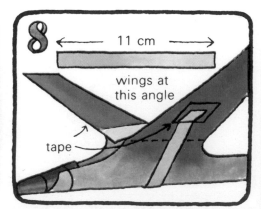

Cut out a narrow strip of paper
11 cm long. Fold it in half. Hold it
under the plane. Tape it to each
side of the wings so that the wings
tilt up at the same angle.

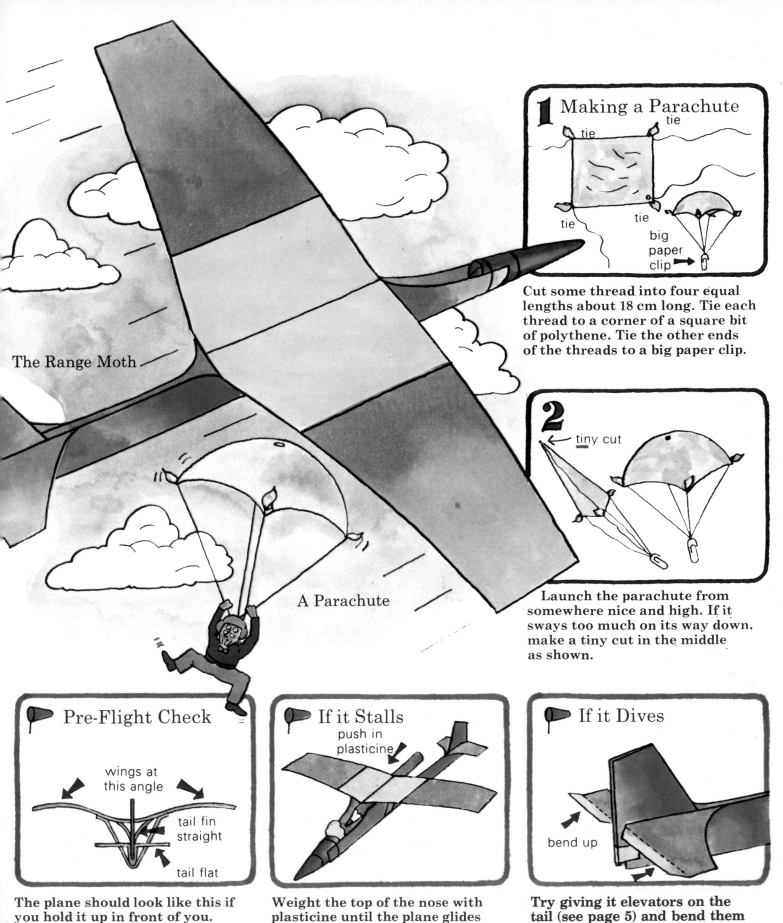

The Range Moth

A Parachute

1 Making a Parachute

tie   tie

tie   tie

big
paper
clip →

Cut some thread into four equal
lengths about 18 cm long. Tie each
thread to a corner of a square bit
of polythene. Tie the other ends
of the threads to a big paper clip.

2

tiny cut

Launch the parachute from
somewhere nice and high. If it
sways too much on its way down,
make a tiny cut in the middle
as shown.

Pre-Flight Check

wings at
this angle

tail fin
straight

tail flat

The plane should look like this if
you hold it up in front of you.
The tail fin must point straight
up with the tail pieces flat. Wings
must be at an angle.

If it Stalls

push in
plasticine

Weight the top of the nose with
plasticine until the plane glides
smoothly. Then push the same
plasticine into the pen cap with a
pencil as shown.

If it Dives

bend up

Try giving it elevators on the
tail (see page 5) and bend them
up, as shown.

The Moon Bug

You will find that the Moon Bug is a very easy aeroplane to make. See page 9 on making a tracing.

You will need
THE MOON BUG PATTERN ON PAGE 28
a sheet of paper 21cm × 29cm
tracing paper and a pencil
scissors and sticky tape
a ruler
a ball point pen for scoring

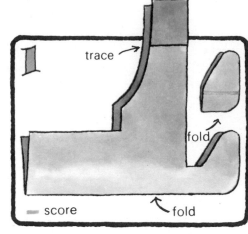

Fold the paper and trace the plane and tail pattern on to it. Cut it out, but do not cut along the fold. Trace the lines on the wings and tail. Score the tail as shown.

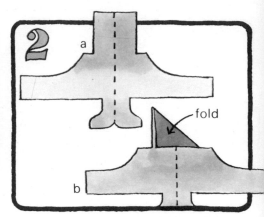

To make the nose of this aeroplane, you will have to make guide lines. Start with the paper opened out (a). Then, fold one of the corners over as shown (b).

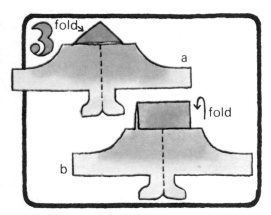

Fold the other corner over (a). Open the paper out and make a third fold (b) like this. Open the paper out for the last time and you have your guide lines.

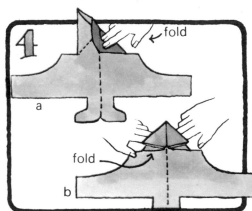

Make a fold like this on one side of the paper (a). Hold this fold down and fold the other side down in the same way (b).

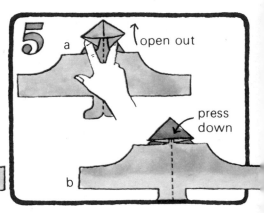

Hold the paper folds in place with one hand and with the other open the paper above them out (a). Then press all the paper down (b).

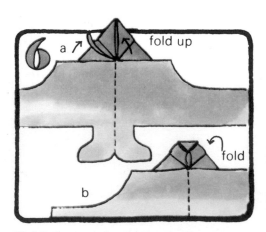

Fold the two bottom corners up as shown (a). Then fold the pointed end down (b).

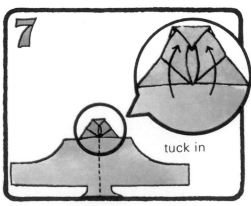

When you folded the pointed end down, you made little pockets at the top of the paper. Tuck the two free corners right into the pockets as shown.

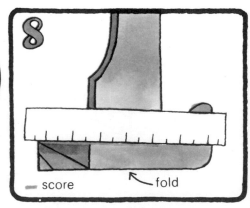

Fold the paper in half. Put your ruler along the top of the fuselage and score a line across the wings.

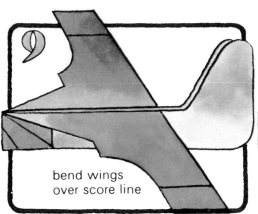

9 bend wings over score line

Bend the wings back along the score line so that they are level.

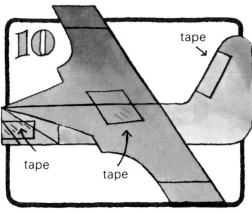

10 tape

tape   tape

Tape the plane together at the nose and across the top of the wings. Tape the tail fin together as shown.

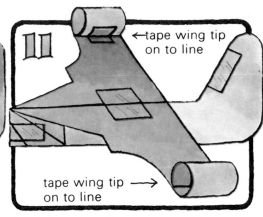

11 ←tape wing tip on to line

tape wing tip on to line

Curl the wing tips over and tape them on to the wings at the traced lines as shown.

12 tape on tail

bend

Bend the tail along its score lines and tape it under the tail fin so that the back of the plane looks like this.

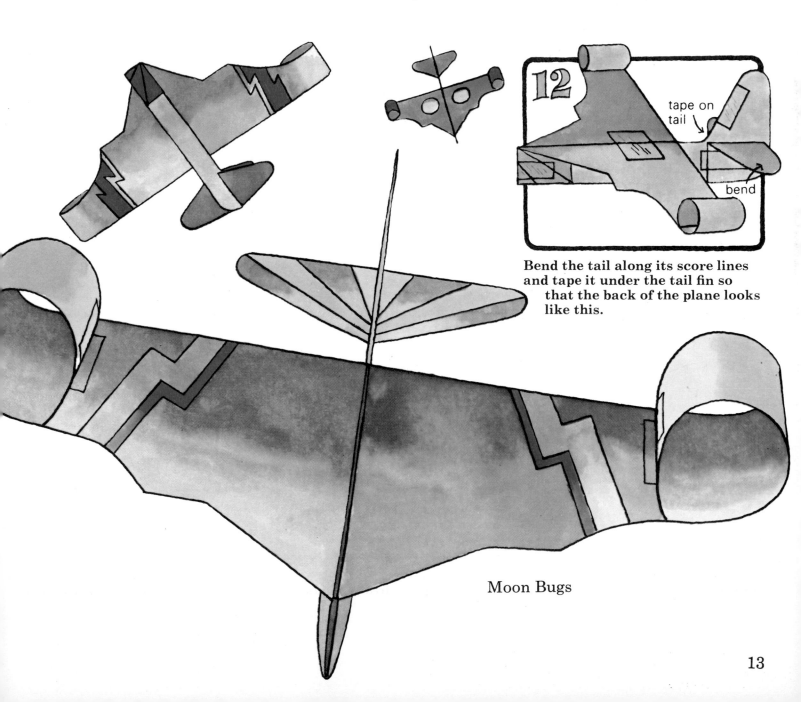

Moon Bugs

The Drinking Straw Glider

The Drinking Straw Glider has a special kind of curved wing. It is called a cambered wing. The camber gives the plane a little more lift. See page 9 on making a tracing

You will need

THE PATTERN FROM
   PAGE 29
a sheet of paper for the wings
   and tail
card from a document folder
2 drinking straws
tracing paper and a pencil
scissors and a ruler
plasticine or silver foil
strong glue and sticky tape

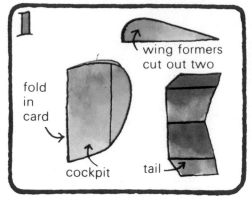

1

Trace and cut out a card cockpit, two card wing formers and a paper tail. Remember to trace all the lines on the patterns.

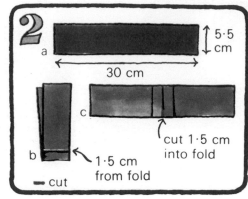

2

Cut out a paper wing as shown (a). Fold the paper in half and draw a line 1·5 cm from the fold (b). Open the wings out and cut a notch into the fold as shown (c).

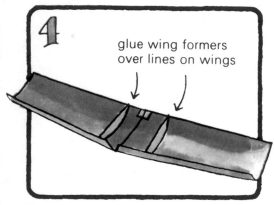

4

Put glue on the curved edge of the wing formers. Glue them on to the wings along the lines you drew each side of the notch.

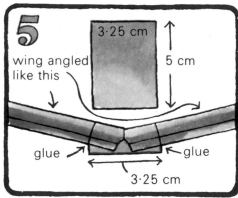

5

Cut out a piece of card 5 cm × 3·25 cm. Glue its long edges to the bottom edges of the wing formers so that the wings become angled like this.

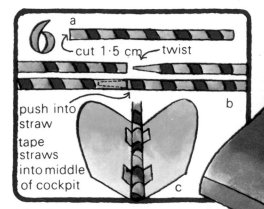

6

Slit the end of a straw (a). Twist the slit end into a point, push it into another straw to make one long straw (b). Tape the middle of this long straw into the cockpit (c).

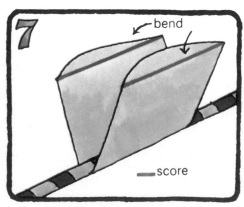

7

Score the cockpit along the lines you traced. Bend the cockpit along the score lines as shown.

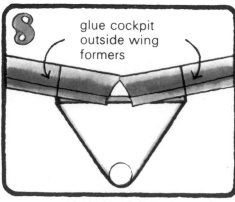

8

Glue together the wings and cockpit with the cockpit outside the wing formers as shown.

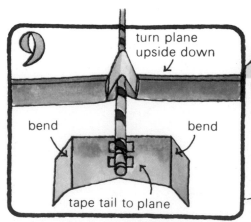

9

Put the plane upside down and tape the tail on to it like this with the straw lying along the line down the middle of the tail. Bend the sides of the tail as shown.

14

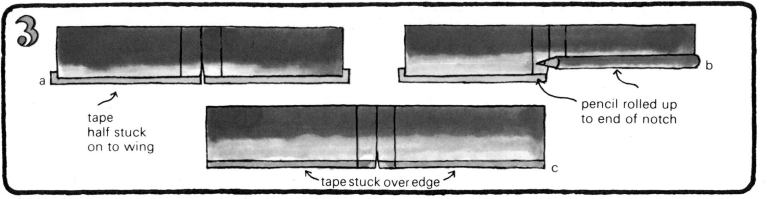

3

a

b

pencil rolled up
to end of notch

c

tape
half stuck
on to wing

← tape stuck over edge →

Half stick some tape along the
notched edge of one wing as shown
(a). Then put a ROUND pencil on to
the unstuck half of the tape in
line with the front wing edge.

Roll the pencil up the wing as far
as the end of the notch (b). Then
unroll the pencil and take the
tape off it very carefully. Do it
again on the other wing.

Fold the free edge of the tape up
over the wing edge like this (c).
The curve you have just made is
called a camber.

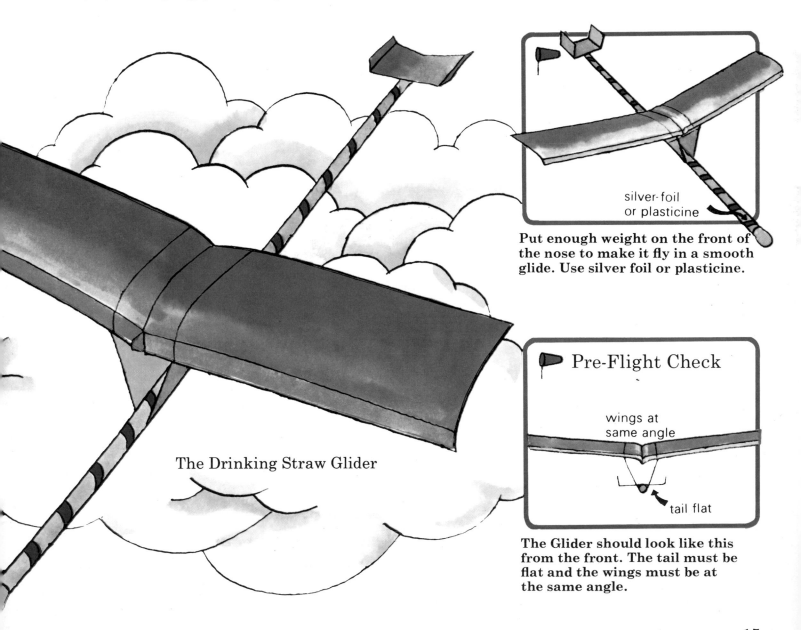

The Drinking Straw Glider

silver-foil
or plasticine

Put enough weight on the front of
the nose to make it fly in a smooth
glide. Use silver foil or plasticine.

Pre-Flight Check

wings at
same angle

tail flat

The Glider should look like this
from the front. The tail must be
flat and the wings must be at
the same angle.

Jungle Fighter KH20

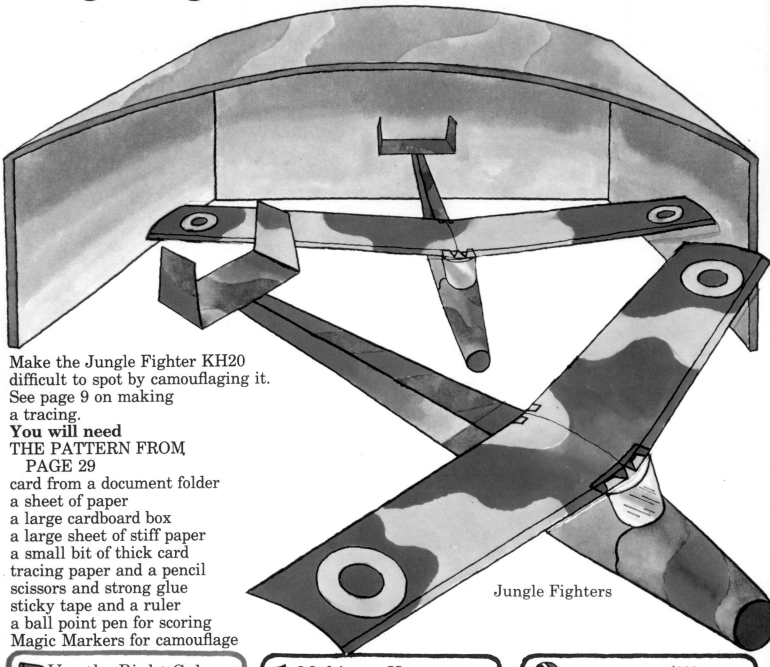

Make the Jungle Fighter KH20
difficult to spot by camouflaging it.
See page 9 on making
a tracing.
You will need
THE PATTERN FROM
   PAGE 29
card from a document folder
a sheet of paper
a large cardboard box
a large sheet of stiff paper
a small bit of thick card
tracing paper and a pencil
scissors and strong glue
sticky tape and a ruler
a ball point pen for scoring
Magic Markers for camouflage

Jungle Fighters

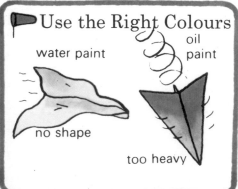

Use the Right Colours

water paint

oil paint

no shape

too heavy

Do not use water-based paints on
the planes. The paper will crumple
up and lose its shape. Oil paints
are too heavy. Colour them with
Magic Markers.

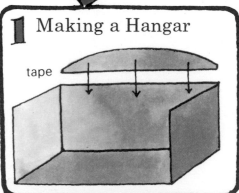

1 Making a Hangar

tape

Put a large cardboard box on its
side. Cut off the top side. Cut
out a curved shape from the extra
cardboard as shown. Tape the
shape on to the back of the box.

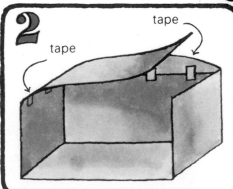

2

tape

tape

Make a roof by laying some stiff
paper over the curved shape and
taping it to the sides of the box.
Camouflage it by painting it the
same colour as its surroundings.

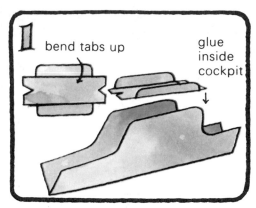

1
bend tabs up
glue inside cockpit

Trace and cut out a card cockpit and cockpit top. Score and bend the cockpit top as shown and glue it into the top of the cockpit.

2
a
glue to cockpit
glue to tab
b
c

Trace and cut out a paper nose (a). Bend the nose piece round, dab glue on its tab and join it up (b). Glue it to the front of the cockpit (c).

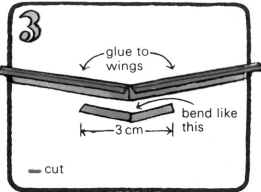

3
glue to wings
bend like this
3 cm
— cut

Trace and cut out its paper wings. Make a small snip as shown and camber them (page 14). Cut out a narrow strip of thick card. Bend it, glue the wings on to it as shown.

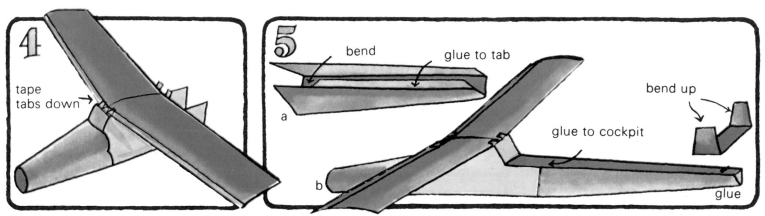

4
tape tabs down

Put the wings on top of the cockpit. Bend the front and back cockpit top tabs over the wings and tape as shown.

5
bend
glue to tab
a
b
glue to cockpit
bend up
glue

Trace and cut out a paper fuselage. Bend it as shown. Put glue on its tab and glue it together (a). Trace and cut out a paper tail. Bend the tail sides up where shown.

Glue the fuselage into the back of the cockpit like this. Glue the tail on top of the end of the fuselage as shown (b).

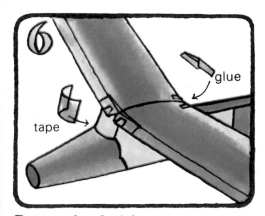

6
glue
tape

Put a strip of sticky tape over the front of the cockpit. Trace and cut out a card cockpit back. Score it and glue it into the back of the cockpit.

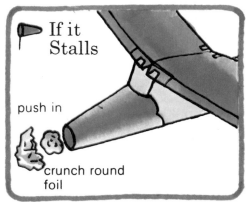

If it Stalls
push in
crunch round foil

If it stalls it means that the nose is not heavy enough. Make the nose heavier by squeezing plasticine into it or crunching silver foil around it.

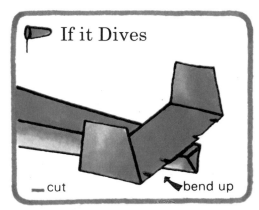

If it Dives
— cut
bend up

If it dives, it means that the nose is too heavy. Take some weight off the nose or make tail elevators (page 5). Bend them up as shown.

17

The Hawkeye Devastator

The Hawkeye Devastator flies out of doors. Launch it against the wind. Its propeller spins round when it flies. See page 9 on making a tracing.

You will need
THE PATTERN ON PAGES 30 AND 31
card from a document folder
a big sheet of paper
tracing paper and a pencil
a rubber band and a straw
a 3cm long big-headed pin
2 ball point pens
scissors and a ruler
sticky tape and glue
a needle and thread

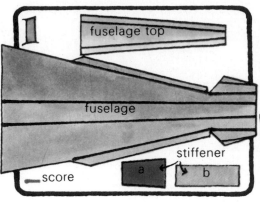

Trace and cut out a paper fuselage, a paper fuselage top and two card stiffeners. Score the fuselage as shown.

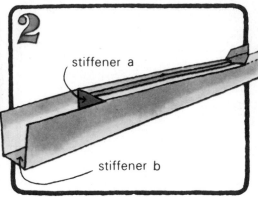

Bend the fuselage sides up along the score lines. Glue stiffener (a) and (b) into the fuselage as shown. Stiffener (b) should touch the bottom edge of stiffener (a).

The Hawkeye Devastator

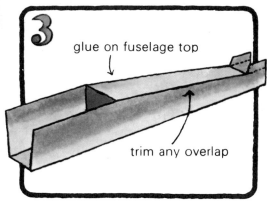

3 glue on fuselage top

trim any overlap

Bend the fuselage tabs in and glue the fuselage top on to the fuselage like this. When the glue is dry, trim off any overlapping paper.

4 bend

score   bend

Trace and cut out two card cockpit pieces. Score them both like this. Bend the bottom cockpit tabs up so that they lie flat on a table.

5 stiffener

fuselage and cockpit pieces level

glue on cockpit pieces

Glue the cockpit pieces on to the sides of the fuselage. Do this on a flat surface so that the bottom edge of each cockpit is in a straight line with the fuselage.

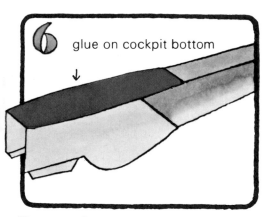

6 glue on cockpit bottom

Trace and cut out a card cockpit bottom. Turn the fuselage over. Put glue on the tabs at the bottom of the cockpit and glue the cockpit bottom on as shown.

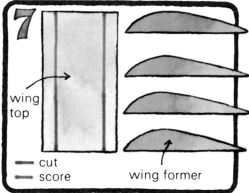

7 wing top

cut
score

wing former

Trace and cut out a card wing top and four card wing formers. You must trace the score and cut lines on the wing top. Then score and cut it like this.

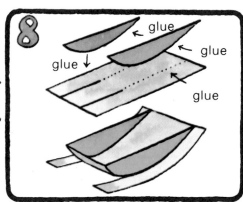

8 glue

glue

glue

glue

Put glue on to the curved edges of two of the wing formers. Glue them to the wing top along the score and partly cut lines as shown.

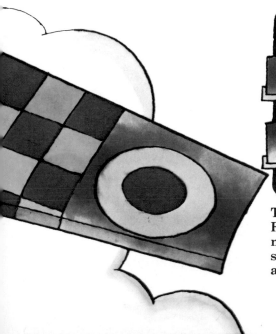

9 underside of wings   wing strut mark

tape   wing strut mark

Trace and cut out two card wings. Remember to trace the wing strut marks. Put sticky tape on the straight edge of each wing as shown.

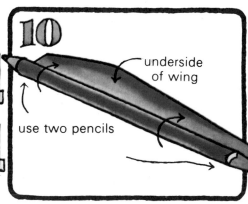

10 underside of wing

use two pencils

Camber each wing (page 14). You will have to use TWO round pencils instead of one. Make sure that they touch each other. Roll them both forward at the same speed.

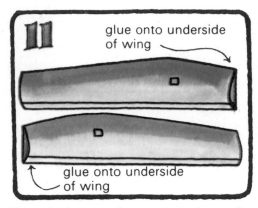

11 glue onto underside of wing

glue onto underside of wing

Put glue on to the curved edges of the other two wing formers and glue them on to the wings so that they look like this.

12 glue wings to wing top

glue here

glue here

wings and wing top in straight line

Glue the wing formered edges of the wings under the wing top flaps as shown. Make sure that the front edges of the wings and wing top lie in a straight line.

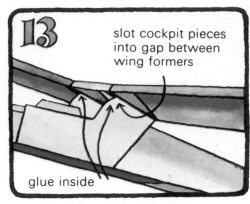

13 slot cockpit pieces into gap between wing formers

glue inside

Put glue on the inside of the curves at the top of the cockpit pieces and slip them up into the wing top so that each piece slots between two wing formers.

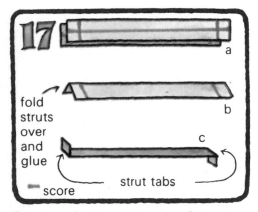

17 a

fold struts over and glue

b

c

score

strut tabs

Trace and cut out two card struts. Score each one as shown (a). Fold each one down the middle score line and glue (b). Bend along the other score lines as shown. (c).

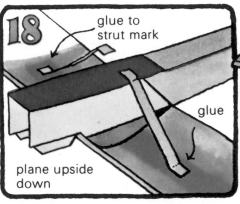

18 glue to strut mark

glue

plane upside down

Turn the plane upside down. Glue one of the strut tabs on to the wings over the wing strut mark. Do the same with the other strut on the other wing.

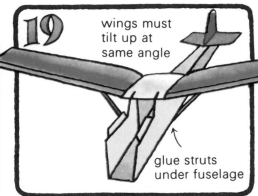

19 wings must tilt up at same angle

glue struts under fuselage

Turn the plane over. Move the free end of each strut tab up and down the fuselage base until both wings are at the same angle. Then glue the strut tabs on to the base.

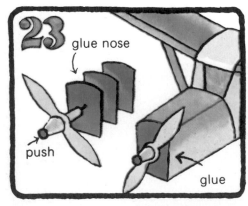

23 glue nose

push

glue

Trace and cut out three card noses. Glue them together. Push the long propeller pin firmly through them as shown. Glue them into the nose like this.

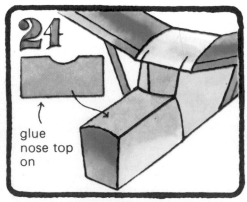

24 glue nose top on

Bend the tabs at the front of the cockpit pieces inwards. Trace and cut out a paper nose top. Glue it round the front of the cockpit.

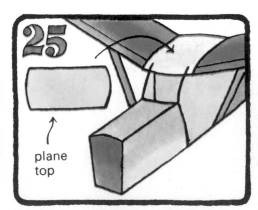

25 plane top

Trace and cut out a paper plane top. Put glue on to it and glue it over the middle of the wings so that it hides the score and cut marks on the wing top.

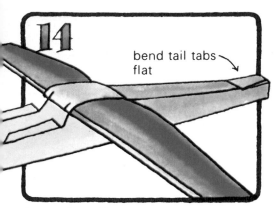

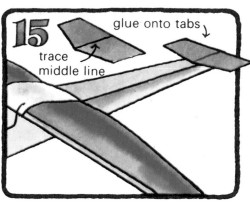

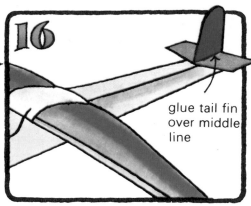

Bend the tail tabs at the end of the fuselage down on to each other so that they form a flat and level surface on which to glue the tail.

Trace the tail and the line going across it on to card. Cut it out. Put glue on the tail tabs and glue the tail on to them with the line going exactly down the middle.

Trace and cut out a card tail fin. Glue it down on to the middle line on the tail as shown.

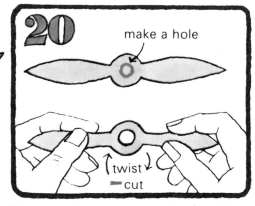

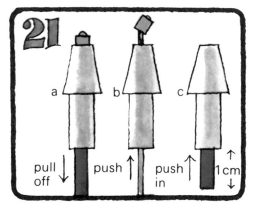

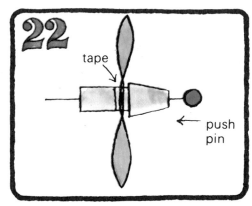

Trace and cut out a card propeller. Make a hole with a knitting needle where shown. Gently twist one blade in one direction and the other in the other direction.

Pull out the inside tube of a ball point pen (a). Push the ball point out of the bearing with a long pin (b). Cut 1 cm off the inside tube, push it back into the bearing (c).

Push the bearing through the hole in the propeller as shown. Tape the propeller to the bearing. Push the long big-headed pin through the hole in the middle of the bearing.

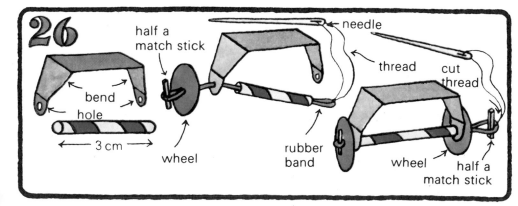

Trace and cut out two card wheels and a card undercarriage. Make holes where shown. Score the undercarriage and bend its sides. Cut a straw as shown. Push a

needle, thread and rubber band through undercarriage, wheels and straw as shown. Stop the rubber band ends with half a match stick. Cut the thread.

Turn the plane upside down again. Glue the undercarriage on to the base of the cockpit just in front of the struts as shown.

Flying Tips

If you have managed to make your aeroplanes glide smoothly in a straight line, you might like to try making them fly in other ways. On this page you can find out how to make the different controls on an aeroplane that make it fly in different directions and perform flying tricks. Some of these, like looping-the-loop and S-bends take a lot of practice.

Making a Plane with a Keel turn left and right

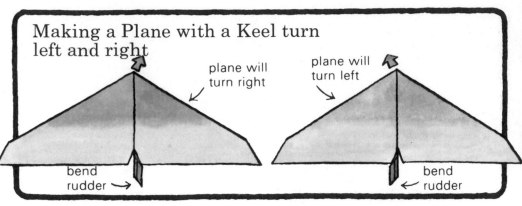

Planes with a keel like darts and Air Scorpions can be made to turn left and right by making a short snip through the keel just at the back under the wings and sticking the two sides together with tape. This is a rudder. Bend the rudder left to make the plane turn left, bend it right to make the plane turn right.

Making a Plane without a Keel turn left and right

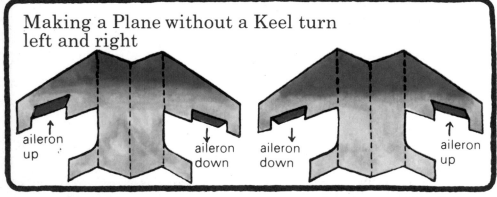

To make these planes turn you can give their wings ailerons. Make two cuts on each wing as shown. To make a plane fly to the left, bend the left aileron up and bend the right aileron down. To make a plane fly to the right, bend the right aileron up and the left one down.

Planes with Tail Fins

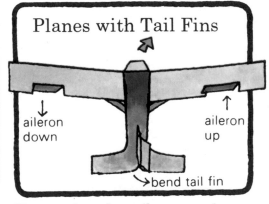

If your plane has ailerons and a tail fin, bend the ailerons in the usual way and bend the end of the tail fin to point in the direction you want the plane to fly.

Turning by Launching

A plane set to fly straight can be made to fly left by launching it at this angle. Tilt it in the other direction to make it turn right. This is launching it in a bank.

S-Bends

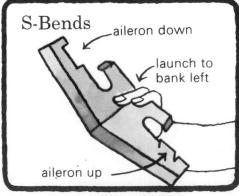

If you find it easy to launch your plane in a bank, try making it do an S-Bend. Set the controls to make it fly one way then launch it in a bank in the opposite direction.

Looping-the-Loop

Some people can make their planes loop-the-loop. Bend the tail elevators up, point the plane down and launch it very hard. This takes a lot of practice.

Flying out-of-Doors

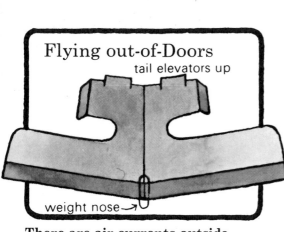

tail elevators up

weight nose →

There are air currents outside which make it more difficult for a paper plane to fly. Try making your plane heavier by weighting the nose. Bend the elevators up.

1 Flying in a Wind

Aeroplanes can do strange things in a wind. If you launch a plane so that it flies in the same direction as the wind, it will fly much faster than it would inside.

2

If you launch a plane in the opposite direction to the way the wind is blowing, it may fly backwards like this.

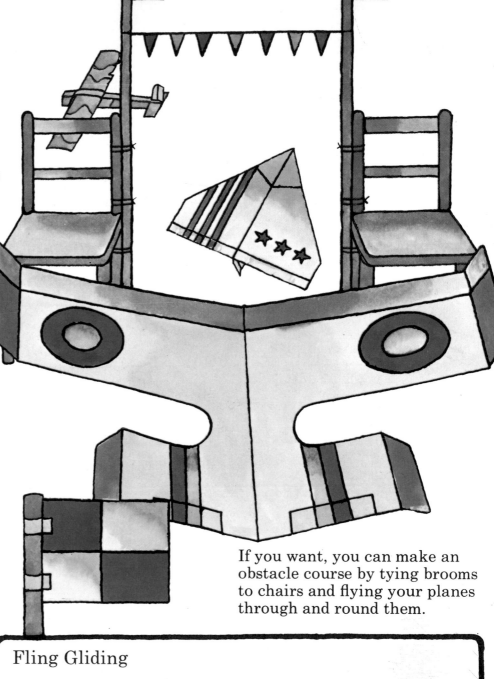

If you want, you can make an obstacle course by tying brooms to chairs and flying your planes through and round them.

Fling Gliding

Heavier planes can be exciting to fly by fling gliding. Tie one end of a piece of string to the edge of a wing, tie the other end to a strong stick or ruler. Bend the tail elevators up a bit. Hold the stick and turn round and round facing the stick all the time. See how long you can make the string without losing control.

23

Air Race

This is a game to test your skill at flying paper planes. Any number of players can play it. Everybody will need a paper plane and a counter. What you do is to make yourselves an aerobatics course like the one on page 23. You fly your plane on the course and then you move your counter along the board. The number of spaces you move your counter depends on how you fly your plane. Each flying trick is worth a different number of points. If you fly your plane to the left, it is worth 2 points, so you move your counter on 2 spaces on the board. Have a look at the score board and see what each trick is worth. Fly your planes in turn. When your counter lands on a space, you have to do what it says on the box. Try not to let your counter land on the hazard boxes. The player whose counter gets to the airport at the end of the course first is the winner. If you want, you can play the game with dice and counters only.

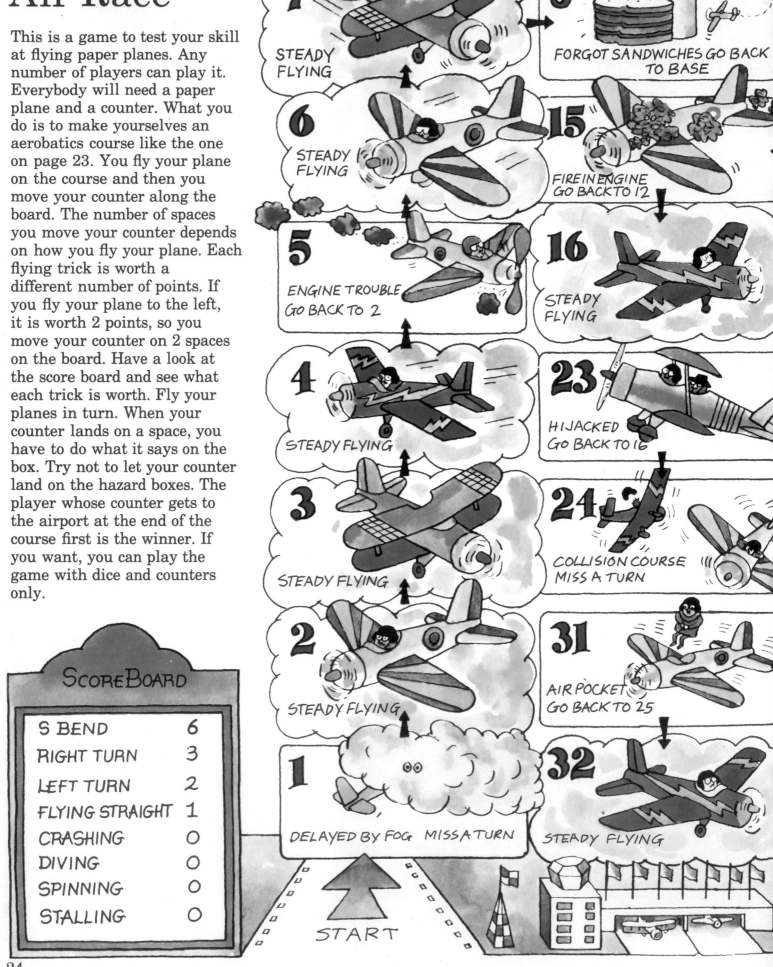

7 STEADY FLYING

8 FORGOT SANDWICHES GO BACK TO BASE

6 STEADY FLYING

15 FIRE IN ENGINE GO BACK TO 12

5 ENGINE TROUBLE GO BACK TO 2

16 STEADY FLYING

4 STEADY FLYING

23 HIJACKED GO BACK TO 16

3 STEADY FLYING

24 COLLISION COURSE MISS A TURN

2 STEADY FLYING

31 AIR POCKET GO BACK TO 25

1 DELAYED BY FOG MISS A TURN

32 STEADY FLYING

SCORE BOARD

S BEND	6
RIGHT TURN	3
LEFT TURN	2
FLYING STRAIGHT	1
CRASHING	0
DIVING	0
SPINNING	0
STALLING	0

START

Hang Gliders

One of the first aeroplanes was a Hang Glider. It was invented by a German called Otto Lilienthal in 1891. He was a very successful pioneer of flying. He had no controls on his glider. He hung by his arms under it and changed its direction by swinging his body.

You will need

a polythene bag at least
  20 × 20cm
4 drinking straws
a small, light, plastic figure
  or plasticine and a paper clip
scissors, thread and sticky tape

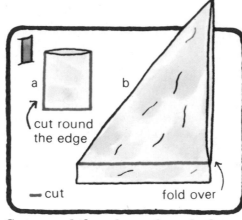

Cut round the edges of a polythene bag (a). Fold one piece as shown to make a square (b).

Tape two straws along the edge of the polythene as shown. Turn it over and tape the straws on from the other side too.

The Hang Glider

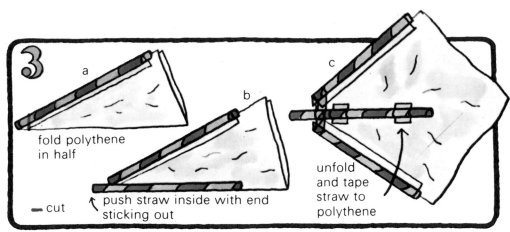

3

a

fold polythene
in half

— cut

b

push straw inside with end
sticking out

c

unfold
and tape
straw to
polythene

Fold in half and snip 1 cm off its front (a). Push another straw inside the polythene with its end sticking out at the front (b).

Unfold very gently. Try to keep the third straw exactly in the middle. Then tape it on to the polythene as shown (c).

4

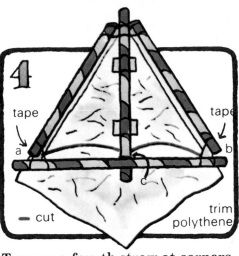

tape

tape

a

b

c

— cut

trim
polythene

Tape on a fourth straw at corners (a) and (b) only. Trim off middle straw (c). Trim the polythene as shown.

5

tape to
middle of
back
straw

Tape the middle straw to the fourth straw as shown. Your polythene should be a little baggy, and not taped at the back.

6

tape

Tie or tape a small, light plastic figure to the centre straw as shown to balance the plane. A plasticine weighted paper clip will balance the plane if you have no toy.

How Lilienthal changed his Glider's Direction

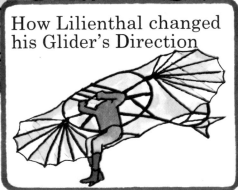

Lilienthal swung his body in different directions to make his glider fly differently. To raise the nose, he made the glider tail heavy by swinging his legs back.

Figure too far Forward

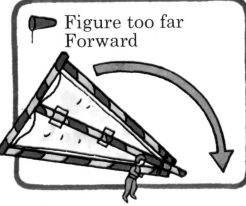

Your glider's nose will be too heavy and the glider will dive. Move the figure back until your Hang Glider flies smoothly.

Figure too far Back

Your glider's tail will be too heavy and the glider will stall. Move the figure forward bit by bit until the plane glides smoothly.

27

Patterns for Tracing

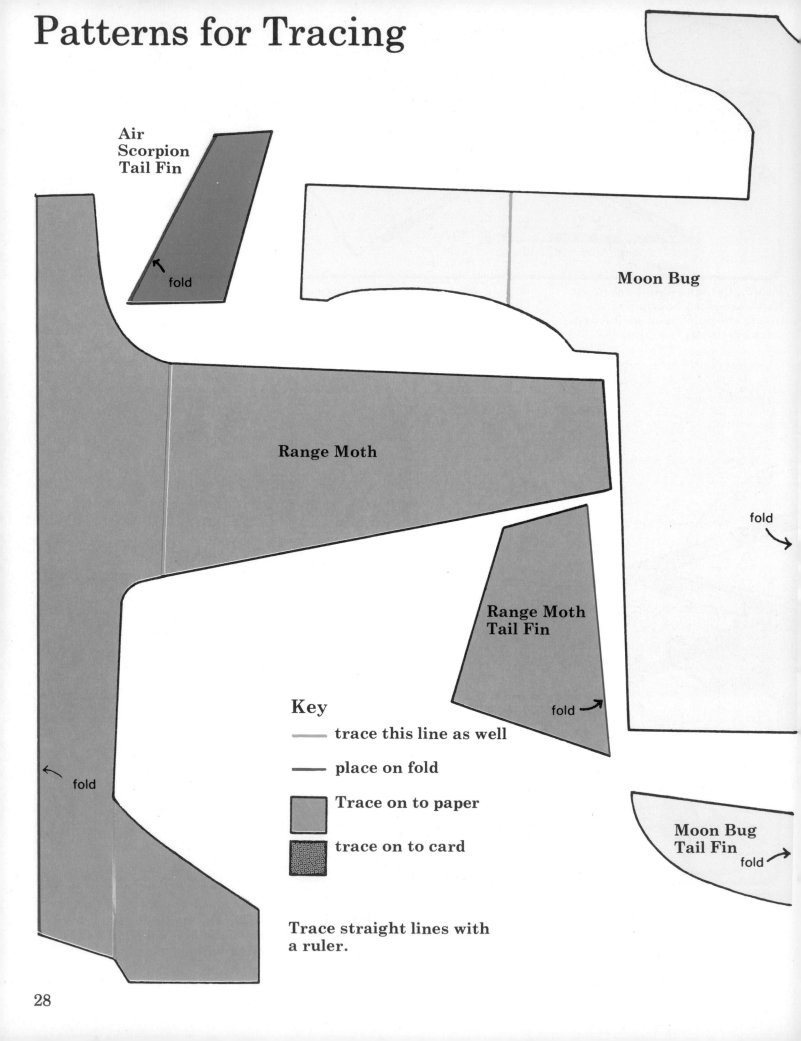

Air Scorpion Tail Fin

fold

Moon Bug

Range Moth

fold

Range Moth Tail Fin

fold

fold

Key

—— trace this line as well

—— place on fold

Trace on to paper

trace on to card

Moon Bug Tail Fin

fold

Trace straight lines with a ruler.

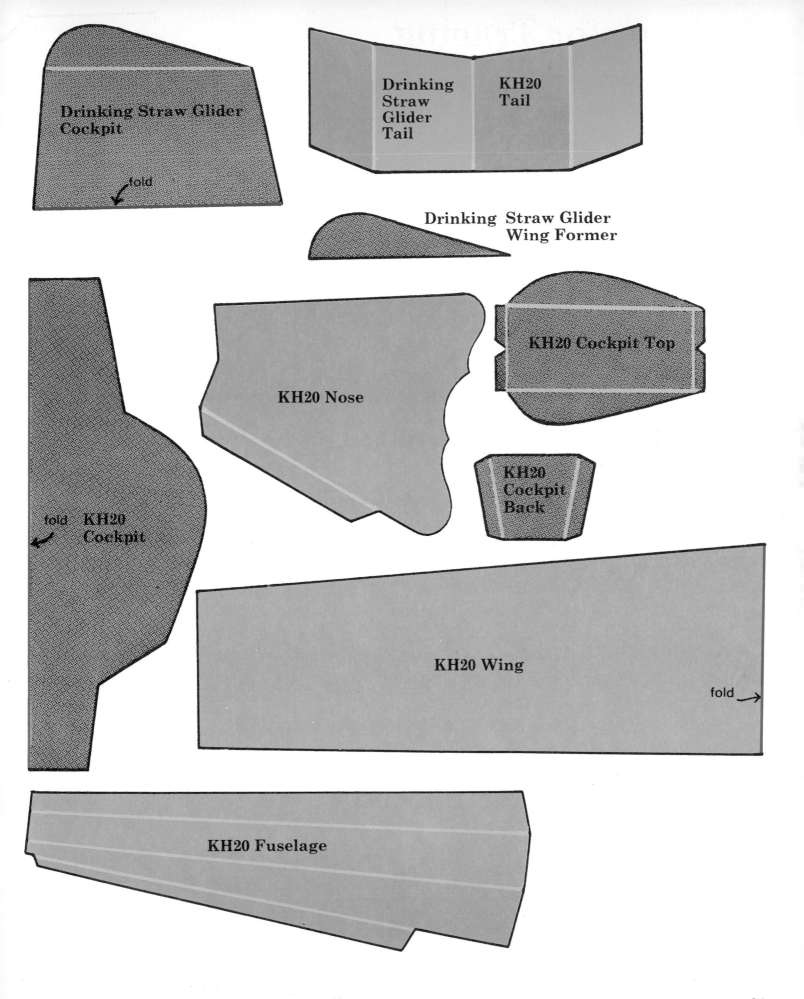

Drinking Straw Glider Cockpit

fold

Drinking Straw Glider Tail

KH20 Tail

Drinking Straw Glider Wing Former

KH20 Nose

KH20 Cockpit Top

KH20 Cockpit Back

fold KH20 Cockpit

KH20 Wing

fold

KH20 Fuselage

Patterns for Tracing
Hawkeye Devastator

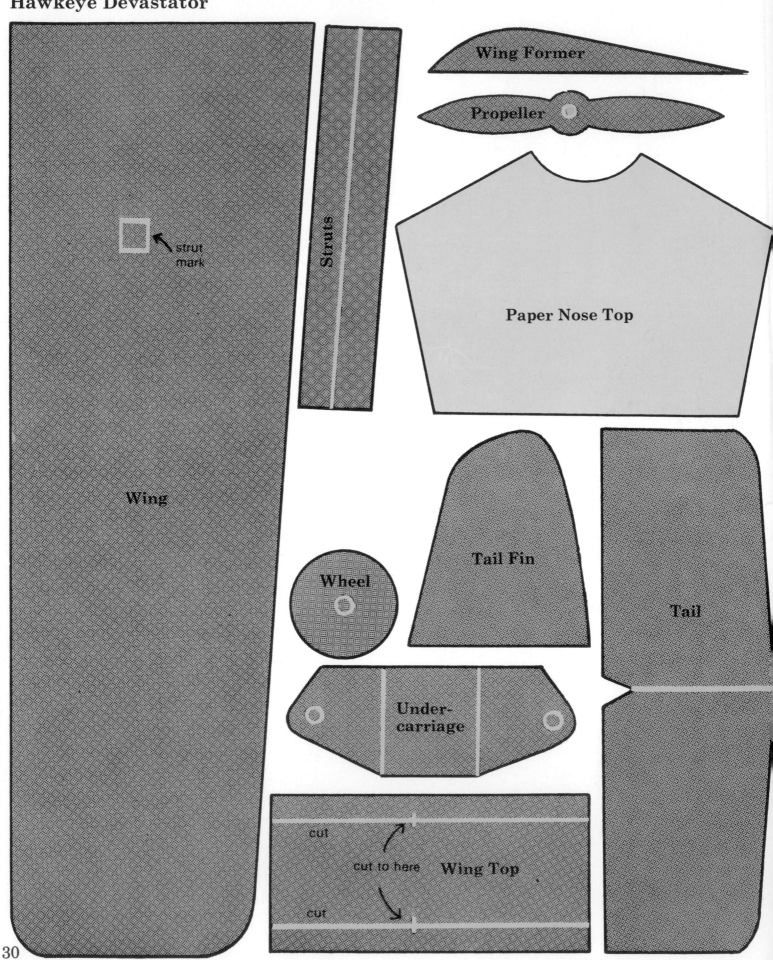

Wing Former

Propeller

Struts

Paper Nose Top

Wing

strut
mark

Wheel

Tail Fin

Tail

Under-
carriage

cut

cut to here

Wing Top

cut

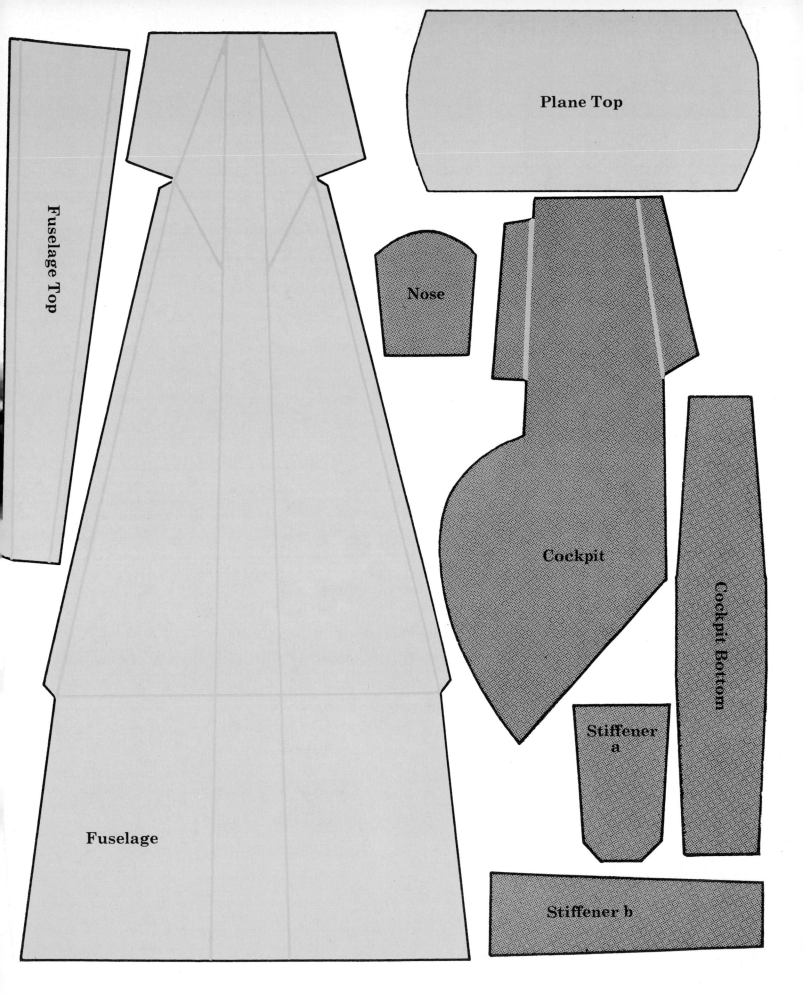

Fuselage Top

Plane Top

Nose

Cockpit

Cockpit Bottom

Fuselage

Stiffener a

Stiffener b

Going Further

Microfilm Model

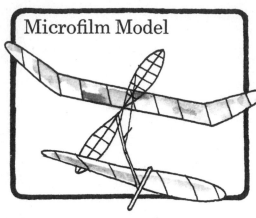

This model is made of balsa wood covered with very thin microfilm, It flies indoors and only weighs one gramme.

Simple Gliders for you to Make

If you want to try making a plane from balsa wood, you should start with a simple balsa glider which you can buy quite cheaply.

Where to Shop

If you look at the last pages of an aeromodelling magazine you will find a list of model shops. They are listed town by town so that you can go to the nearest one.

Finding out More

You should be able to find out more about model aeroplanes by writing to any of the following addresses:

Model Aeronautical Association of Australia, Hon. Sec. Gordon Burford, Witton Street, Flagstaff Hill 5179, South Australia.
Model Aeronautical Association of Canada, Box 9, Oakville, Ontario, Canada.
Model Aeronautics Council of Ireland, John McNally, Marieville, Bendermeer Park, Magazine Road, Cork.
Northern Ireland Association of Aeromodellers, Hon. Sec. Maurice Doyle, 28 Carlston Avenue, Holywood, Co. Down.
New Zealand Model Aeronautical Association, Hon. Sec. John Malkin, 51 Clyma Street, Upper Hutt.
Scottish Aeromodellers' Association, Hon. Sec. P. Malone, 105 Sighthill Loam, Edinburgh FH11 4NT.
South African Model Aeronautic Association, P.O. Box 4, Howard Place, Pinelands, Cape.
Society of Model Aeronautical Engineers, Dept MS, 116 Pall Mall, London SW1Y 5EB.

Books about Planes

How to Make and Fly Paper Aircraft	Captain Ralph S Barnaby	(Piccolo 1973)
Jet-Age Jamboree	Yasuaki Ninomiya	(Japan Publications Inc. 1968)
Aircraft	K. Munson	(MacDonald Visual Book 1971)
Aeromodeller Annuals		(Model & Allied Publications 1948)
Aeromodeller Pocket Data Book	P. G. F. Chinn	(Model & Allied Publications 1968)
Model Plane Building from A—Z	Flying Models Staff	(Carstens Publications U.S.A. 1969)
A Beginner's Guide to Building and Flying Model Aircraft	Robert Lopshire	(Harper & Row 1967)
Model Airplane Handbook	Howard McEntee	(Thomas Y Crowell U.S.A.)
Control-Line Manual	R. G. Moulton	(Model & Allied Publications 1973)
The World of Model Aircraft	Guy R Williams	(Andre Deutsch 1973)

Magazines about Planes

Aero	46, Porter Street, Prahan, Victoria 3181, Australia.
Aero Modeller	P.O. Box 35, Bridge St., Hemel Hempstead, Herts, England.
Airborne	P.O. Box 205, Blacktown 2148, Australia.
Free Flight News	11, Parkside Rd., Sunningdale, Ascot, Berks SL5 0NL, England.
Model Aeroplane Gazette	12, Slayleigh Ave., Sheffield, England.
NON News of the North	R. Magill, 1852 Great North Rd., Auckland 7, New Zealand.
Radio Modeller	64, Wellington Rd., Hampton Hill, Mddx. England.
Wings	113, Winchester House, Loveday St., Johannesburg, S. Africa.

The KnowHow Book of Puppets

Violet Philpott and Mary Jean McNeil

Illustrated by Malcolm English
Designed by John Jamieson
Photographs by Brian Marshall

With the help of Deva Cook and
Sally Chaplin (Educational Adviser)

Contents

About This Book

This is a book which tells you how to make lots of different kinds of puppets and how to work them properly when you have made them. You will find that the puppets at the beginning are easier to make than those at the end.

At the end of the book there is a puppet play. We have started it, leaving you to make up the rest of the story yourself.

The puppets are made from things you will probably be able to find at home. A lot of them are made with glue. When you buy glue, remember to buy strong, quick drying glue like Bostik 1 and UHU.

Boxes with a sign like this show you how to do things which you may need to know on other pages as well.

First published in 1975

Usborne Publishing Ltd
Usborne House, 83-85 Saffron Hill,
London EC1N 8RT

©Usborne Publishing Ltd 1989, 1975

Printed in Belgium.

Puppets for Beginners

You will need
a pair of gloves for each puppet
rubber bands and tissue paper
sticky labels
cloth scraps
scissors and strong glue
paints and crayons

Here are three little puppets which are very easy to make. Look at the boxes carefully and you should be able to make them very quickly. The finger mice are called finger puppets. You can make a whole family of mice on the finger tips of one glove. When you've made them, put them on. Put your other hand in front of your palm and make them move up and down behind it.

All the puppets on this page can be used in a puppet play. Have a look at the last two pages of this book and see the kind of thing they can do.

From now on, don't throw anything away. You may be able to make a puppet with it. The most surprising things can be turned into puppets.

Finger Mice

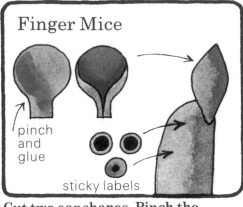

Cut two ear shapes. Pinch the bottoms with glue. Glue the ears to the fingertip tops. Put on sticky labels for their snouts and eyes. Colour them.

Rabbit

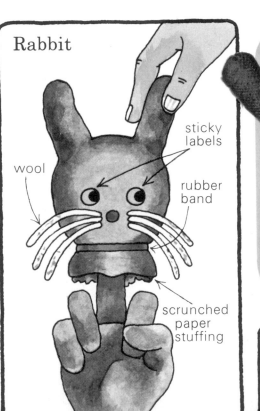

wool
sticky labels
rubber band
scrunched paper stuffing

Turn an old woollen glove inside out. Push the first and little fingers up. Stuff the head with tissue paper. Glue on wool whiskers and sticky label eyes and nose. Use a rubber band for the neck. Put your gloved middle finger into the head. Your thumb and other fingers are legs.

Finger Puppets

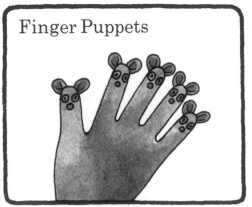

Always make finger puppets on the fingertips of whole gloves. It's much easier to put gloves on during a play than lots of tiny puppets.

Spider

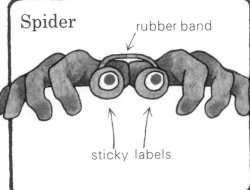

rubber band
sticky labels

Put on your gloves. Fix a rubber band around your thumbs. Put sticky labels on the thumbs of your gloves to make spiders' eyes. Now make him move.

The Earth Chief

You will need
a card flower pot
a paper cup
pipe cleaners and beads
2 squeezy bottle tops
sticky labels
scissors and strong glue
a cork bottle top
card and sticky tape
paints and crayons

The Earth Chief Monster puppet and his private army of Himlings are not very nice puppets to know. Their feelers wobble up and down. Look at the things they get up to on page 30

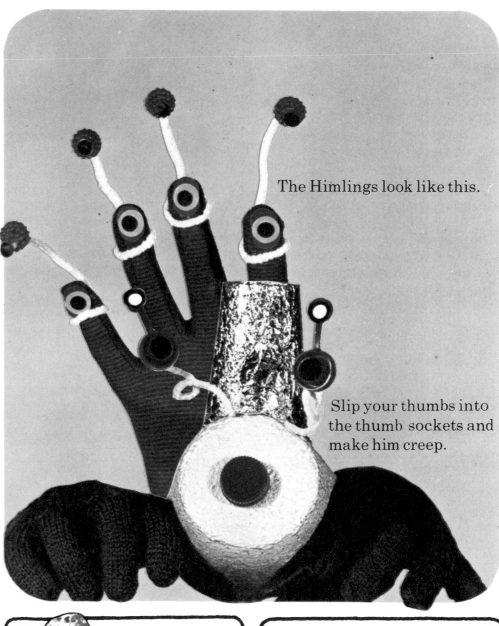

The Himlings look like this.

Slip your thumbs into the thumb sockets and make him creep.

1 Making the Earth Chief

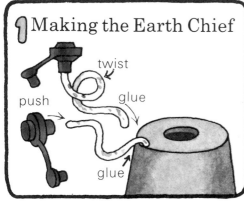

twist
push
glue
glue

Twist and curl two pipe cleaners. Push squeezy bottle tops over the ends. Glue the other ends to the top of a card flower pot.

2

glue
make hole
push cork in

Cut a half circle out of a paper cup. Glue it over the feelers on the front of the pot. Make a hole in the middle of the pot and push in a cork bottle top, so that it looks like this.

3

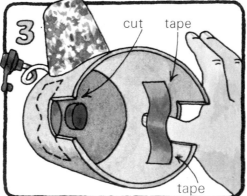

cut
tape
tape

Cut two bits off the sides of the pot for your thumbs. Tape two strips of card each side of the holes to make thumb sockets. Paint the Earth Chief now.

Making Himlings

wrap around
push bead over

Twist a pipe cleaner round a glove's finger tip. Bend it and push a bead over its top. Do this to each finger tip. Put sticky labels on for eyes.

Sock Animals and Creatures

You will need
a sock for each puppet
sticky labels for their eyes
For Funny Nose
a sponge for his nose
fur fabric for his hair
a scarf
For a Moose
rubber bands for his ears
scrunched paper to stuff his
    head
strong glue and scissors

Here are three little puppets
you can make from old socks.
Before you use glue have a good
look at the box under here.

Making Slithery Snake

sticky labels

Put a sock over your hand and arm.
Put sticky labels where you think
his eyes look best. Make him wave
up and down over a table.

Rearing Snake

Put your elbow on a table. Put your
arm up straight and bend your hand
over like this.

Look First, Glue Later

When you're sticking on eyes and
hair, just put a little bit of glue on,
see what it looks like, then add
more and glue it down properly.

1 Making a Moose

rubber band

Put your hand into a sock. Poke
two fingers up just after the heel.
Put rubber bands on them. Take
your fingers away and stuff the
rubber band ears with paper.

2

sticky labels

stuff scrunched paper

Stuff the rest of the sock in front
of his ears with crumpled paper.
Put sticky labels where you think
his eyes look best.

1 Making Funny Nose

Put a sock over your hand and arm.
Put your thumb in the heel so that
it pokes out under the foot of the
sock like this.

2

snip into shape

glue

glue

Push in the front of the sock to
make a hole. Cut a sponge into a
pear shape. Glue it into the hole.
Stick fur fabric on for his hair and
sticky labels for eyes.

Grinning Funny Nose

Move your thumb down and wiggle
it to and fro.

This is Slithery Snake

This is Moose

Funny Nose looks like this.

Thoughtful Funny Nose

Scrunch your hand into a ball and he looks very worried.

Old Lady Funny Nose

Put a scarf over Funny Nose's head and he turns into a very old lady.

Disguise your Voice

Make your mouth into a strange shape. Keep it like that and start to talk. You can't help sounding different when you talk.

Joey the Clown

You will need

a paper plate or card for his
   head
sponge for his nose
cloth for his dress
a ruler for his body
thick wool for his hair
a small strip of card
scissors and strong glue
sticky tape
paints and crayons

This little clown has a magic
neck. When you've made him,
hold his dress, push the ruler
up and his neck will grow
longer and longer.

This is Joey.

1 Making Joey the Clown

cut sponge

hole

push

wool

Cut out a sponge nose (page 12)
**Make a hole in the centre of a paper
plate or card circle, push the nose
in, draw the rest of his face and glue
on wool hair.**

2

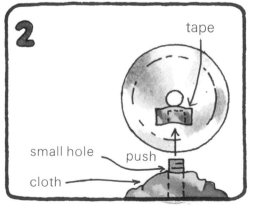

tape

small hole

push

cloth

Snip a hole just big enough to
slip the ruler through in the
middle of the cloth. Slip the
ruler through it and tape the
ruler to the back of his head.

Wandering Puppets

Puppets travelled all over the
world. Wandering puppet showmen
would carry their puppets from
country to country, town to town.

They would set up their booths, call
all the people to come and watch,
give a show and then move on to the
next town.

All about Punch and Judy

In some countries, like England, Punch has been bashing puppets on the head for centuries. In other countries, like Germany, he takes the side of law and order. But, whatever he is doing, nearly every country has its Punch. You can see him in France and Germany, in Italy where he came from and in Russia. If you want a Punch puppet, you will have to ask someone to buy you one, or you will have to make one. Punch is a glove puppet, so have a look at the pages on glove puppets in this book.

1 Punch and Judy Story

Punch dances around singing to himself. Judy comes on and asks him to look after the baby. But the baby won't stop crying, so he throws the baby away.

2

Judy wants to know where the baby has gone. The audience says he has thrown it out of the window. She gets a stick. He grabs it, throws her after the baby and rides off.

3

Punch falls off his horse and calls for a Doctor. He kicks the Doctor in the eye and the Doctor gets a stick. Punch grabs it and knocks the Doctor out of the way.

4

A policeman, an Officer and Jack Ketch, the Hangman, come on to arrest Punch for murder. After a fight they get the better of him and drag him off to jail.

5

Instead of Punch getting hung for three murders, he manages to get Jack Ketch to put his head into the noose, pulls the rope and hangs Jack Ketch instead.

6

On comes the Devil brandishing a stick. After chatting for a bit they have a great duel which Punch wins and he whirls the Devil around on top of his stick.

Swazzles

Punch and Judy men put a Swazzle into their mouths. They force their breath through the swazzle and their voices sound squeaky. This is how they get Punch's hooting voice.

Punch's Birthday Cake

In 1962 Punch and Judy men gave a huge birthday party for Punch to celebrate his 300th year in England. Snakes and dragons came out of his cake.

Boy and Girl Glove Puppets

You will need
2 bits of cloth twice as big as
your hand and forearm
an artificial sponge for her
a sock for him
cardboard for their necks
fur fabric
different material for her hair
old tights or cotton wool
needle and thread
scissors
paper and a pencil
a ruler
strong glue
sticky labels
paints and crayons

Making Bodies

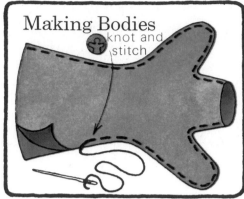

knot and stitch

Cut round it. Turn the cloth bits
the other way round and sew them
together with tiny stitches. Pull it
inside out. Now its inside's the
outside.

Making the Girl's Head

glue

snip hole

dab glue

Make a card tube which is thinner
at the top. Snip a hole in the sponge
large and deep enough for half the
tube. Glue the tube into the sponge
hole like this.

Making Bodies

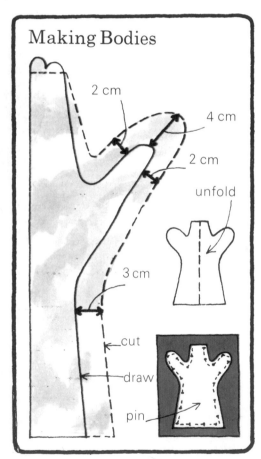

2 cm

4 cm

2 cm

unfold

3 cm

cut

draw

pin

Fold a long piece of paper and put
your second finger on the fold like
this. Draw round your hand and
forearm as far down as your elbow.
Measure and mark where shown
and join the marks up. Cut it out,
unfold it and pin to a double layer of
cloth as shown.

1 Making the Boy's Head

stuff sock loosely

Loosely stuff the foot of a sock
with old tights or cotton wool.
Make a card tube which is thinner
at the top for the neck.

2

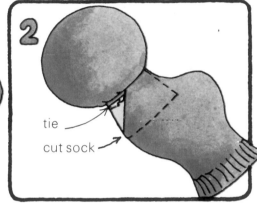

tie

cut sock

Use a piece of wool to hold the
stuffing and half the neck tube in
the sock. Then cut the sock off at the
heel like this.

Joining Heads and Bodies

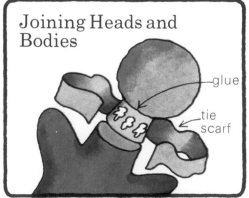

glue

tie scarf

Dab glue on to the inside top of the
body and the bottom of the neck
tube. Glue them both together. Tie
a strip of cloth round the neck to
make it neat.

Making his Hair

sticky labels

Stick fur fabric all over the back of
his head. Use sticky labels, buttons
or felt for his eyes and mouth.

This is what they look like.

Making her Hair

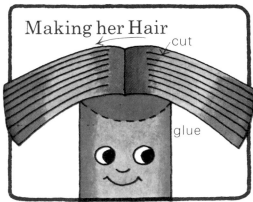

cut

glue

Cut a band of cloth into strips from both sides. Don't cut all the way through the centre. Glue it on to her head. Trim it if it's too long.

Making Knots and Stitching

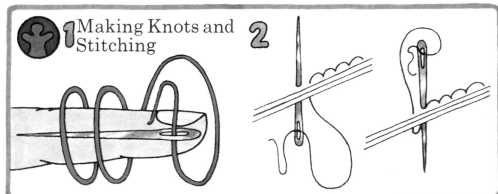

1 Twist the end of a thread twice round your finger. Push the needle under the loops you've made. Pull the thread through, ease the knot off your finger.

2 Hold the material. Push the needle up through it and then down where your last stitch ended. Keep on doing this. Make the stitches as small as you can.

Puppet Action

You will need
your puppets
a yoghurt pot
silver foil
string
scissors and glue
a bundle of small twigs
a larger twig, rod or pencil

Puppet Action is all about
giving your puppet life. Once
you know how to hold him
properly he will do the rest.
Just relax and think what kind
of character he is.

Don't keep the puppet's arms in
the air all the time. Put them
up when there's a good reason
for it – when your puppet is
afraid or surprised, for
instance. To make him go to
sleep turn his head away and let
his head rest on his arms. He
can't close his eyes so the only
way to show that he's asleep is
to hide his face.

Holding a Puppet

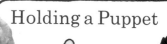

Put your middle fingers into the
puppet's neck. Your two end fingers
go in one arm. Your thumb goes in
the other. This is the proper way to
hold him.

Making a Bucket

Cover a yoghurt pot completely
with silver foil. Make two holes with
your scissors near the top for a
string handle. Tape it in.

Carrying Loads

To make a puppet carry something on his back, bend your middle fingers down and use your other fingers to hold the load behind his head like this.

Just Standing

Bend your thumb and outer fingers on to his chest. We don't stand around with our arms in the air all the time, so why should puppets?

Bowing

Your wrist is the puppet's waist. Bend your whole hand forward and he can bow.

Turning his Neck

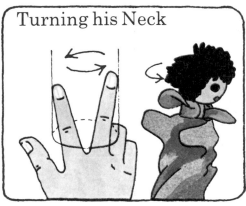

Push your two neck fingers hard against the edge of the neck tube. Keep them there. Move your fingers round and he turns his neck.

Making a Broom

Tie some small twigs to one end of a thicker twig or old pencil. Use cotton or thin string to do this.

Using Things

See how many things you can make your puppet do. Give him pens and pencils to play with.

Can you make him carry the bucket and sweep with the broom?

Faces and Hair

On this page there are lots of little tips on how to make different kinds of faces for your puppet. If you look at the boxes carefully you should be able to give your puppet any kind of face you like. You must remember that your friends will be watching from a distance, so always use bright colours. Don't worry about too much detail either. It won't show up from far away and it takes a long time to do. Can you think of any other odds and ends that would made good faces?

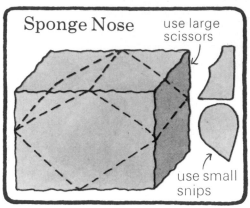

Sponge Nose

use large scissors

use small snips

Cut the nose shape with large sharp scissors. Then trim it with small scissors. Use small snips at a time. Try different nose shapes.

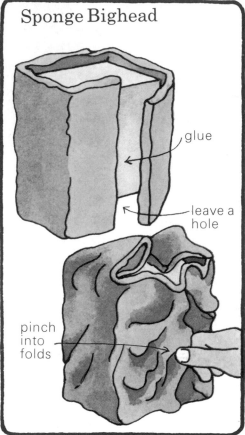

Sponge Bighead

glue

leave a hole

pinch into folds

Glue a sheet of sponge to an old box. Immediately slide, push and pinch the sponge to make folds of skin. The glue must still be wet. Even plastic containers will do. You can make really good wrinkles like this.

This is what a Sponge Bighead looks like

This witch has a pointed nose and fingers.

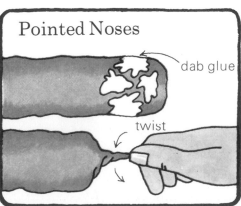

Pointed Noses

dab glue

twist

Dab the end of a sponge nose with a rubber solution glue. Pinch and twist it between your thumb and fingers to make it pointed. Make fingers too.

You can make this little pig by giving him a sponge face, nose and ears. His eyes are made from buttons.

1 Wool Hair

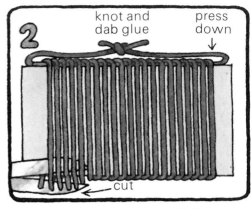

clip   dab glue   clip
wind

Paper clip some wool or tape along the top of a long piece of card. It must be twice as long as the card. Wind more wool round tightly. Dab glue on top.

2

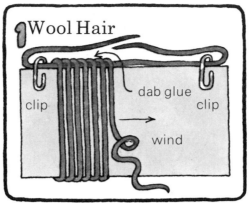

knot and dab glue   press down
cut

Knot the top strand. Cut all the way along the bottom. Dab glue along the top again and press down the knotted strand. This will be the puppet's parting.

3

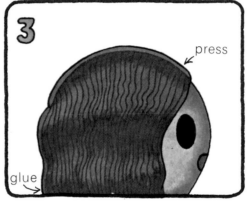

press
glue

Put glue over the back of the puppet's head. Take the wool hair off the card and press it on to the puppet like this.

Beards and Hair

scrunched paper
sticky labels
fur fabric

Scrunch up tissue paper and glue it to the puppet. Fur fabric makes a good beard as well.

Sticking on Hollow Noses

slice it level   glue in paper   glue to puppet

If you want a hollow bottle top nose and you want to stick it to something slippery, glue sponge or crumpled paper into it and trim any paper that sticks out.

Eyes

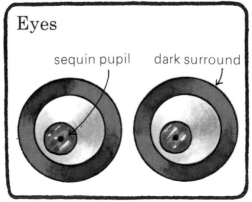

sequin pupil   dark surround

When you're making eyes, it's a good idea to draw a dark circle around them and to give them a pupil. This makes them show up well from far away.

Tips for Small Puppets

The lower down on a puppet's face that you stick its eyes and mouth, the younger it will look. Small puppets do not always need noses to make them look real.

Mouth Monsters

You will need
For a Cake Box Monster
a cake box and a thimble
2 bits of cloth wide enough to
    wrap a cake box in and as long
    as your arm
2 yoghurt pots for his eyes
paper to cover them
For an Egg Box Monster
2 egg boxes
an old woollen sleeve
2 bottle tops and sticky labels
scissors and glue

Cake Box Monster

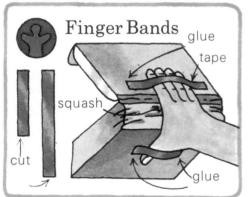

Finger Bands

Tape box hinge. Squash the back
of the box until you can hold it. Cut
two strips of card and glue the strip
ends to the box as shown to make
into finger bands.

1 Making the Cake Box Monster

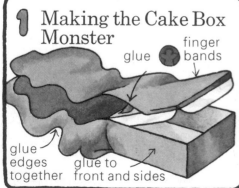

Make finger bands. Glue one bit of
cloth to the front and sides of the
box. Glue the other to the front and
sides of the lid. Glue the cloth edges
together.

2

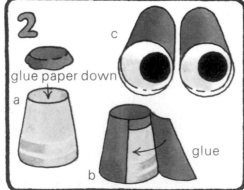

Put paper over the open ends of
two yoghurt pots. Glue it down over
the sides (a). Then cover the sides
with paper (b). Paint a blob on the
other ends (c).

3

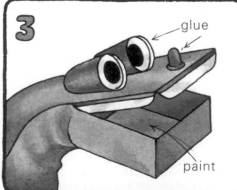

Glue the pots to the top of his head.
Stick a thimble to the front of his
head for his nose. Paint the inside
of his mouth.

Floating Monsters

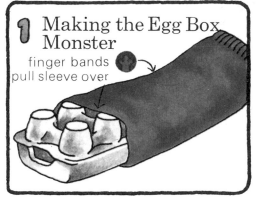
Sometimes there are puppet shows where the puppets and the people who work them are on the stage together. But you can't see the people because they're dressed in black and the background is black

too. All you see are bright and colourful puppets which look as if they're moving by magic. They just float in mid-air. It's called the Black Theatre.

Make finger bands (see opposite page). Shut the box and pull the sleeve of an old woollen jumper right over it until it is completely covered.

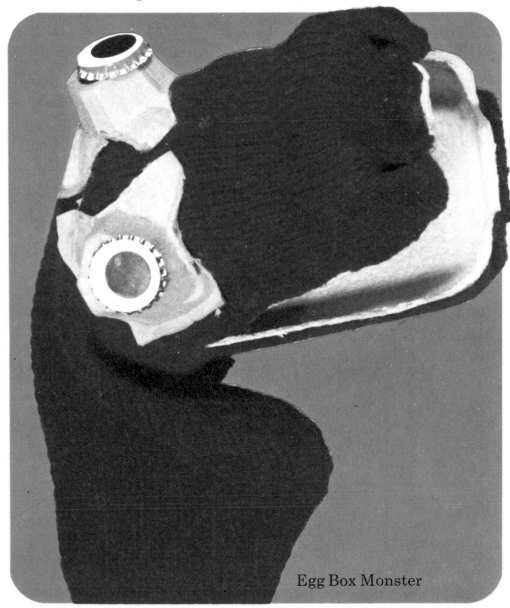

Egg Box Monster

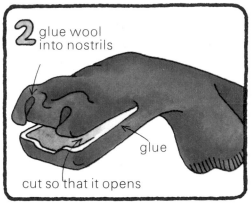

2 glue wool into nostrils

glue

cut so that it opens

Cut the wool along the sides of the egg box so that it opens. Glue the cut edges of the wool over the box's sides and front. Pinch and glue the nostrils like this.

3 glue

Cut two egg holders from another egg box and stick a bottle top to the top of each. Glue them to the top of his head and stick labels to the bottle tops for his eyes.

15

OddFrog and GooseBeak

You will need

For OddFrog

a paper plate or circle of card

some cloth twice as wide as the plate and as long as your arm

tissue paper and bottle tops

For GooseBeak

card at least 30 cm long and wide for his beak

an old shirt for his body

about 4 thin plastic bags

any old hat with a brim

cotton wool

sticky labels and buttons

scissors and strong glue

a needle and thread

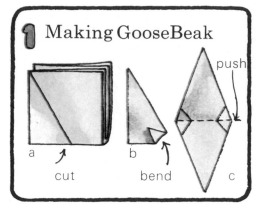

1 Making GooseBeak

Fold some card in four and cut a long triangle shape (a). Bend in the corners (b). Open the card out and push the corner bends inwards (c).

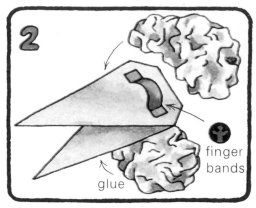

2

Make finger bands (page 14). Crunch thin plastic bags into balls. Glue them to the top and bottom of his beak like this.

Asking for Help

Let your puppet ask the audience for help. Hide something and let them see where you hide it. Then, get him to ask them where it is. Make him look in the wrong places.

1 Making OddFrog

Fold a paper plate in half. Bend the corners in (a). Open it. Make finger bands on the outside (page 14) and push the corners in (b). Stick a paper tongue inside (c).

2

fold over and glue

Put the mouth in the material. Fold edges over with an overlap and glue them together. Cut round the curve of the plate and glue the material to its top.

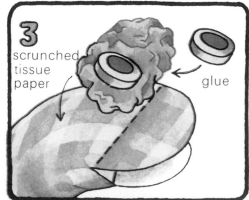

3

scrunched tissue paper

glue

Scrunch tissue paper as shown. Glue it to the top of his head. Make his eyes from bottle tops and sticky labels. Glue them to the top of his head like this.

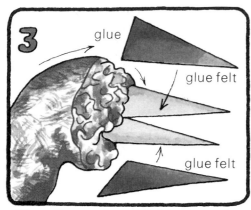

3

glue

glue felt

glue felt

Slip a sleeve of an old shirt over the plastic balls and glue. Glue felt over the outsides of his beak. Paint the inside as shown.

4

tuck in and sew

cut

stuff

Cut off half the other sleeve of the old shirt. Sew the sleeve's frayed edges together. Stuff it with cotton wool to make a tail. Tuck in the collar and sew it.

5

glue on cotton wool

cut

cut

Cut two holes for your arms on each side of an old hat. Cover its top and sides, but not the armholes, with cotton wool. Glue the cotton wool on as shown.

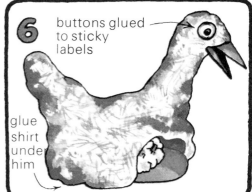

6

buttons glued to sticky labels

glue shirt under him

Pull the shirt down over the hat so that the two hat holes are under the sleeve openings. Glue the shirt's edge under the brim. Stick on eyes as shown.

This is OddFrog

This is GooseBeak

Working GooseBeak

Cross your arms and keeping them crossed, put one arm through one hole up to his head, put the other arm through the other hole up to his tail. Lift your arms up.

Stick Puppet Animals

You will need
1.5 metres of rope
tissue paper for their bodies
a needle, thread and strong glue
scissors and sticky tape
For the Cat
a flat sponge for the cat's head
rubber bands for his whiskers
2 beads, card and safety pins
thin sponge for his ears and nose
For the Wolf
card 30 cm × 60 cm for his head
a rubber glove finger tip for
   his nose
scrunched paper to stuff his jaw
4 straight sticks 1 metre long

This is the Wolf

1 The Cat's Head

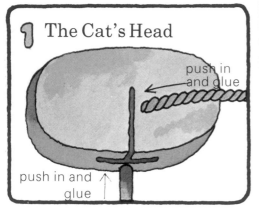

push in
and glue

push in and
glue

Make two slits in a flat sponge as
shown. Glue the insides of the slits
and stick a straight stick and a
piece of long thick rope in as shown.

2

slot in and glue

glue

Glue rubber band whiskers on to his
face. Stick on sponge nose over
them. Make two slots for his ears
and stick two thin sponge ears into
them.

The Cat's Wobbly Eyes

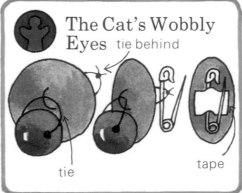

tie behind

tie

tape

Loosely thread a bead. Tie some
more thread through a piece of card
and hang the beaded thread from
this. Tape a safety pin on to the
back like this.

Making the Cat's Body

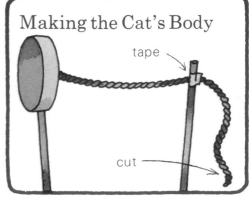

tape

cut

Decide how long you want the body
to be. Tape the rope firmly to a
second straight stick. Cut it off at
the end for its tail.

This is the Cat

1 Making the Wolf

cut

Fold some card. Draw a wolf's head shape, a pointed ear and a jaw. Cut them out where shown. Unfold them and cut the ear only along the fold.

2

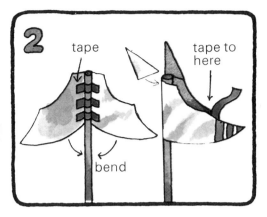

tape

tape to here

bend

Tape the back of the head shape to a straight stick. Bend the sides of the shape round. Tape half the shape together. Tape ears to the back of the head.

3

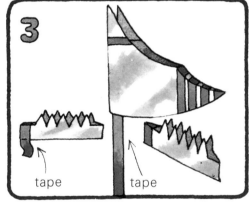

tape

tape

Tape the two ends of the jaw. Stuff it with a little bit of scrunched paper. Tape it firmly to the straight stick just under the head shape.

Making the Wolf's Body

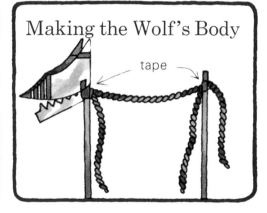

tape

Make his body like the cat's. Cut two bits of rope and tape one to each straight stick as shown. Cover the ropes and sticks with tissue paper like the cat.

Papering the Cat's Body

wrap and glue

Scrunch and twist long strips of tissue paper. Wind the paper strips round the rope leaving a bit of rope free near the head for the neck. Glue the strips to the rope.

Sitting Wolf

Tie a string loop to the bottom of his rope back paw. Hold the back stick and put one of the fingers from the same hand through the loop. Move them up as shown.

Prancing Wolf

push rope up

Tie some rope to his rope front paw. Hold the front stick and push the rope you've just tied on up and out with the fingers of the same hand.

19

Captain Plunder Bones

You will need
a medium sized cereal packet
a cardboard tube from a kitchen roll
a thick stick about 60 cm long
an old T-shirt
2 straight sticks 1 metre long
2 old stockings
card for ears, eye patch and hands
a scarf and old curtain ring
fur fabric or wood shavings
a cork for his nose
scissors and string
strong glue and sticky tape

Captain Plunder Bones is a three stick puppet. Make him nice and big. Make the hand sticks first.

Working Captain Plunder Bones

Captain Plunder Bones is better if two of you work him. One the main stick, the other the hand sticks. Stand facing each other.

Speaking and Moving

The person working the main stick speaks for the puppet. He also turns the puppet's head and moves the puppet from one part of the stage to another.

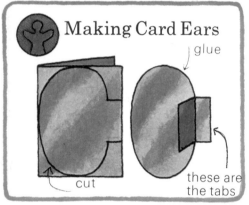

Making Card Ears

glue

cut

these are the tabs

Fold some card. Cut out two ear shapes with tabs as shown. Bend the tabs out. Glue the two ear shapes together, but not the tabs. Glue tabs on to the puppet.

This is what Captain Plunder Bones looks like.

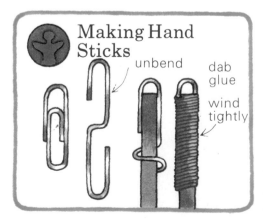

Making Hand Sticks

unbend

dab glue

wind tightly

Hand sticks move the puppet's hands. Unbend a paper clip. Put it on top of a straight stick and glue and wind string round them both very tightly.

Reaching Up

Hold the puppet up high. You must always remember to make the hand sticks long enough for him to reach right above his head without your arms being seen.

Holding the Hand Sticks

If you move his hand sticks behind his back, his arms will look as if they're broken. Keep them in front of him or at his sides.

Working him Alone

If you tilt the main stick forward so that his arms fall in front of him, you won't have to hold the hand sticks. You can work them one at a time then.

1 Making Captain Plunder Bones

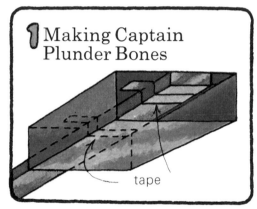

tape

Cut off the bottom of the cereal packet. Tape a thick stick firmly down the centre of the inside of the packet. This is the main stick.

2

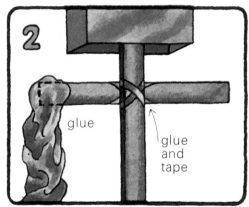

glue

glue and tape

Glue and tape a kitchen roll tube behind the thick stick as shown. Glue an old stocking to each end of the tube. These will be his arms.

3

cover or paint

Cover or paint the cereal packet with one colour. Dress him in an old T-shirt. Always remember to dress stick puppets before you put their hands on.

4

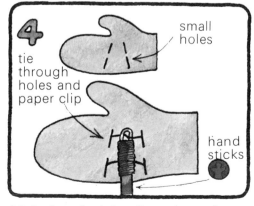

small holes

tie through holes and paper clip

hand sticks

Make hand sticks. Cut two card hand shapes. Make four little holes as shown. Put a hand stick between them and tie string through them and the paper clip.

5

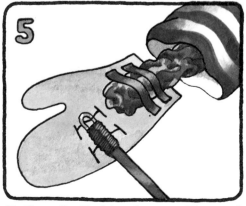

Roll up the T-shirt sleeves. Glue and tape the ends of the stockings to the hands like this. Roll the sleeves down again to hide the joins.

6

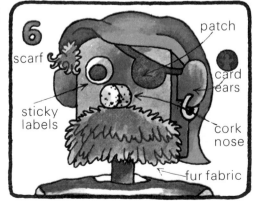

patch

scarf

card ears

sticky labels

cork nose

fur fabric

Glue on a cork nose, card ears and a fur fabric or wood shaving beard. Give him a scarf, a black patch and an ear ring made from an old curtain ring like this.

21

Giants

You will need
For the Giant
a big cardboard box for his head
a thick stick 1 metre long
a cardboard kitchen tube
old stockings for hair
3 paper cups
1 metre of cloth for his clothes
For a Megaphone
thick card 40 cm × 20 cm
For a Treasure Trove
an old box
silver foil and coloured paper
a needle and thread
scissors and sticky tape
strong glue

Cut the bottom off the box. Tape the thick stick up the inside of it and paint the box. Glue on a paper cup nose and eyes and card ears (page 20).

Glue scrunched up old stockings on to his head and under his nose and make little cuts in them. Slip a cardboard tube up the stick, wind tape under it to keep it up.

Working the Giant

You need a helper to work the Giant. Get the helper to put his thumbs into the thumb loops. It'll look as if they're the Giant's hands.

Twisting his Neck

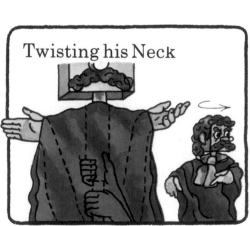

If you twist the stick with one hand and hold the tube without twisting it with the other, he will turn his head without moving his body.

This is the Giant

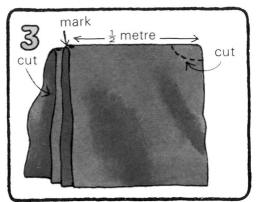

Fold the material you're going to dress him in into four. Cut a hole as shown. Make two marks on the top end of each fold with a felt pen as shown.

Thread a needle and make two thread loops. Put them on the felt pen marks. You work the Giant's hands by putting your own thumbs through the loops.

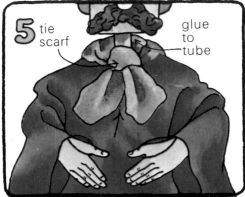

Push the stick and tube down through the hole in the middle of the material. Glue the material round the hole to the tube and tie a scarf round it.

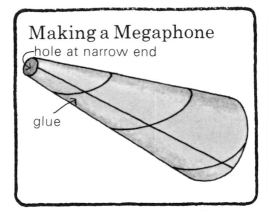

Making a Megaphone

Glue the card for the megaphone into a cone shape. Leave a hole at its narrowest end. Giants have deep, booming voices. Speak down it. Your voice will be loud.

Wellington Boot Giant

If you want to show Giant's feet in a play, put some big boots on to the stage. Other puppets will be much smaller and your Giant will look very big.

Treasure Trove

Paint an old box. Fill it with scrunched up silver foil and coloured paper.

Be a Giant

There's no reason why you should not dress up as a giant yourself and act with the puppets in the play.

Giant Puppets

An American called Remo Bufano made giant puppets. One clown he made was 11 metres high. Some of his puppets were worked from a platform 13 metres up.

Backstage KnowHow

Stage Front

moon on a stick

this is called the playboard

The play has just started. Look at the front of the stage. That's what the audience sees. Look at the picture just below it. This is what it looks like back stage just before a play starts. The puppets are hanging ready and everything that is needed is in its own special place. When you put plays on, you must try to have everything ready like this too.

You will need
4 thick poles 2.5 metres long
4 chairs and some rope
2 sheets and drawing pins

Back Stage

lights

lights

place for sound effects

plank across chairs for putting things

place for props

puppet hook

puppets hanging from rope

Stage Plan

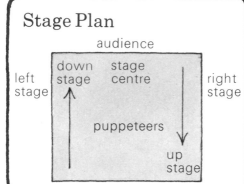

audience

left stage

down stage

stage centre

right stage

puppeteers

up stage

Real puppeteers often use written stage plans on bits of paper to help them remember where puppets are supposed to be.

Puppet Hook and Line

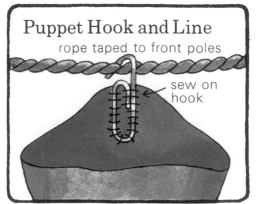

rope taped to front poles

sew on hook

It's a good idea to make a hook from an unbent paper clip sewn to the hem of a puppet's dress. Then you can hook him to a rope taped across the front poles.

Making a Stage for Hand and Stick Puppets

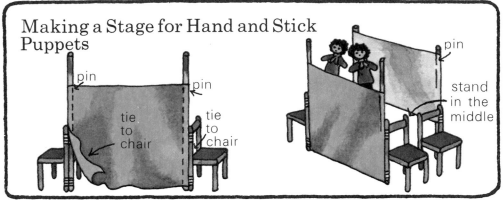

For String Puppets

Tie four poles to four chairs as shown. Stretch the top of an old sheet across the two front poles just above your head. Pin it to the poles as shown.

Pin the top of another sheet to the top of one of the back poles. Stretch it across to the other back pole and pin it to the top of that one. Stand in the middle.

Turn the whole stage round so that the lower sheet is now at the back. Lower this sheet and re-pin it so that you can work a string puppet over it easily.

Scenery

Lights

If you have scenery, don't make it too complicated or people won't be able to see your puppets clearly in a play.

For hand and stick puppets, put your lights each side of the front of the stage pointing towards it. Look at it on the audience side to make sure it's

bright enough. For string puppets put the lights between the sheets pointing on to the puppets. Don't put your stage in front of a window.

Hold them High

Even Higher

Talking to Each Other

Always hold the puppets up high on stage. If you work them so that their hem lines are about $2\frac{1}{2}$ cm below the playboard they will be just the right height.

The further away from the front of the stage you hold your puppet, the higher up you're going to have to hold him.

If your puppets are having a conversation with each other, you must make them face each other. Hold one on each hand.

KnowHow Special Effects

Sound Effects are very exciting because they sound so real. But don't use them too much. Real puppeteers only use them when they're needed to make a play more alive.

Anything a puppet uses in a play is called a prop. Don't worry if a puppet drops a prop over the front, make him ask one of the audience for it back.

You will need
card 60 cm × 30 cm for the boat
a straight stick 60cm long
scissors and strong glue

Horses' Hooves

Knock first one side and then the other of two empty yoghurt pots on to the top of a table. Clop one pot after the other and get faster and faster.

Bird Song

Wet a cork and rub it over the side of a glass bottle. Then you can get a chirpy bird song effect.

Crackle of Flames

Crumple cellophane paper into a ball and it'll sound as if there is a large fire nearby.

Thunder

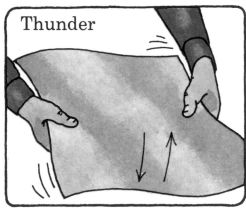

Take a large sheet of card or tin and shake it violently backwards and forwards. It'll sound as if there's a terrible storm outside.

Rain

Sprinkle uncooked rice on to a tin or baking tray. It'll sound as if rain is beating against the window.

Eerie Lights

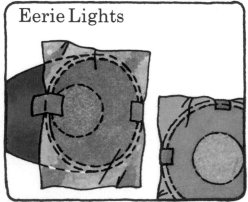

Cover the front of your stage lights with coloured cellophane. Make sure that it doesn't touch the bulb. The whole of your stage set will change colour.

Marching Feet

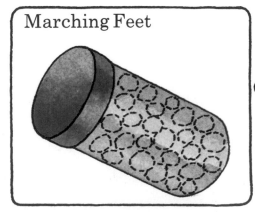

Fill a tin with stones. Put the lid back on and shake it up and down. If you put a lot of stones in, it'll sound as if there's a really big army approaching.

Handling Things

Puppets can use almost anything they like as a prop. But make sure they're not too slippery. Be sure they're big enough, too, or they won't be seen.

Making a Boat

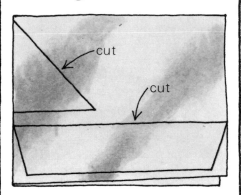

Fold a piece of card. Draw a boat shape and sail. Cut them out. Do not cut the sail along the fold.

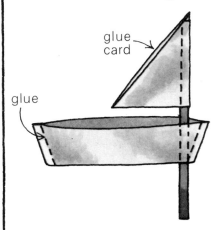

Glue a stick to the end of one of the boat shapes. Lay the other one on top and glue them together at both ends. Glue the sail around the top of the stick.

A Puppet Going for a Boat Ride

Hand Puppet Props

When your puppet has to put a prop down during a play, try holding it for him like this.

Stick Puppet Props

Stick puppet props have to go on sticks as well. You will have to be careful to move both together at the same speed.

Going on a Boat Ride

Hold the boat stick in one hand and push the puppet up through the middle of the boat. Then move them both along.

The Serpent and the Phantom Wafter

These are string puppets. Sometimes people call them marionettes. They are worked from above.

You will need
For the Phantom Wafter
1 metre of almost transparent cloth for his body
2 hangers
For the Serpent
about 30 paper cups
about 30 buttons or beads
a thin hollow plastic ball
2 bottle tops and sticky labels
2 hangers
a needle and some strong thread
strong glue and sticky tape

1 Making the Phantom Wafter

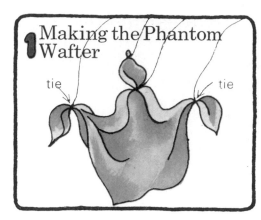

Cut four threads 1 m long. Tie three to three of the cloth's corners. Tie the fourth thread to the cloth 6 cm underneath the centre thread as shown.

2

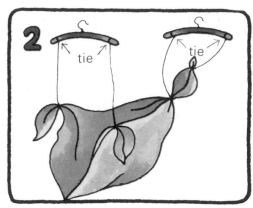

Tie the ends of the two side threads to a hanger as shown. Tie the two middle threads to another hanger as shown. When you're not using it hang it up.

1 Making the Serpent

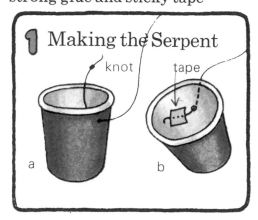

Thread a needle with 1 m of thread. Knot it. Push the needle through a side of a paper cup (a). Tape the knot (b). Do same again with another cup and thread.

2

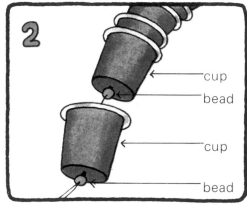

Thread a needle with 6 m of double thread. Knot. Push it through the bottom of another cup from the inside. Tape. Push it through a bead, cup, bead, cup 30 times.

3

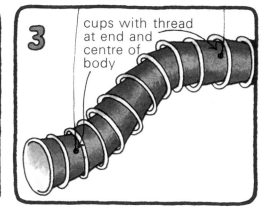

Thread the two cups with thread in them to the line of cups and beads. Put one near the end and one in the middle. See that their strings are on the same side.

4

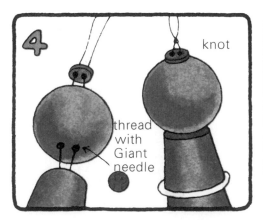

Make two holes on opposite sides of the ball. Make a Giant needle. Thread the two strands through the holes and on through a button or bead. Tie knot as shown.

5

Glue on paper cup eyes decorated with bottle tops and sticky labels. Make a big bow and glue it between the eyes as shown.

6

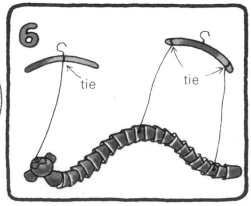

Tie the thread that comes out of the head to the middle of one hanger. Tie the two threads in the cups to different ends of another hanger as shown.

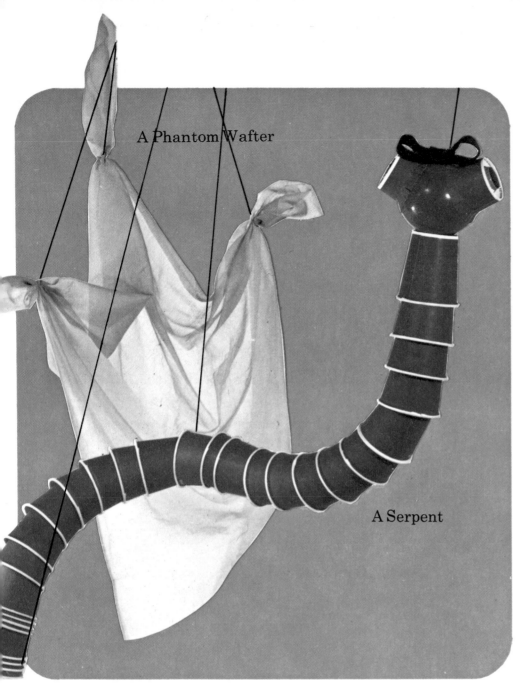

A Phantom Wafter

A Serpent

1 Making a Serpent Slither

head hanger

cup on its open end

Hold the hangers in different hands. Tip the body hanger down and make the end cup stand on its open end as shown.

2

Gently lower the rest of his cup body on to the bottom cup. Bring the head hanger towards the body hanger. Move the hanger up and he comes out again.

Battling Puppets

There are puppeteers in Sicily who use puppets dressed in shining armour like these puppets here. The puppet plays show the adventures of medieval knights.

They fight great duels and battles. Even St. George appears with a dragon belching fire and smoke.

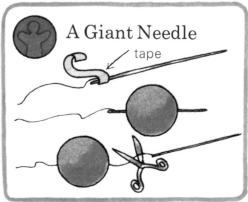

A Giant Needle

tape

If you want to pass a thread through something that is wider than the length of your needle, tape the thread to a piece of wire, push through and cut.

The Invasion of the Earth Chief

Scene 1

The Girl is crying because she's lost her goose. Her brother, the Boy says he'll go and look for it.

Scene 2

He looks for it everywhere. At last he finds it. It was hiding. 'I can't even hide in peace. Don't you know that they're coming?' says Goose. 'Who are?' asks the Boy, very puzzled. They hear a noise.

Scene 3

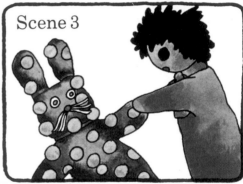

Rabbit comes on crying for help. 'I'm covered with the Himlings' sticky stuff. If I don't get it off I'll die,' says Rabbit. 'My sister will wash it off,' says the Boy.

Scene 4

They wash him. 'The Earth Chief is wandering around. He has a strange ship and an army of Himlings. He sniffs the air with his wobbly feelers,' says Rabbit.

Scene 5

Suddenly they hear an eerie sniffing sound. 'Hide. It must be the Earth Chief' says Rabbit. They hide behind a rock just as the Earth Chief comes on with his Himling Army behind him.

Scene 6

'What's happening?' cries the Boy. 'I'm being moved towards it. I can't stop. Help.' The Earth Chief sends out his thought waves and the Boy is dragged nearer and nearer the Earth Chief's ship . . . .
(*Finish the story your way.*)

If you have never put on a puppet play before, you might like to base your first play on the one we have here. We give you only half the story. It stops at an exciting point but the programme on the right gives you a hint for Scene 7. You have to make up the ending. Do not let too many people work the puppets at the same time, or you will bump into each other. You must have room to turn round in. Have the puppets and props ready (page 24). Decide who is going to work each puppet. Decide what is going to happen in each scene and what each puppet is going to say. Write it down. When you have done a few plays you will not have to write everything down.

This is a story about what happens to a little girl, her brother, Goose and Rabbit when the Earth Chief Monster invades the Earth with his army of Himlings and captures the Boy with his powerful thought waves. Make up the end of the story of how the little girl and her friends outwit the Monster. You will find the Earth Chief and his Himling Army on page 3, Little Girl and Boy on page 8, Rabbit on page 2, Goose on page 16.

Making a Programme

Fold some paper into a programme for the audience. Make a list of scenes on one side. Put a list of characters and who works them on the other, like this one here.

Having a Good Wash

The person working the Girl can blow bubbles with her free hand from underneath the stage front. Someone else has the Boy on one hand and Rabbit on the other.

Advancing and Sniffing

The person who worked the Girl now works the Earth Chief with both hands. You'll need another helper to work the Himlings.

Sticky Stuff

Cover Rabbit with coloured sticky labels. The Boy will be able to pull them off easily and then stick them to something else under the stage.

Index

Going Further

If you have enjoyed finding out about puppets, here are some more books you might like to read.

Art of the Puppet by Bill Baird (Plays, Inc. USA)

Bandicoot and His Friends by Violet Philpott (Dent)

Caspar and His Friends by H. Baumann (Dent)

Dictionary of Puppetry by A. R. Philpott (Macdonald)

Eight Plays for Hand Puppets by A. R. Philpott (Garnet Miller)

Exploring Puppetry by Stuart and Pat Robinson (Mills and Boon)

Let's Look at Puppets by A. R. Philpott (Muller)

Modern Puppetry by A. R. Philpott (Michael Joseph)

Let's Make Puppets by A. R. Philpott (Evans)

Punch and Judy by P. Fraser (Batsford)

Punch and Judy by G. Speaight (Studio Vista)

St George and the Dragon by D. John (Penguin)

Finding out More

You should be able to find out more about puppets by writing to any one of the following addresses:

Puppet Centre,
Battersea Town Hall,
Community Arts Centre,
Lavender Hill,
London, S.W.11.

Mrs. E. Murray,
UNIMA,
'Moonahwarra',
Lawson Road,
Springwood 2777,
Australia.

Puppetry Guild,
Mrs. Clarke,
28, Baal Street,
Palmyra 6157,
West Australia.

Lilian Herzberg,
19, Saldhausen Avenue,
Claremont,
Cape Town,
South Africa.

Action Toys

Heather Amery

Illustrated by Neil Ross
Designed by David Armitage and Patricia Lee

Contributors: Andrew Calder, Diane Dorgan
Educational Adviser: Frank Blackwell

Contents

About Action Toys

This book is about lots of toys, machines, models and games to make and work. For most of them, all you need are paper, card, plastic bottles, pots and straws. You can probably find most of them at home. The measurements we have given are only a guide. You can make the things any size you like.

When you make the models and toys, you can cover them with coloured paper as you go along, or paint them when finished.
Remember to use quick-drying strong glue or gum, except for sticking expanded polystyrene tiles. For them you need a rubber-solution glue.

First published in 1975
by Usborne Publishing Ltd
Usborne House
83-85 Saffron Hill, London EC1N 8RT

©Usborne Publishing Ltd 1989, 1975

The name Usborne and the device are
Trade Marks of Usborne Publishing Ltd.

Creeping Moon Bug

Wind up the motor on this Moon Bug. Put the Bug down and watch it creep along very slowly.

You will need
an empty cotton reel
a used matchstick
a strong rubber band
a candle
a stick, about 10 cm long
a sheet of thick paper
thick cardboard
corrugated cardboard
thin, bendy wire
a table knife
a pencil and scissors

1 Cotton Reel Motor

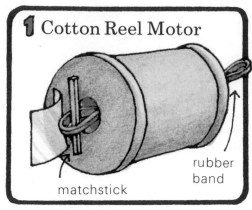

Push the rubber band through the cotton reel. Push a short bit of matchstick through the loop at one end. Stick the matchstick down with a bit of tape.

2

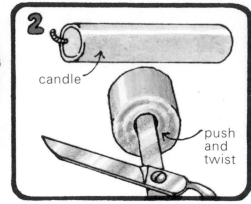

Slice a ring, about 1 cm wide, off the end of a candle with a table knife. Make a hole through it with one blade of the scissors.

3

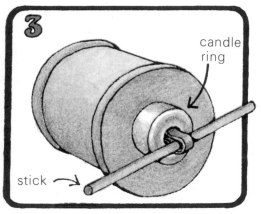

Push the free end of the rubber band through the candle ring. Then put the stick through the loop.

1 Moon Bug

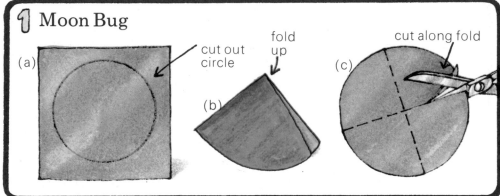

Draw a circle on thick paper (a). Cut it out. Fold the circle in half and then in half again (b). Unfold the paper and cut along one crease to the middle (c).

2

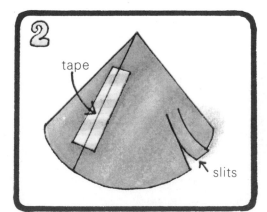

Curl the paper round to make a cone. Stick the edges together with tape. Cut two slits in the cone to make a flap.

3

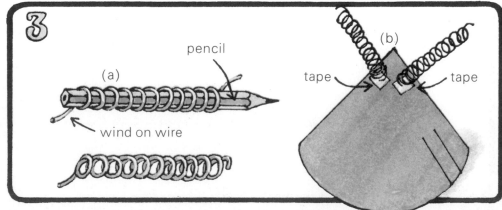

To make the antennae, wind a piece of bendy wire round a pencil (a). Slide it off. Curl up a second piece and stick them on the paper cone with tape (b).

Wind up the cotton reel motor. Put the cone of the Moon Bug over it, with one end of the stick poking out through the flap.

1 Climbing Bug

draw round

cardboard

Put a cotton reel down on a piece of thick cardboard. Draw round it. Draw a second circle.

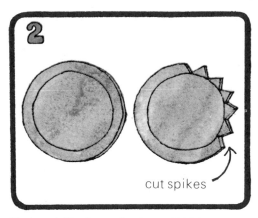

2

cut spikes

Cut out the two circles a bit bigger than the drawn lines. Cut out little bits all round both circles, like this.

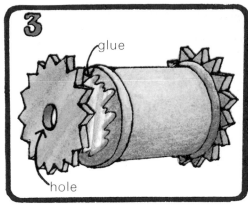

3

glue

hole

Glue a circle to each end of the cotton reel. Leave it to dry before making it into a Moon Bug.

4

Cut a long strip of corrugated cardboard about 5 cm wide. Make it into a steep road by putting things under it. Put the Bug at the bottom and let it climb.

Winding Up

wind round

Wind up the cotton reel by turning the stick round and round lots of times. Put the reel down. Put the cone over it with one end of the stick poking through the flap.

3

Rollers and Rockers

Jumping Bean

Make this Jumping Bean and stand it at the top of a gentle slope. Let it go and watch it jump and roll.

You will need
a ping pong ball
a piece of thick paper, about
    10 cm long and 5 cm wide
a marble
scissors
sticky tape

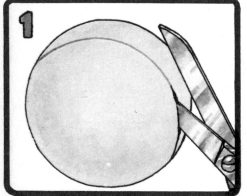

1 Push one blade of the scissors into the ping pong ball on the join line. Cut all the way round on the line.

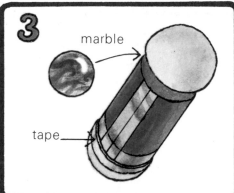

2 Roll the paper into a tube to fit just inside one half of the ping pong ball. Stick the tube with tape (a). Stick the tube to one half of the ball with tape (b).

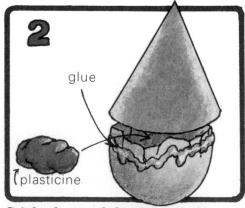

3 Put the marble in the tube. Stick the other half of the ball on the end of the tube with tape.

Rocking Egghead

Knock and push this Egghead in any way you like but he will always stand upright again.

You will need
a clean, dry eggshell with the
    top taken off
a lump of plasticine
a sheet of paper
a pencil
glue
paints
scissors

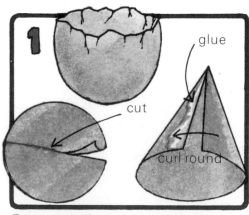

1 Draw a circle on a piece of paper, using a saucer as a guide. Cut out the circle and fold it in half. Cut along the fold. Roll one half into a cone and glue the edges.

2 Stick a lump of plasticine in the bottom of the eggshell. Glue the cone to the top of the shell. Paint a funny face on it.

Floppy Hound Dog

Push the rubber bands hard to make the Dog flop about.

You will need
a strong plastic carton
2 strong rubber bands
a piece of kitchen foil rolled
    into a small ball
a drinking straw
4 pieces of very strong thread,
    each about 20 cm long
a big needle
a piece of thin cardboard,
    about 4 cm long and 4 cm wide
7 small buttons
sticky tape and scissors

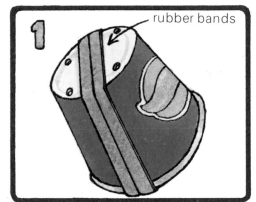

Put two rubber bands round the plastic carton. Poke four holes in the bottom of the carton, near the edges, with a needle.

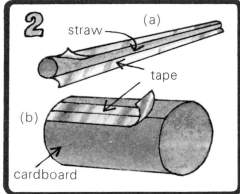

Roll the straw tightly in sticky tape (a). Cut it into 12 pieces, all the same length. Roll up the piece of cardboard into a tube. Stick it with tape (b).

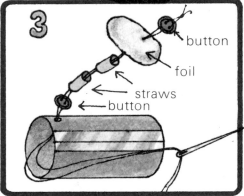

Knot two threads together. Thread the ends through a small button, the foil ball, two straw bits, another small button, and then the cardboard tube, like this.

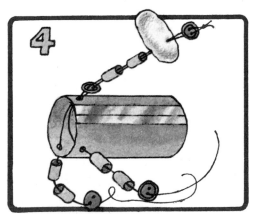

Pull one thread out of the needle eye. Push the other one through the other side of the tube, two straws and a button. Do the same with the other thread.

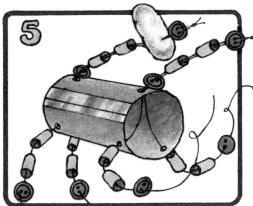

With two more threads, do the same at the other end of the tube to make the tail and the back legs, like this.

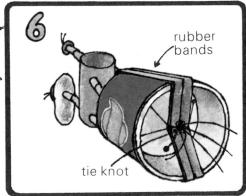

Push a thread through each hole in the bottom of the carton. Pull two threads down on each side of the rubber bands. Tie all the threads together very tightly.

Noisy Toys

Twirling Tweeter

Hold the end of the string and twirl the Tweeter round and round your head.

You will need
a very small plastic pot or tube with a lid
a piece of string, about 1 metre long
a used matchstick
sticky tape and scissors

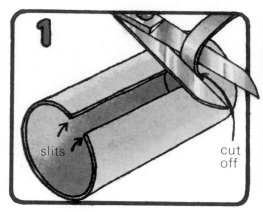

1

Take the lid off the plastic pot or tube. Cut two slits down one side, about ½ cm apart. Bend back the flap and cut it off.

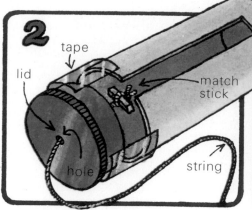

2

Make a hole in the lid. Push one end of a piece of string through and tie it round a matchstick. Put the lid on the pot and stick it down with tape.

Wailing Whirler

Hold the stick and swing the Whirler round and round it. Make sure the string is on the rosin. The faster the Whirler goes, the louder it will wail.

You will need
a thin stick or a pencil
a piece of nylon string or fishing line, about 30 cm long
a lump of rosin (this is sold in music shops)
a plastic carton or yoghurt pot
a used matchstick
glue and scissors

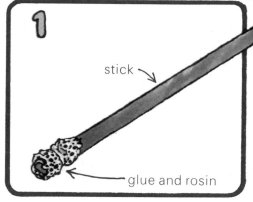

1

Break a small piece of rosin into bits by banging it with the handle of the scissors. Put glue on one end of the stick and dip it in the bits of rosin. Leave to dry.

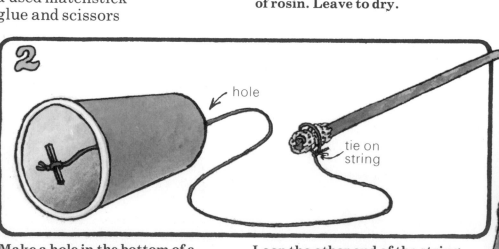

2

Make a hole in the bottom of a plastic carton. Push one end of the string through and tie a matchstick to the end, like this.

Loop the other end of the string loosely round the rosin on the end of the stick. Tie a knot.

Hanger Clanger

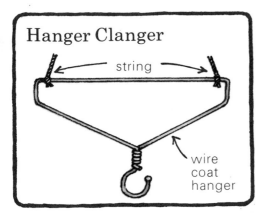

Tie the two pieces of string to a wire coat hanger, like this. Hold the other ends of the string in your ears. Bang the hanger against something and listen.

Roaring Ruler

Thread a piece of string through the hole in the end of a ruler or a thin, flat piece of wood. Tie a knot. Spin the ruler round your head to make a roaring noise.

Singing Bottle

Dip a cork in water and rub it on the side of a glass bottle. Try rubbing it gently and then hard to make bird singing noises.

Clucking Hen

Hold the carton in one hand. Hold the string very tightly between your fingers and thumb of the other hand and jerk them down the string.

You will need
2 plastic cartons or yoghurt pots
a piece of string, about 20 cm
    long
a used matchstick
a lump of rosin
quick-drying glue
scissors

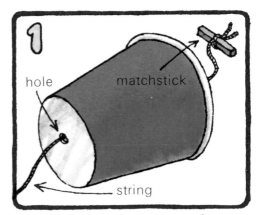

Make a hole in the bottom of a plastic carton. Push a piece of nylon thread through the hole. Tie it round a matchstick.

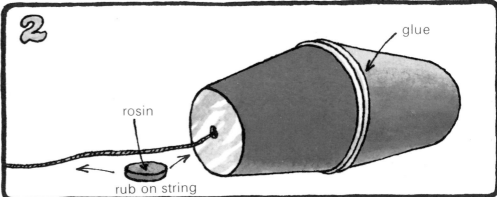

Glue a second carton to the first one, like this. Rub the string up and down on a piece of rosin.

When you have used the clucker a few times, rub on more rosin. Try making cluckers with smaller or larger plastic cartons to make different clucking noises.

Titan Traction Engine

You will need

a strong cardboard box, about 27 cm long, 9 cm wide, 9 cm deep
thick cardboard
corrugated cardboard
2 small boxes, each about 12 cm long and 4 cm wide
a small, open cardboard box
5 cotton reels and 3 pencils
a cardboard tube, about 10 cm long
6 thin sticks or garden canes
a small polystyrene tray
1 egg holder cut from an egg box
sandpaper
scissors, glue, sticky tape, string, a saucer, a yoghurt pot

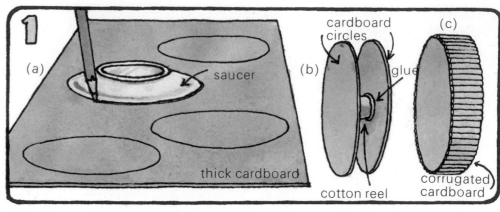

Draw four circles on cardboard, using a saucer as a guide (a). Cut them out. Glue one circle to each end of a cotton reel (b). Glue the other two circles to a second reel.

Glue a strip of corrugated cardboard round the edges of two of the cardboard circles, like this (c). Do the same to the other two cardboard circles.

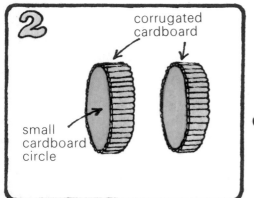

Make the front wheels in the same way as the back ones, but much smaller. The cardboard circles should be about the same size as the top of a small yoghurt pot.

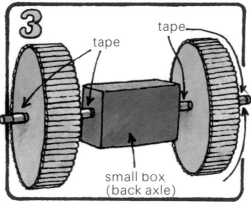

Push a thin stick, about 28 cm long, through the middle of a small box. Push one back wheel on to each end of the stick. Wrap sticky tape round the stick each side of both wheels.

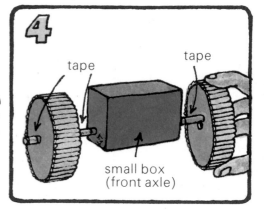

Push another stick through another small box, about 1 cm from the base. Push one front wheel on to each end of the stick. Wrap sticky tape round the stick each side of the wheels.

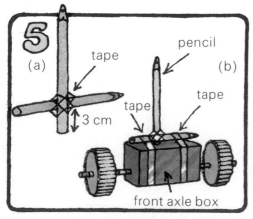

Tape two pencils together (a). Push the upright pencil into the front axle box, like this. Tape the other pencil firmly to the axle box (b).

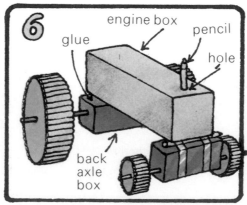

Glue the back axle box underneath one end of a strong cardboard box. Push the upright pencil on the front axle box through a hole at the other end of the box.

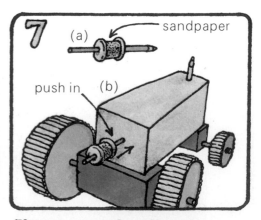

Glue corrugated cardboard or sandpaper round the middle of a cotton reel. Push a pencil through the reel (a). Push the pencil point into the back of the engine box (b).

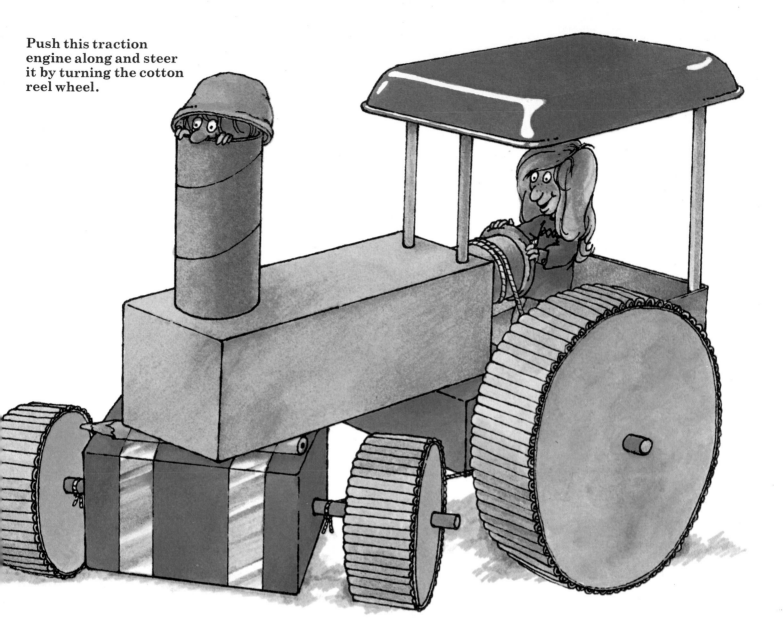

Push this traction
engine along and steer
it by turning the cotton
reel wheel.

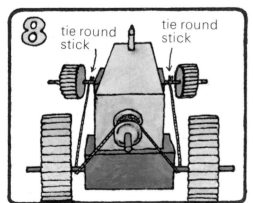

8

tie round
stick

tie round
stick

Wrap a piece of string round the
reel, like this. Tie one end to one
side of the front axle. Pull the
other end tightly and tie it to the
other side of the axle.

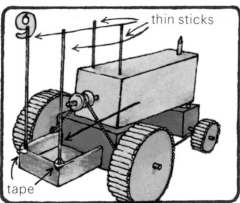

9

thin sticks

tape

Glue the open box to the back axle
box, like this. Tape two sticks,
about 26 cm long, to two corners.
Push two sticks, about 15 cm long,
into the engine box, as shown.

10

tray

egg holder

tube

glue

Put a polystyrene tray on top of the
four sticks, like this. Glue a
cardboard tube over the pencil at
the front of the engine box. Put
the egg holder on top of it.

9

Delta-Wing Jet

You will need
an expanded polystyrene ceiling
    tile, 30 cm square
glue for sticking material, such
    as Copydex
a small lump of plasticine
a strip of cardboard, about
    10 cm long and 5 cm wide
3 long, big-headed pins
a big sheet of paper
a strong rubber band
a long cardboard box
a ruler and a ball-point pen
scissors and paints

Launch your jet and see how far and
how fast you can make it fly. Or
make two jets and have indoor or
outdoor races.

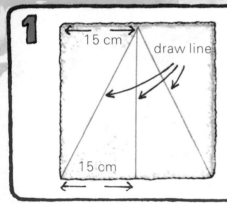

Measure 15 cm along the top and
bottom of the tile and make marks.
Draw a line between the two marks.
Draw lines from the top mark to the
two bottom corners (a).

Carefully cut along the two lines
from the top to the corners with
scissors (b). Be careful not to break
the cut-off pieces.

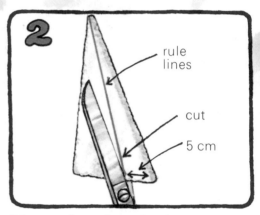

Measure 5 cm along the short edge of
one cut-off piece. Draw a line from the
mark to the point. Cut along the drawn
line. Throw away the small cut-off
piece.

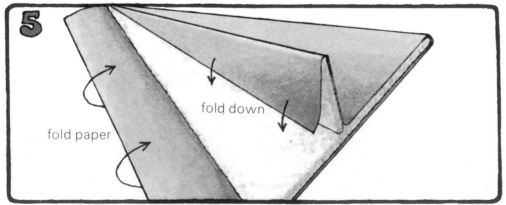

Put the jet down on a large sheet of
paper. Fold the paper round the
wings very neatly. Press it up the
fin and glue the edges of the paper
together.

Trim the edges of the paper on the
fin. When the glue is dry, paint the
paper in different colours.

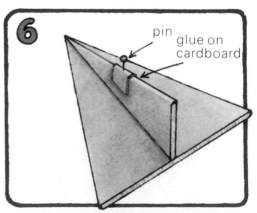

Fold the strip of cardboard in half.
Glue it to the fin, about half-way
along. Push a big-headed pin into
the middle of the cardboard strip,
like this.

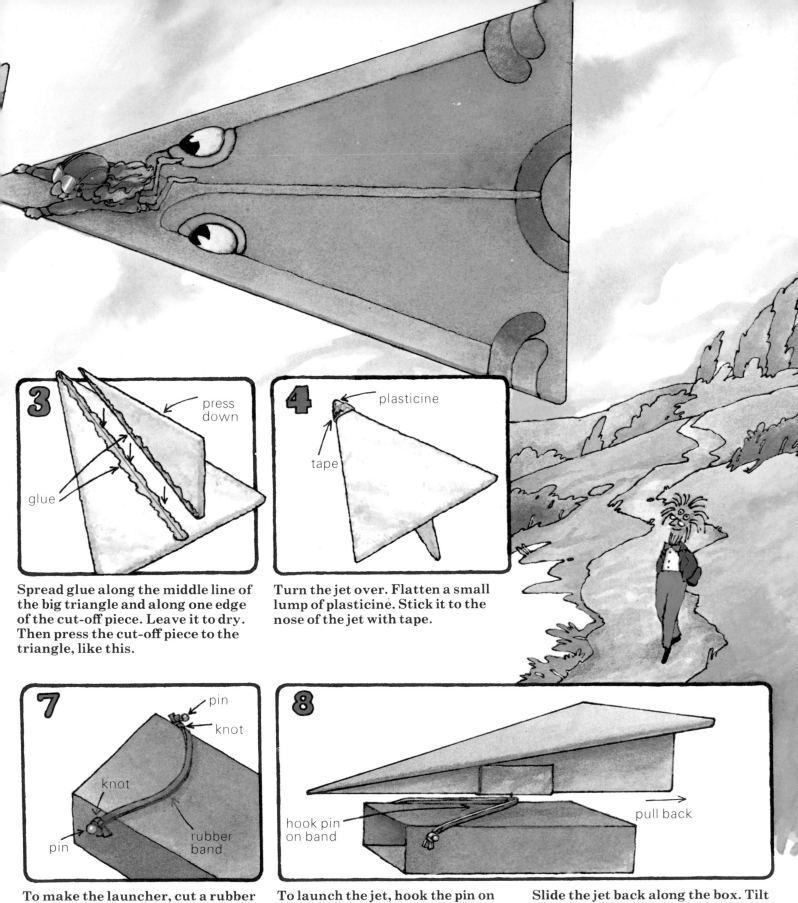

3
press down

glue

Spread glue along the middle line of the big triangle and along one edge of the cut-off piece. Leave it to dry. Then press the cut-off piece to the triangle, like this.

4
plasticine

tape

Turn the jet over. Flatten a small lump of plasticine. Stick it to the nose of the jet with tape.

7
pin

knot

knot

pin

rubber band

To make the launcher, cut a rubber band in half. Push a big-headed pin into each side of a long cardboard box. Tie the ends of the band to the big-headed pins.

8
pull back

hook pin on band

To launch the jet, hook the pin on the jet fin on to the band on the launcher. Hold the jet fin and pull it gently backwards.

Slide the jet back along the box. Tilt the box slightly upwards. Point the jet and let it go.

11

Dizzy, the Dashing Dragon

Pull up the curtain ring on the Dragon's head and let it go to make him rush along.

You will need
a piece of cardboard, about 12 cm
　　long and 12 cm wide
a lump of modelling clay
a rubber band
a plastic drinking straw
a piece of nylon thread or very
　　thin string, about 70 cm long
a small curtain ring
a big hairpin
a piece of thin paper, about
　　12 cm wide and 60 cm long
sticky tape and glue
scissors

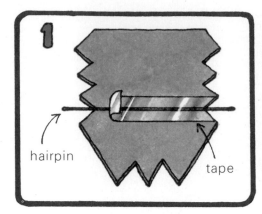

1 Cut a head shape out of cardboard, like this. Straighten a hairpin. Stick the pin with tape across the head, quite close to one end.

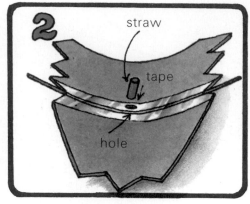

2 Make a hole in the middle of the head, just behind the hairpin. Push a short piece of straw into the hole. Glue it in place. Bend the head into a curved shape.

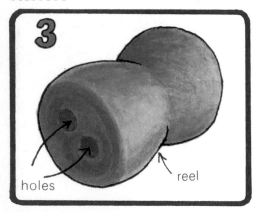

3 Make a reel, about 4 cm long and 3 cm across, out of modelling clay in this shape. Make two holes right through it, like this.

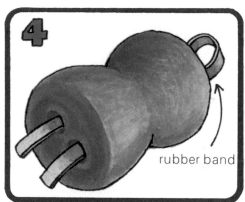

4 Cut a rubber band. Push the ends through the two holes in the clay reel, like this. Leave the reel until it is dry.

5 Knot the ends of the rubber band. Tie one end of the nylon thread on to the reel. Wind all the thread on to the reel. Push the free end through the straw.

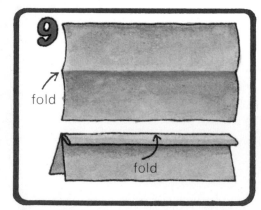

9 To make the dragon's body, fold the long piece of paper in half (a). Fold over the folded edge to make a flap about 1 cm wide (b).

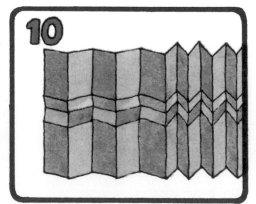

10 Open out the paper. Make folds, about 2 cm wide, all along it, like this. Turn the paper over and crease all the folds the other way.

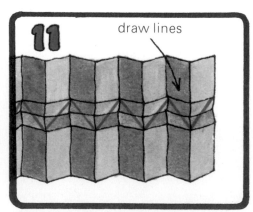

11 Open the paper again. Draw zig-zag lines from the top fold line to the bottom fold line, like this.

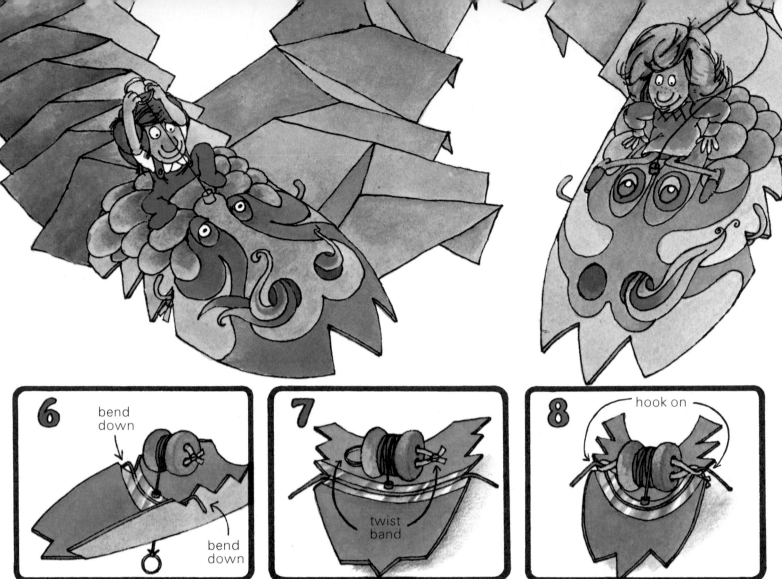

6 bend down · bend down

Tie one end of the thread to a curtain ring on top of the head. Bend the ends of the hairpin down.

7 twist band

Turn the reel round and round to wind the thread very tight. Give one twist to each end of the rubber band.

8 hook on

Hook each end of the rubber band on to the ends of the hairpin. Bend the head again to make sure the reel will not rub on it.

12

Fold the paper along all the drawn lines. Pinch together all the drawn lines and pleat the paper with your fingers, like this.

13 tape

Stick one end of the paper body to the edge of the cardboard head, like this. Paint the dragon's head with lots of different colours.

To make a longer tail, fold up a second strip of thin paper in the same way as the first one. Glue it to the end of the first strip.

Two-Stage Saturn Rocket

You will need
a long cardboard tube
2 short cardboard tubes
3 paper clips
2 rubber bands
a piece of string, about as long
    as the long tube
a piece of very thin cloth,
    about 20 cm long and 20 cm
    wide
4 pieces of cotton thread, each
    about 25 cm long
a small curtain ring
thick and thin cardboard
sticky tape and glue
scissors and a pencil

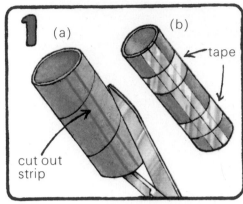

Slide a short cardboard tube into the long one. If it is too big, cut out a strip (a). Hold the cut edges together and stick them with tape to make a smaller tube (b).

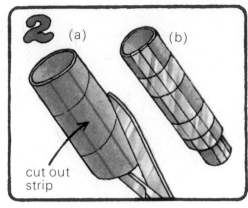

Cut a wider strip out of a second short tube (a). Stick the edges together with tape. Slide it inside the first tube (b).

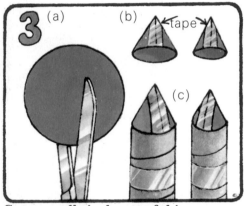

Cut a small circle out of thin cardboard. Cut it in half (a). Curl both halves into cones and stick with tape (b). Glue one cone to the top of each tube (c).

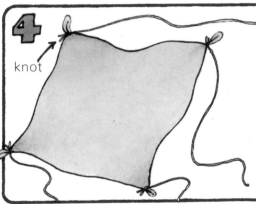

To make a drogue parachute, tie a piece of cotton thread tightly to each corner of the piece of cloth.

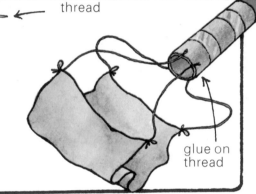

Glue the ends of the four pieces of thread to the end of the small rocket, like this. Make sure the threads are not twisted together.

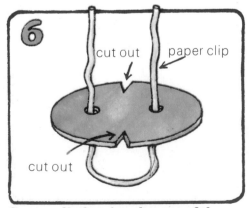

Cut two little triangles out of the edge of the cardboard circle. Straighten a paper clip. Push the ends through the holes in the circle, like this.

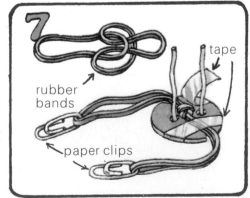

Loop two rubber bands together (a). Put them on the circle over the cut-out triangles (b). Stick them down with tape. Hook a paper clip on to the end of each band.

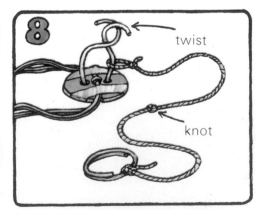

Twist the ends of the paper clip together and bend back. Tie the string on to the paper clip. Make a knot in the middle. Tie the curtain ring on the other end.

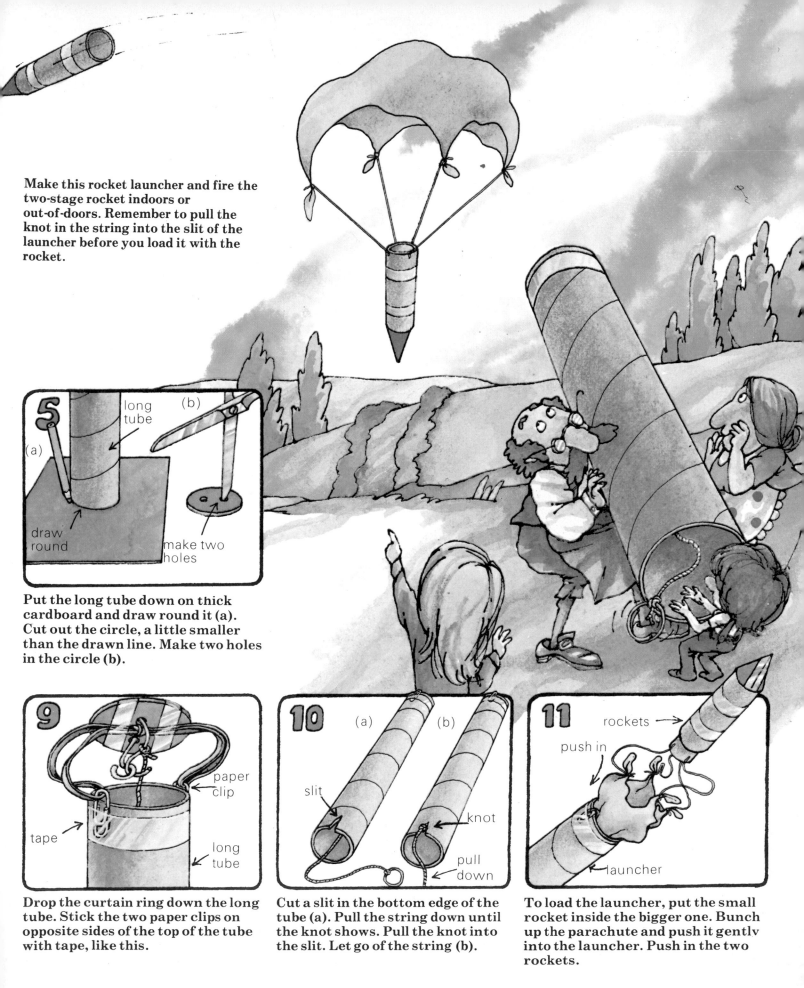

Make this rocket launcher and fire the two-stage rocket indoors or out-of-doors. Remember to pull the knot in the string into the slit of the launcher before you load it with the rocket.

5
(a) (b)
long tube
draw round
make two holes

Put the long tube down on thick cardboard and draw round it (a). Cut out the circle, a little smaller than the drawn line. Make two holes in the circle (b).

9
paper clip
tape
long tube

Drop the curtain ring down the long tube. Stick the two paper clips on opposite sides of the top of the tube with tape, like this.

10
(a) (b)
slit
knot
pull down

Cut a slit in the bottom edge of the tube (a). Pull the string down until the knot shows. Pull the knot into the slit. Let go of the string (b).

11
rockets
push in
launcher

To load the launcher, put the small rocket inside the bigger one. Bunch up the parachute and push it gently into the launcher. Push in the two rockets.

High-Wire Walker

Tie a very long piece of string across a room. Put the Walker on it. Push the plasticine to make it swing and move the Walker.

You will need
a matchbox
4 plastic drinking straws
a sheet of paper
a piece of thin cardboard
a piece of string, about 60 cm
    long
a long big-headed pin
plasticine
sticky tape and glue
scissors

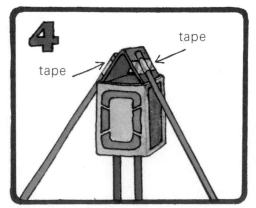

Cut a straw in half and then in half again. Push the tray half out of the matchbox. Stick two pieces of straw to the tray with tape to make legs. Push in the tray.

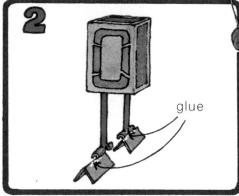

Cut two little slits in the end of each leg. Bend back the ends. Fold two small pieces of cardboard in half. Glue one to the end of each leg to make feet.

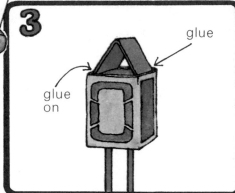

Cut a strip of cardboard about twice as long as the top of the matchbox. Fold it in half. Glue the ends to the top of the matchbox, like this.

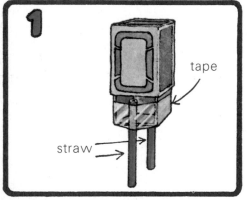

Stick a straw on each side of the folded cardboard with tape, like this, to make arms.

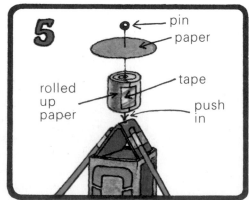

Roll up a thin strip of paper to make a head. Stick it with tape. Cut out a paper circle. Push the pin through it and into the head. Pin it to the top of the body.

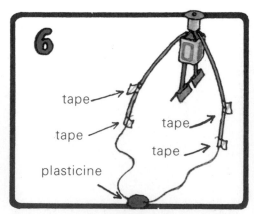

Cut a straw in half. Stick one half to each arm with tape. Stick the ends of the string on to the straws with tape. Put a lump of plasticine in the middle of the string.

Trick Cyclist

Balance the Cyclist on a very long piece of string. Tilt the string downwards to make the wheel roll round.

You will need
a piece of cardboard, about
   30 cm long and 15 cm wide
a cardboard tube
a drinking straw
a hairpin
a sheet of paper
plasticine
a pencil
glue and scissors

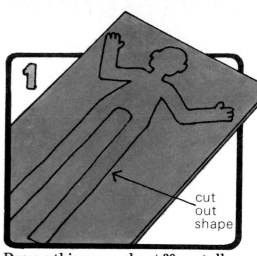

Draw a thin man, about 30 cm tall, on cardboard. Make the legs about twice as long as the body. Cut out the shape, with a wide space between the legs, like this.

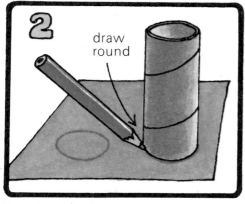

Put the end of a cardboard tube on some cardboard and draw two circles. Cut out the circles, about 1 cm wider than the lines.

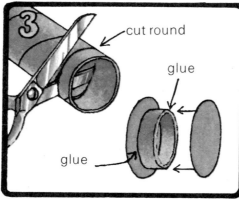

Cut a band, about 1 cm wide, off the end of the tube (a). Glue a circle on each side of the band to make a wheel (b).

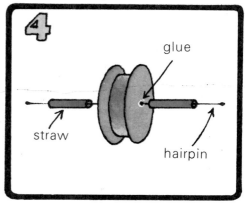

Straighten a hairpin and push it through the middle of the wheel. Glue it to the wheel. Push a short bit of straw on the hairpin on each side of the wheel.

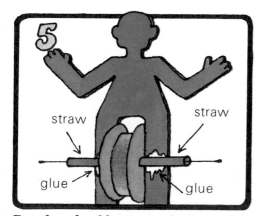

Put the wheel between the legs of the cardboard man, with a gap at the top. Make sure the wheel turns easily. Glue the two bits of straw to the legs, like this.

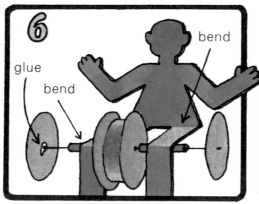

Bend the man's legs round the straw and bend him again at the top of his legs. Cut out two small paper circles. Glue one to each end of the hairpin.

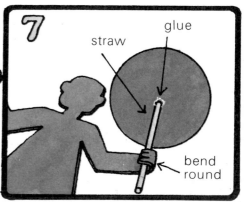

Cut out a paper circle. Glue it to the end of a bit of straw. Glue the other end to the man's hand. Glue a small lump of plasticine to the ends of the man's legs.

Fire-Fighting Truck

You will need

a shoe box, or an oblong
   cardboard box
a small cardboard box
4 empty cotton reels
very thin string
3 rubber bands
3 strips of thick cardboard, each
   about 30 cm long and 6 cm wide
2 paper fasteners
2 used matchsticks
3 pencils or thin sticks
a ball-point pen, without the
   ink tube, and a balloon
a plastic carton
scissors and glue

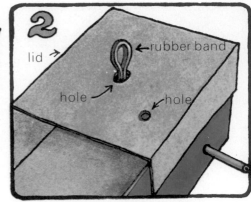

Cut four square holes in the shoe box bottom. Make two holes in each side. Push two pencils through one side. Slide two cotton reels on to each pencil and push out the sides.

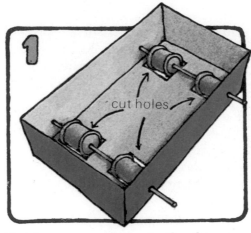

Cut the box lid in half. Make a hole in the middle of one half. Push a rubber band end through and slide on a matchstick underneath. Make a second hole. Put on the lid.

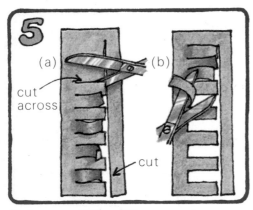

Cut up one side of the second cardboard strip. Then cut across (a). Cut out every other piece (b) to make a ladder. Cut a second ladder in the same way.

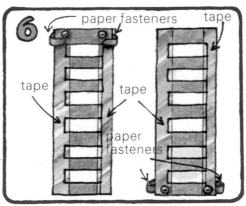

Put sticky tape down the sides of each ladder. Push two paper fasteners through the top of one ladder and the bottom of the other. Bend over the ends, like this.

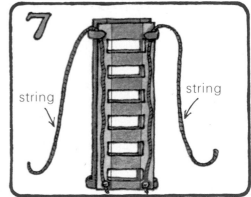

Cut two strings, each twice as long as the ladders. Put the two ladders together, like this. Tie a string to each bottom fastener and loop it over the top ones.

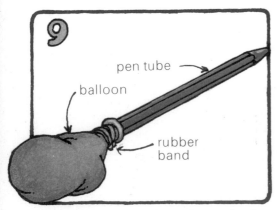

Push the pen tube into the neck of the balloon. Wind a rubber band round the balloon neck several times to make it very tight.

To fill the balloon, put the pen tube up a water tap. Turn on the tap. When the balloon is about as big as an orange, put the pen top on very quickly.

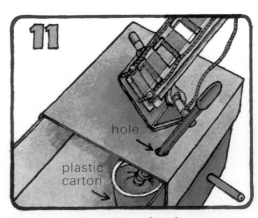

Put the balloon in a plastic carton to catch the drips of water. Push the pen tube through the hole in the box lid from the inside.

18

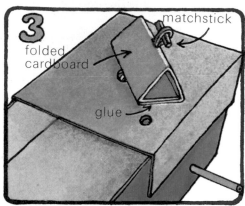

3 Fold a strip of cardboard up to make a triangle, like this. Make a hole in one flat side and one fold. Push the band through. Slide a matchstick through loop of the band.

matchstick
folded cardboard
glue

Put a pencil through the cardboard triangle. Loop a rubber band over one end of the pencil. Twist it in the middle and hook it over the other end of the pencil.

pencil
rubber band

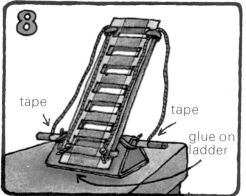

8 Glue the underneath ladder to the triangle on the box lid. Wind the end of each string round the pencil and stick it with tape.

tape
tape
glue on ladder

Push the fire engine to a pretend fire. Twist the pencil to wind up the ladder and take off the pen top to squirt the water.

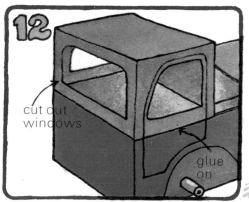

12 To make a cab, cut out the sides of a small box for the windscreen and side windows. Glue the box to the front of the fire truck.

cut out windows
glue on

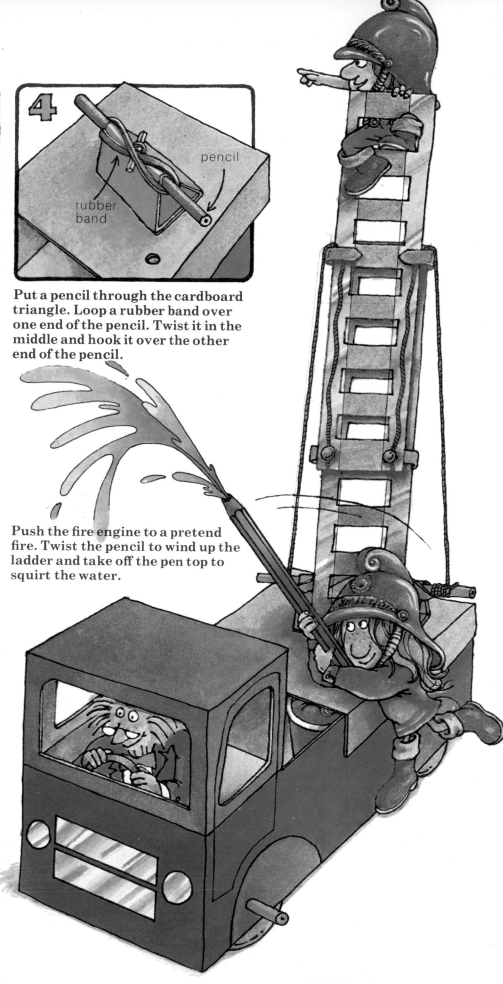

Power Pacer

Wind the propeller on this boat about 20 times. Put the boat in water and let it go.

You will need
a plastic squeezy bottle
a piece of plastic cut from the side of a plastic bottle
a ball-point pen, with the ink tube taken out
3 strong rubber bands
a piece of thin bendy wire, about 10 cm long
a used matchstick
kitchen foil
scissors

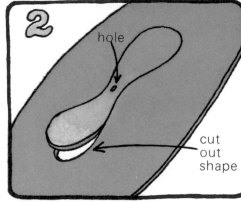

Push a rubber band through the pen tube. Push a matchstick through the loop at one end. Hook a piece of bendy wire through the other end.

To make the propeller, draw the shape of a figure eight, about 6 cm long, on the plastic piece. Cut it out. Make a small hole in the middle.

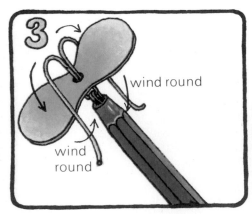

Push the ends of the wire through the hole in the propeller. Wind them tightly round, like this.

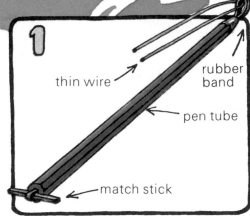

Hold the ends of the propeller like this. Twist the right side towards you and the left side away from you.

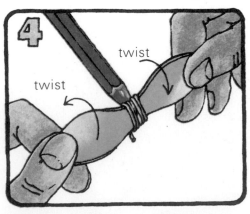

Wrap the plastic bottle tightly in foil. Put the pen tube against one side, with the propeller sticking out from the flat end. Put on two rubber bands, like this.

Balloon Record Breaker

Try making two boats and have races with them. The bigger you blow up the balloon, the faster and farther the boat will go.

You will need
a plastic squeezy bottle
a ball-point pen, with the
   ink tube taken out
a balloon
a small rubber band
plasticine
scissors

1

cut out

Push one blade of the scissors into one side of the plastic bottle. Cut out a long, wide strip, like this.

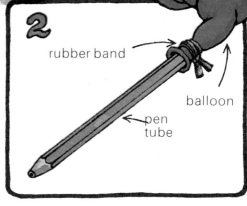

2

rubber band

balloon

pen tube

Push the pen tube into the neck of the balloon. Wind a rubber band very tightly round the neck of the balloon.

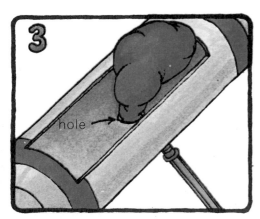

3

hole

Make a hole in the plastic bottle on the opposite side to the cut-out side. Push the balloon through the hole from the outside.

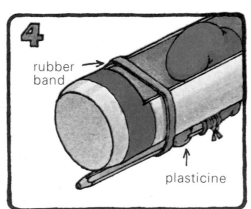

4

rubber band

plasticine

Bend back the pen tube towards the flat end of the bottle. Put a rubber band round it, like this, to keep it in place. Press some plasticine round the pen tube.

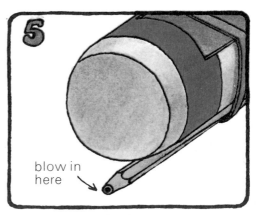

5

blow in here

To make the boat go along, blow up the balloon through the pen tube. Put the boat quickly in water and let it go.

Eager Weaver

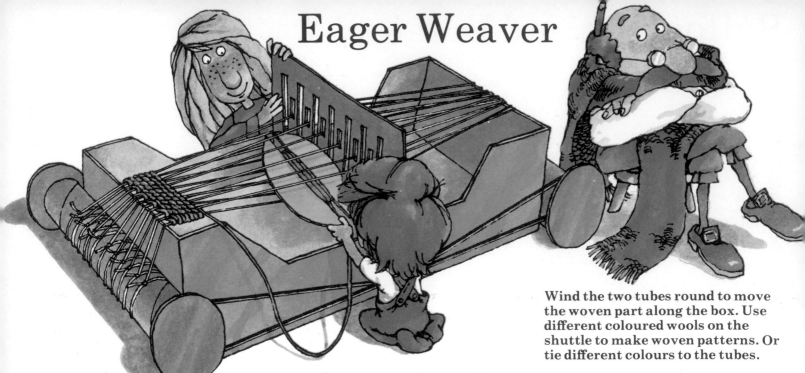

Wind the two tubes round to move the woven part along the box. Use different coloured wools on the shuttle to make woven patterns. Or tie different colours to the tubes.

Make this loom and use it to weave small scarves, ties and belts. Or weave long pieces and sew them together to make patchwork blankets.

You will need
a cardboard shoe box or strong
    cardboard box
thick cardboard
2 long cardboard tubes
4 large rubber bands
coloured wools
a pencil and a ruler
glue and sticky tape
scissors

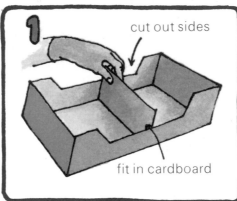

1

cut out sides

fit in cardboard

Cut out the sides of the box, like this. Cut a piece of cardboard for the handle, about 9 cm wide and as long as the width of the box. Make sure it fits the box.

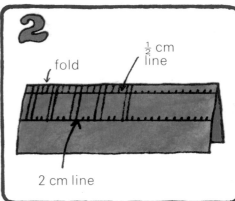

2

$\frac{1}{2}$ cm line

fold

2 cm line

Fold the cardboard in half. Rule lines $\frac{1}{2}$ cm and 2 cm from the fold. Mark every $\frac{1}{2}$ cm along both lines. Rule long and short boxes, with a space between them, like this.

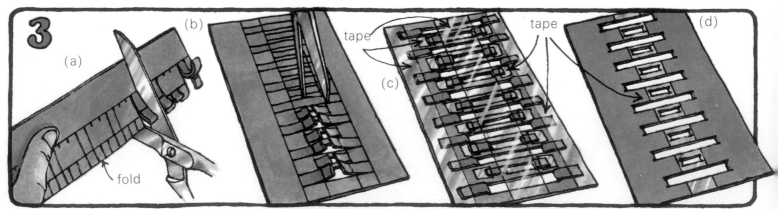

3

(a)

(b)

fold

tape

(c)

tape

(d)

Cut along all the lines from the fold (a). Unfold the cardboard. Snip every other cut bit along the fold (b).

When all the bits have been cut, fold them back. Fold the short cuts back to the $\frac{1}{2}$ cm line and the long cuts to the 2 cm line. Stick all the flaps down with tape (c).

Stick tape along the fold on both sides of the cardboard (d). Snip out all the bits of tape in the spaces. This piece of cardboard is the heddle.

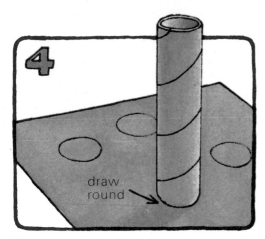

4

Using the end of a tube as a guide, draw four circles on cardboard. Cut out the circles a little larger than the lines. Glue a circle to each end of the tubes.

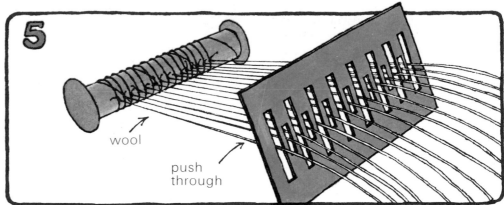

5

Cut 15 pieces of wool at least 50 cm long. Knot one piece round one end of a tube. Push the other end through the first hole in the end of the heddle.

Tie on another piece of wool. Push it through the second hole in the heddle. Tie on the rest of the wool, pushing it through the holes in the heddle, like this.

6

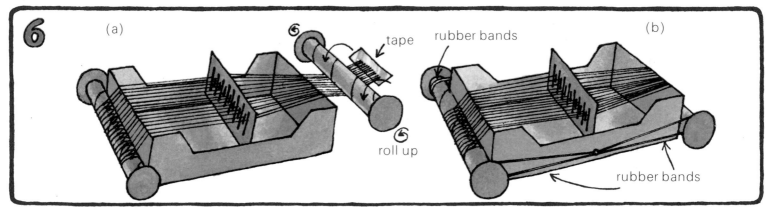

Put the heddle in the middle of the box. Put the tube with the wool on the outside at one end. Pull all the free ends of the wool over the other end of the box.

Put a second tube over the ends of the wool. Stick the ends to the tube with tape (a).

Knot two rubber bands together. Hook them over the tubes on one side of the box (b). Knot two more bands and hook them on to the other ends of the tubes.

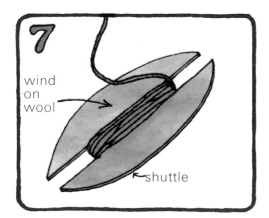

7

Cut out a piece of cardboard a little longer than the width of the box. Cut it into this shape. This is the shuttle. Wind on a very long piece of wool, like this.

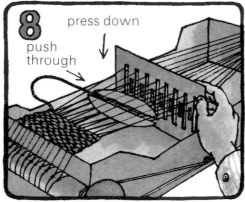

8

Tie the end of the wool on the shuttle to a strand of wool on the loom. Press the heddle down and push the shuttle through between the strands of wool.

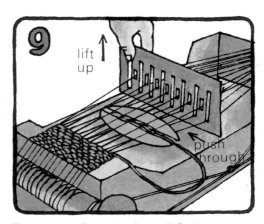

9

To weave the next line, lift the heddle up. Push the shuttle through from the other side. Push the heddle against the woven part each time you weave a new line.

Mr Twitch

Turn Mr Twitch upside down to make his arms go round. When they stop, turn him up again.

You will need
2 plastic cartons or yoghurt pots
a piece of thin cardboard
4 used matchsticks
2 long needles
table salt
a drinking straw
glue and sticky tape
a needle and thread
a pencil and scissors

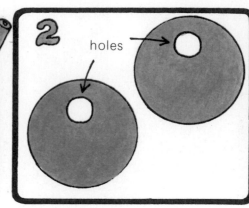

Draw four circles on thick cardboard, using the top of a plastic carton as a guide. Cut out the circles.

Cut a round hole in each of the cardboard circles, near one edge, like this.

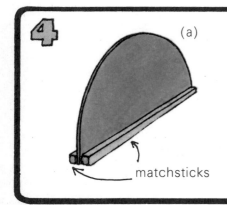

Fold a third cardboard circle in half. Cut along the fold. Glue a matchstick on each side of one half-circle (a). Glue matchsticks to the other half-circle.

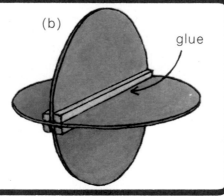

Glue the uncut circle to the matchsticks on one half-circle. Glue the second half-circle to the circle, like this (b).

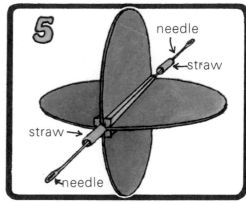

Push a needle into each end of the matchsticks. Slide a very short bit of straw on to the end of each needle.

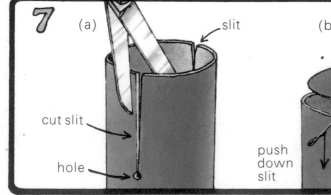

Stand the tube on end and cut two slits about half-way down it on both sides (a). Make a small hole at the end of each slit.

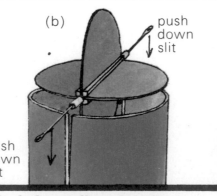

Push the cardboard circles down inside the tube with the needles in the slits (b). Spin the circles to make sure they turn easily. If not, trim a bit off the circles.

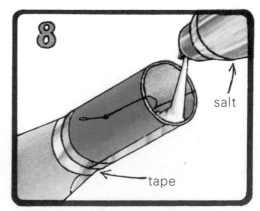

Pour some table salt into the tube. Put in enough to almost fill the plastic carton.

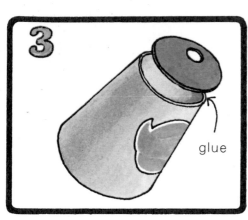

Glue one cardboard circle to the top of each of the plastic cartons. Use lots of glue to stick them very firmly.

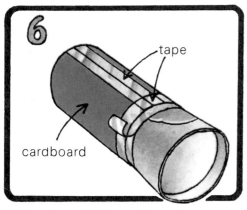

Roll a piece of thin cardboard very tightly round the top of a plastic carton. Stick it with tape to make a tube. Tape the tube very firmly to the carton.

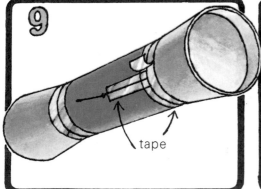

Push the top of the second plastic carton into the top of the tube. Wrap sticky tape very tightly round the end of the tube to stick it to the carton.

Cut the shape of two long arms out of thin paper. Cut them at the elbows. Cut out fingers and thumbs. Use a needle and thread to join the arms and fingers, like this.

Push the top of each arm on to the ends of the needles in the cardboard tube. Put one arm up and the other down. Glue them to the needles.

Formula XF Bullet

You will need

a sheet of paper, 29 cm long
    and 21 cm wide
2 ball-point pens without
    the ink tubes
a ball-point pen top
2 plastic drinking straws or
    very thin sticks
a bead
bendy wire and a paper clip
a matchbox cover
thick cardboard
stiff plastic cut from a
    plastic bottle
a strong rubber band
glue and sticky tape
a pencil and scissors

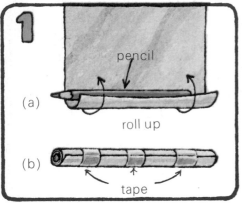

1

(a) pencil

roll up

(b) tape

Put the pencil on one edge of the paper. Roll the paper very tightly round the pencil (a). Stick the end of the rolled paper with tape (b). Shake out the pencil.

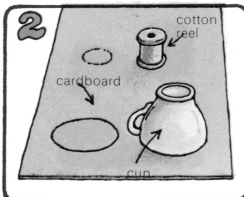

2

cotton reel

cardboard

cup

Cut two small circles out of cardboard, for the front wheels. Use a cotton reel as a guide. Cut out two big circles for the back wheels. Use a cup as a guide.

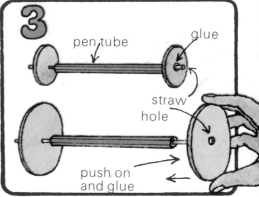

3

pen tube

glue

straw hole

push on and glue

Make a hole in the middle of each wheel. Push a straw through a pen tube. Push a small wheel on each end and glue them on. Do the same with the back wheels.

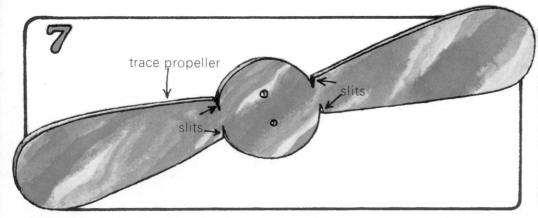

7

trace propeller

slits

slits

Trace this propeller shape on thin or see-through paper. Cut out the shape. Hold it down on a piece of plastic. Draw round the shape.

Cut the shape out very carefully. Cut two little slits on each side of the round part. Make two holes in the round middle part.

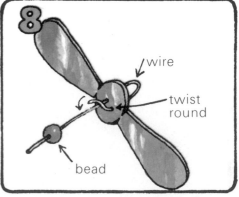

8

wire

twist round

bead

Loop a piece of bendy wire through the holes in the propeller. Twist one end round the other end, like this. Push the long end through a bead and pull it tight.

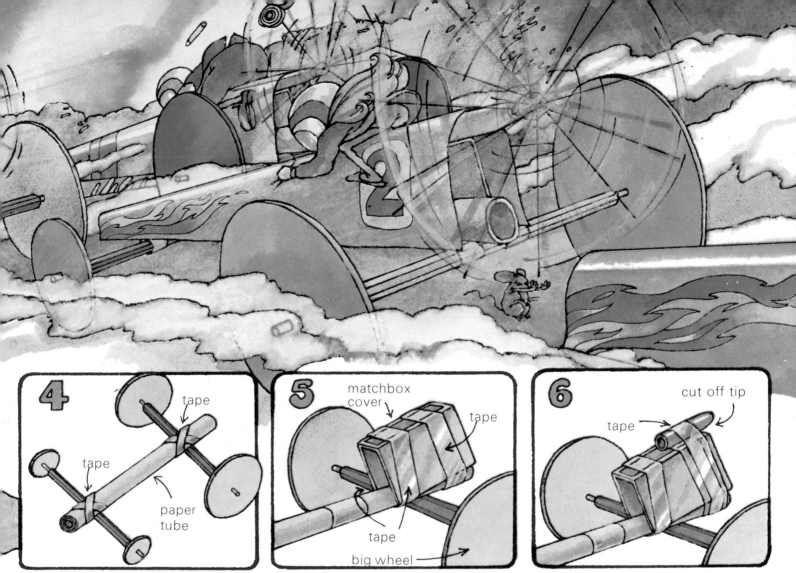

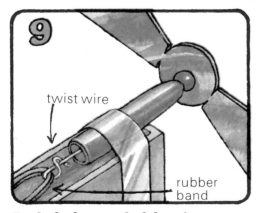

4 Put the paper tube across the two pen tubes, like this. Wind sticky tape round the paper tube and each pen tube to fix them in place.

tape *tape* *paper tube*

5 Cut one side off a matchbox cover. Put it, cut side down, on the paper tube at the end with the big wheels. Tilt it forward a little, like this, and stick it to the tube with tape.

matchbox cover *tape* *tape* *big wheel*

6 Cut the end of a pen top with scissors. Put it on top of the matchbox cover, like this. Stick it down very firmly with tape.

cut off tip *tape*

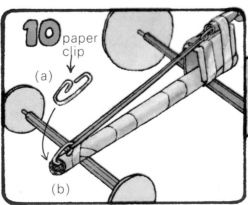

9 Push the long end of the wire through the pen top on the car. Loop a rubber band on to the wire and twist the wire round, like this.

twist wire *rubber band*

10 Bend open a paper clip (a). Push one loop into the end of the paper tube. Hook the end of the rubber band on to the other loop of the paper clip (b).

paper clip *(a)* *(b)*

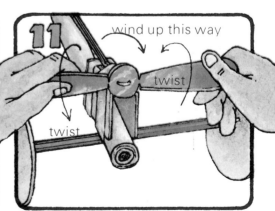

11 Hold the propeller like this. Twist the right side towards the front of the car. Twist the left side the other way. Wind up the propeller this way about 20 times.

wind up this way *twist* *twist*

Water Clock

Make this water clock and use it to tell the time. If the hand goes round too fast, drop a drawing pin or big-headed pin into the bottom of the plastic bottle. Or push a thin piece of stick into the hole. If the cork does not go down with the water, put a bit more plasticine on the string. Remember to empty the pot or bowl in the bottom of the box when it is full of water.

You will need
a plastic squeezy bottle
a large, strong cardboard box,
   about 40 cm high
2 knitting needles
2 corks
4 pieces of string, each about
   as long as the width of the box
a sheet of paper
a piece of cardboard
plasticine
a pot or bowl
a pencil
scissors and glue

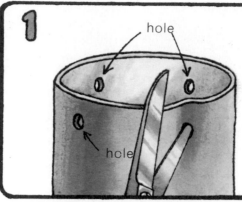

Cut the bottom off a plastic bottle. Make four holes in it, near the bottom edge (a).

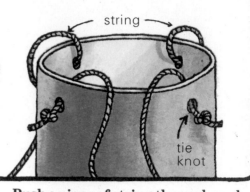

Push a piece of string through each hole. Tie a knot on the end of each string on the outside of the bottle (b).

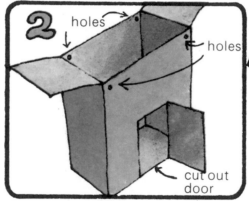

Open the top of the box. Cut a door in one side, near the bottom. Make a hole in each corner near the top of the box.

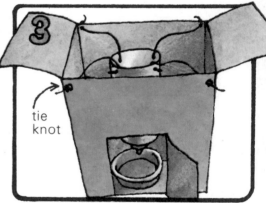

Put the bottle inside the box. Push one string through each hole in the top of the box and tie a knot on the end. Put a pot or bowl in the bottom of the box.

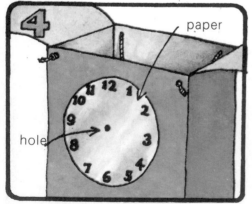

Cut out a paper circle. Write on it the numbers 1 to 12, like the face of a clock. Stick it to the front of the box, near the top. Make a hole in the middle of the circle.

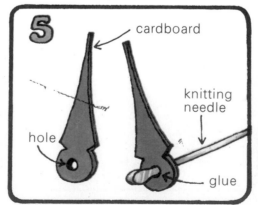

Cut a clock hand from a piece of cardboard. Make a hole in the round end (a). Push a knitting needle through the hole and glue the hand to the end (b).

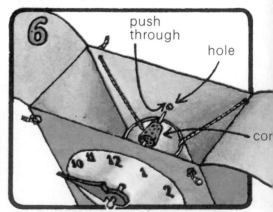

Make a hole through a cork with scissors. Push the knitting needle through the clock face. Push the cork on to the needle and push the needle out the back of the box.

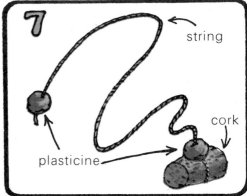

Cut a string a little longer than the height of the box. Tie a cork on one end. Put some plasticine on the string near the cork. Put another lump on the other end.

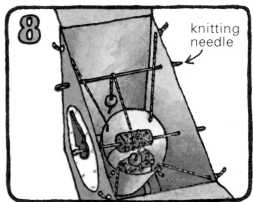

Put the string round the cork, like this. Drop the cork end into the bottle. Push a second knitting needle through the box near the first one. Loop the string over it.

Pour some water into the plastic bottle. Pull up the plasticine end of the string so that the cork just rests on the water.

Grand Prix Car Races

Make this track and race your toy cars all round the floor. It will work best on a floor without a carpet. You can make the circuits any shape you like by putting the strings round more chair legs. If the strings slip on the wheels, push the chairs away from the wheels to make them tight again.

Before a race, decide how many times the cars should go round the tracks. It could be twice for a short race or ten times for a long one. The winner is the first car to reach the finishing line.

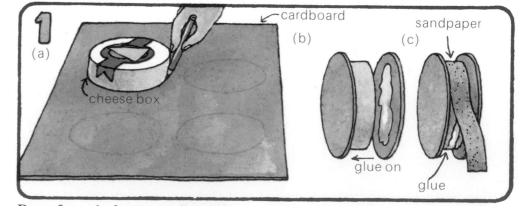

You will need
2 small, toy cars
a round, cardboard cheese box
2 pieces of thick string, each
   about 5 metres long
2 horseshoe magnets
a sheet of sandpaper
2 big nails
2 pencils
2 ball-point pen tops
cardboard
4 empty tins
strong glue

1
(a)
cheese box
cardboard
(b)
sandpaper
(c)
glue on
glue

Draw four circles on cardboard, using the cheese box as a guide (a). Cut out the four circles, making them about 1 cm bigger than the drawn lines.

Glue two circles on each side of the cheese box lid and bottom to make two wheels (b). Glue a strip of sandpaper round the wheels (c).

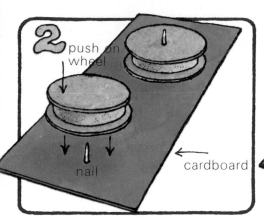

Push two nails through each end of a large sheet of cardboard. Stick a piece of tape over each nail head. Push a nail through the middle of each wheel, like this.

Glue a ball-point pen top over each nail. Make sure no glue goes on the nails. Push a pencil through each wheel near the edge. Glue them in place.

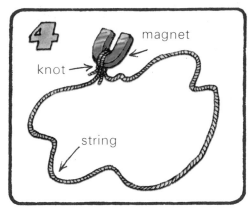

Tie the ends of each piece of string together. Tie a magnet to the knot in each piece of string.

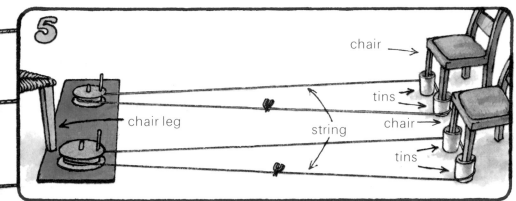

Put the cardboard with the wheels down on the floor. Put a table or chair leg on it. Loop one string round each wheel. Put the front legs of two chairs in tins.

Put two chair legs over each string, like this. Push the chairs gently away from the wheels until the strings are stretched tight.

Try sticking the cars to the magnets. If they will not stick, put a small, fat, iron screw or bit of iron on the front of each car. Stick it firmly in place with tape.

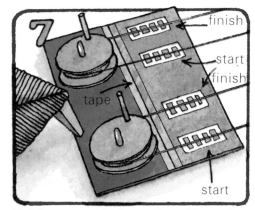

Stick a second piece of cardboard in front of the first one with tape. Draw or paint a starting and finishing line under each string.

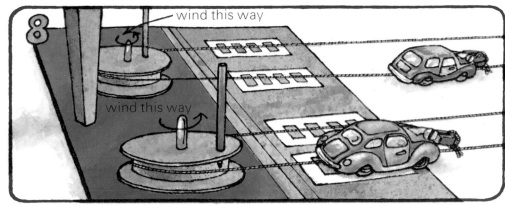

To race the cars, wind the magnets back to the starting lines. Stick a car to each magnet. When someone says 'go', two players each wind a handle to move the cars forward.

If a car comes off a magnet, wind the handle the other way to move the magnet back again to the car. Or go to the car and stick it on the magnet again.

Snow Storm

Make a mountain with little houses, or a hill, and stick on little plastic animals and people. Shake the jar to start the snow storm and watch it slowly settle.

You will need
a short glass jar with a
   screw-on lid
different coloured plasticine
waterproof inks
waterproof glue
french chalk (this is sold in
   chemist shops)
cold, boiled water

press in plasticine

glue

Take the lid off the jar. Spread glue on the inside. Press some plasticine on the glue, keeping it away from the edge of the lid.

Press on more plasticine to make a high mountain. Shape small blocks for houses. Draw in doors and windows with waterproof ink. Press them to the mountain.

french chalk

cold boiled water

Pour cold, boiled water into the jar, almost to the top. Put in one heaped teaspoon of french chalk. Stir it until all the lumps have been mixed in.

screw on lid

When the glue on the lid is dry, turn the lid over. Screw it on to the jar very tightly. Some of the water may run over.

Try making different scenes in other glass jars with lots of coloured plasticine.

You could make a Christmas scene and put gold and silver glitter bits in the water.

The KnowHow Book of Action Games

Anne Civardi

Illustrated by Malcolm English
Designed by John Jamieson

Contributors:
James Opie, Andras Ranki and Christopher Carey

Contents

About This Book

This book shows you how to make and play lots of different kinds of games. There are board games, dice games, table games, races, battle games and paper games. Most of the games are made from things you can probably find at home. There is a list on page 2 which tells you what things you need and where to get them.

At the end of the book there are five pages of party games, treasure hunts and party races.

The measurements given are only a guide. You can make the games any size you like.

Read the rules of each game carefully so you know how to play it before you begin.

First published in 1975
by Usborne Publishing Ltd
Usborne House, 83-85 Saffron Hill,
London EC1N 8RT, England

©Usborne Publishing Ltd 1989, 1975

This abridged edition contains the best projects from the original 48-page version.

Printed in Belgium

The name Usborne and the device are Trade Marks of Usborne Publishing Ltd.

Getting Ready

These are the things you need to make the games in this book:

Thick cardboard – cut from strong cardboard boxes which you can get in supermarkets.
Thin cardboard – cut from empty cereal packets, backs of writing pads, or document folders which you can buy in stationery shops.
Glue – use Bostik 1 or UHU.
Sheet sponge – artificial sponge sold in sheets in Woolworth's and department stores.
Plasticine – sold in toy shops.
Tiddly wink counters – flat, round plastic counters sold in packets in toy shops.
Draught counters – wooden or plastic counters used to play draughts and sold in toy shops.
Garden canes – buy in gardening shops or florists'.
Eye screws – buy in hardware stores.
Paint – use poster paint or water colours.
Tracing paper – use greaseproof paper or very thin, see-through paper.

Ask your friends to help you collect things like:
Plastic and cardboard cartons, such as empty yoghurt, cream and cheese pots.
Cardboard tubes – from kitchen and lavatory rolls.
Cardboard or plastic egg boxes.
Bag ties – used to tie up freezer and garbage bags.
Cardboard boxes in lots of sizes.
Thin and thick cardboard.
Empty squeezy bottles.
Corks, empty matchboxes, hairpins, pipe cleaners, marbles and cardboard cheese boxes.

Home-made Boxes

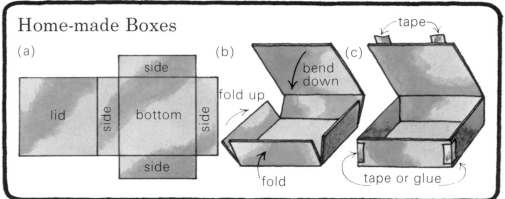

If you cannot find a box, make one out of cardboard. Use a ruler to draw the lines. The lid and bottom are the same size and the sides are all the same size (a).

Fold the cardboard, like this, to make the lid, bottom and sides (b). Stick the side and the bottom together with glue or tape (c). Try making a box without a lid.

1 Who Begins?

There are lots of ways to choose the starter of a game. One is for all the players to throw a dice. The one with the highest number starts (a). Play clockwise from the starter.

Another way is for one player to hold different length straws. Each player picks one. The one with the longest straw starts (b). Or cut up slips of paper. Draw an X on one.

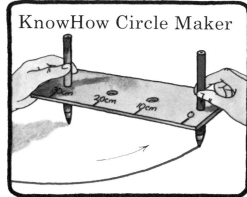

KnowHow Circle Maker

Measure and punch holes every 10 cm on a strip of thin cardboard, like this. Stick pencils through two holes. Holding both pencils firmly, swing one round in a circle.

Cardboard Dice

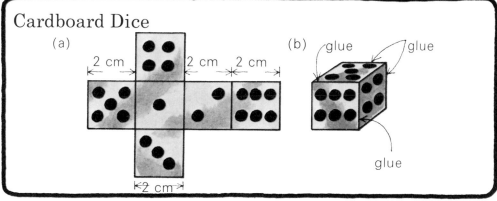

(a) 2 cm 2 cm 2 cm 2 cm

(b) glue glue glue

To make a cardboard dice, draw this shape, with all the sides 2 cm long, on some thin cardboard. Paint the dots in each square, like this (a).

Fold inwards along the lines and glue the sides and the top together (b). On bought dice the two sides opposite each other always add up to seven.

Plasticine and Sugar Dice

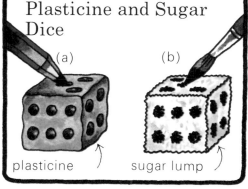

(a) (b)

plasticine sugar lump

To make a dice, shape a lump of plasticine into a cube and mark in the dots with a pencil point, like this (a). You can also ink dots on a sugar lump to make a dice (b).

2 (c) (d)

Fold them in half and jumble them up. Everyone takes a slip. The player with the X starts (c).When there are only two players, toss a coin to see who starts (d).

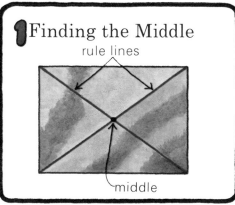

1 Finding the Middle

rule lines

middle

To find the middle of a box, a piece of cardboard or a sheet of paper, rule lines across it from the four corners, like this. The middle is where the lines cross.

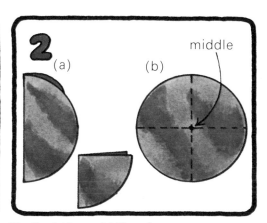

2 (a) (b) middle

To find the middle of a paper or thin cardboard circle, fold it in half twice, like this (a). Open the circle out again. The middle is where the two folds cross (b).

3

Beetle Bugs
(for 2 or more players)

Make enough Beetle Bug parts to build a complete Bug for each player. If you do not have any plasticine, try using clean potatoes for the head and body.

You will need
a dice and a yoghurt pot for a
    dice shaker
For each Beetle Bug
plasticine or 2 potatoes
a toothpick or matchstick and
    some silver foil
2 paper fasteners
thin wire (about 10 cm long)
tissue paper, a pencil and
    some strong glue
6 used matchsticks

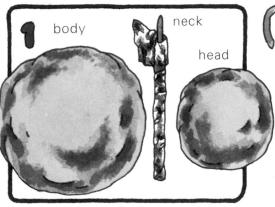

1 body   neck   head

Shape two lumps of plasticine into a round body and a smaller round head. Wrap silver foil round a toothpick or used matchstick to make the neck.

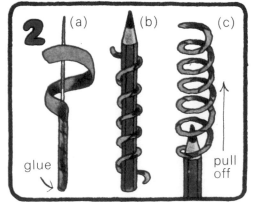

2 (a)   (b)   (c)

glue   pull off

To make a curly tongue, wrap a strip of tissue paper round the thin wire. Glue the paper at both ends (a). Twist the wire round a pencil, like this (b), and slide it off (c).

How to Play

The idea is to build a complete Bug by throwing the dice for each part of the body. Each number on the dice matches a part of the body. If you throw a number you do not need, wait until your next turn.

To start, each player must throw a 1 for the body. Then throw a 2 for the neck or a 6 for each leg. When he has the neck, he throws for the head and the eyes and tongue. The winner is the first player to make up a Beetle Bug with a body, neck, a head, 2 eyes, a tongue and 6 legs.

Numbers to Throw

body	⚀
neck	⚁
head	⚂
eye	⚃
tongue	⚄
leg	⚅

Frog Leaps

(for 2 or more players)

This is a frog race. Each player needs a cardboard frog. The frogs start at one end of the strings and jump along to the other. The finishing line can be a mark on the floor or ponds made out of cardboard for the frogs to jump into.

You will need
thick cardboard
a piece of string (about 2 metres long) for each player
tracing paper
a pencil and some paint
scissors
thin cardboard to make the cardboard ponds

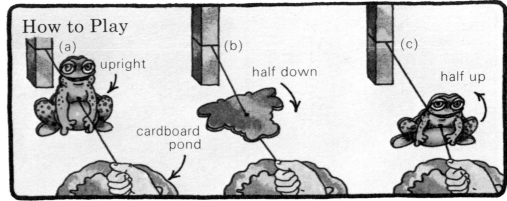

How to Play

(a) upright
(b) half down cardboard pond
(c) half up

Fasten one end of each string to a chair leg so the frogs stand in a line with their feet just touching the floor. Put a cardboard pond at the other end of each string.

Each player holds the end of a string and jerks it up and down to make the frog leap along it. The first frog to get into its pond or past the finishing line wins.

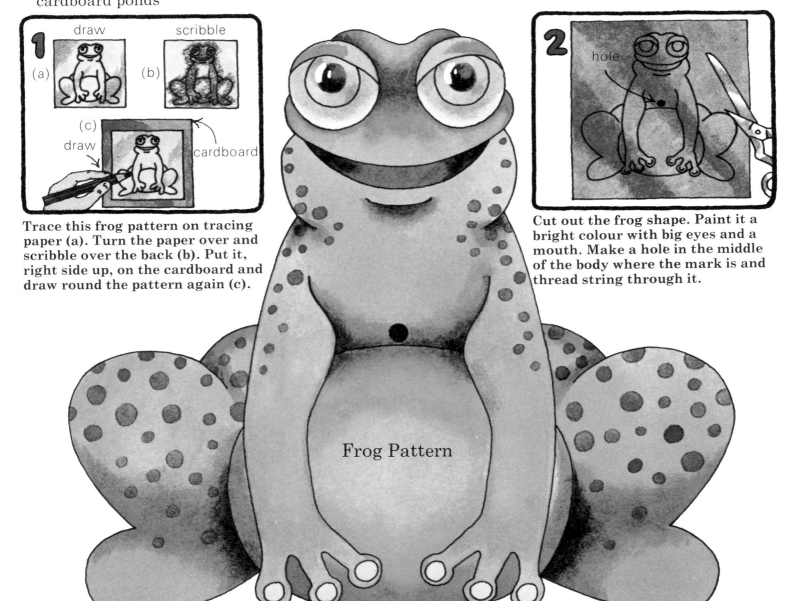

1
draw (a)
scribble (b)
draw (c) cardboard

Trace this frog pattern on tracing paper (a). Turn the paper over and scribble over the back (b). Put it, right side up, on the cardboard and draw round the pattern again (c).

Frog Pattern

2
hole

Cut out the frog shape. Paint it a bright colour with big eyes and a mouth. Make a hole in the middle of the body where the mark is and thread string through it.

Five Minute Games

(for lots of players)

The games on these two pages are very easy to make and only take a few minutes to play.

You will need
For Egg Flip
2 cardboard egg boxes and a fork
For Catchball
2 tall plastic cartons
a ping pong ball
8 rubber bands
thin and thick cardboard
For Blow Football
2 small cardboard boxes
plasticine and 2 straws
a ping pong ball
For Ribbon Roll
1 tall, plastic carton
5 small yoghurt pots
ribbon (about 3 cm wide and 90 cm long)
a pin
thick cardboard and white paper
5 marbles
For Matchbox Bullseye
thin cardboard and a matchbox
For all the games
paint, glue, scissors, a pencil and sticky tape

1 Egg Flip

Cut the tops off both egg boxes and throw them away. Cut the six egg holders out of the bottom of one (a). Paint each egg holder a different colour (b). Leave to dry.

Paint the six holes in the bottom of the second egg box. Make them the same colours as the egg holders, like this (c).

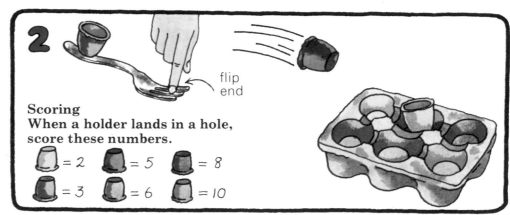

2

Scoring
When a holder lands in a hole, score these numbers.

$\square$ = 2 $\square$ = 5 $\square$ = 8
$\square$ = 3 $\square$ = 6 $\square$ = 10

Put the painted egg box bottom on the floor. Put a fork about 45 cm from the box, like this. To play, balance an egg holder, open end up, on the handle end of the fork.

Push down quickly on the prongs and try to flip the holder into a hole in the egg box. Mark down the score. A holder that lands in the same-coloured hole scores double.

1 Catchball

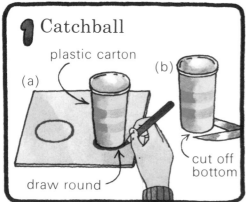

Draw two circles on cardboard, using the bottom of a plastic carton (a). Cut them out ½ cm smaller all the way round. Now cut off the bottom of the carton (b).

2

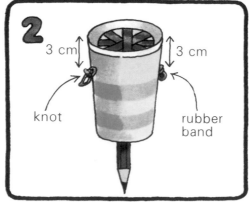

Make a catcher in the same way as you would make a cannon (see page 11). Instead of a cardboard tube, use the plastic carton and the circles you have cut out.

3

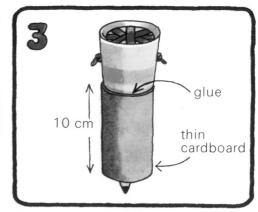

Cut out a strip of thin cardboard, about 23 cm wide and 10 cm long. Glue it round the bottom of the plastic carton catcher, like this. Now make another catcher.

1 Blow Football

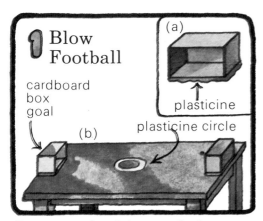

Put some plasticine on the bottom of two small cardboard boxes (a). Push them, plasticine side down, on to the ends of a table (b). Put a plasticine circle in the middle (c).

2

Two people, or four people playing in teams of two, can play. To start, put a ping pong ball in the plasticine circle in the middle of the table, like this.

The players each have a straw and stand on either side of the table. The idea is to blow the ping pong ball, using the straws, into the other team's goal.

1 Ribbon Roll

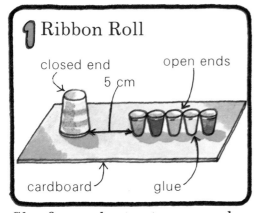

Glue five yoghurt pots, open ends up and touching each other, to cardboard. Glue a tall, plastic carton, open end down, about 5 cm from the first pot, like this.

2

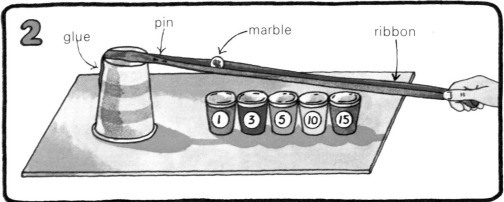

Glue one end of some ribbon, about 3 cm wide and 90 cm long, to the top of the carton. Pin the ribbon together close to the carton, like this, so that it funnels.

Draw these numbers on bits of paper. Glue them on to the pots. Roll marbles, one by one, down the ribbon and try to get them into the pots. Roll five marbles in a turn.

4

Stand 3 metres apart and each hold a catcher. The game is to fire and catch a ping pong ball, using the catchers. The player to catch the ball five times in a row wins.

Matchbox Bullseye

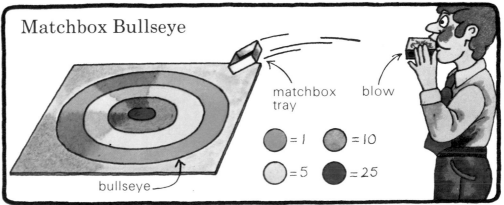

Draw a big circle on some cardboard. Draw three smaller circles inside it, like this. Paint them all different colours. When they are dry paint on the numbers.

Stand 3 metres from the board. Put a matchbox in your mouth and blow hard so that the match tray shoots out on to the coloured circles. Have three blows in a turn.

Mouse Trap

(for 3 or more players)

Each player needs a cork mouse. Instead of making a whirler you can play with a dice.

You will need
a cork for each player
pieces of string (each about 40 cm long)
a hairpin and felt cloth
scissors and strong glue
a big carton or little box
thin cardboard
a used matchstick or a toothpick
tracing paper and a pencil
paint and a paint brush
a circle of cardboard for the cardboard mat

1 Mouse Making

push down

Paint the corks different colours. Leave them to dry. Then make a hole through the middle of each cork, using closed scissors or a knitting needle, like this.

2

(a)

double-knot

(b)

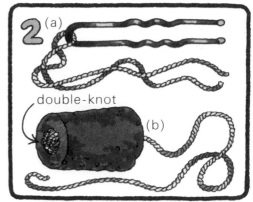

Loop string, about 40 cm long, round a hairpin (a). Push the hairpin through the hole in a cork and double-knot the end of the string (b). Do the same to all the corks.

3

(a)

1 cm

(b)

glue

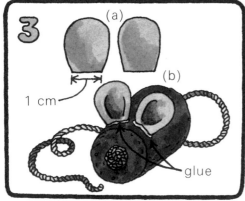

To make the mouse ears, cut out two pieces of felt this shape (a). Glue them to the top of the cork, like this (b). Put two ears on all the cork mice.

Dice Whirler

3 cm

(a)

trace pattern

(b)

paint on numbers

sharpened matchstick

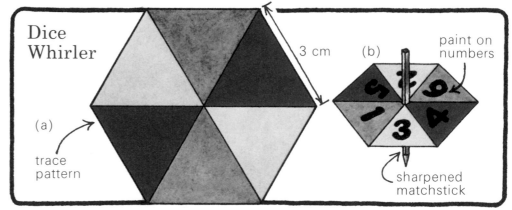

Trace this pattern (a) on to thin cardboard. Rule lines from corner to corner, like this. Cut the shape out very carefully.

Paint the triangles and paint on the numbers. Sharpen a used match with a pencil sharpener. Push it through the middle of the whirler, where all the lines meet.

How to Play

Players spin the whirler in turn. The one with the highest number is the mouse trapper. The others are the mouse holders. Each holder puts his mouse on the cardboard mat and holds its tail. The trapper spins the whirler. When it stops on a 6 or 4 he tries to trap the mice under the carton. The holders try to pull them away before being trapped. If the trapper catches a mouse he scores 5 points. A holder scores 5 points if he pulls his mouse away in time.

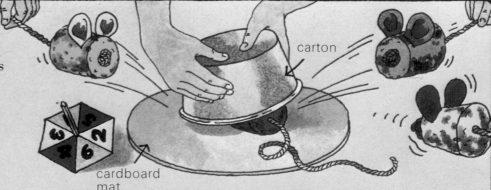

carton

cardboard mat

A holder loses 5 points if he pulls his mouse away when the whirler stops on a number other than a 6 or 4. The first player to score 50 points wins.

When the trapper has spun a 6 or 4 three times, he passes the carton to the player on his left who then becomes the new mouse trapper.

Fish Hook

(for 2 or more players)

This is a race against time. Try to hook as many cork fish as you can before all the salt runs out of the timer.

You will need

6 corks
6 eye screws or hairpins
some felt cloth
strong glue and white paper
a stick (about 50 cm long)
string
a hairpin or thin wire
scissors and paint
a plastic squeezy bottle
a glass jar
salt or fine sand

How to Play

Put the fish, screw ends up, on the floor. Take it in turns to hook the fish with the rod. Add up the numbers on the fish you have hooked after each turn.

A turn lasts as long as it takes for the salt to pour out of the squeezy bottle, once the lid has been opened. The first player to score 20 points wins.

1 Fish Making

eye screw

bent hairpin

Paint six corks different colours. Screw an eye screw into the middle of each cork, or push a hairpin into the cork, like this.

2

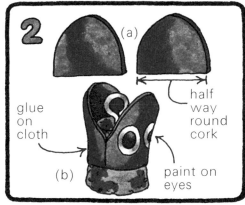

(a)

glue on cloth

half way round cork

(b)

paint on eyes

Cut two pieces of felt, each wide enough to wrap half-way round a cork (a). Glue the felt on to the cork and paint on eyes, like this (b). Do the same to all six corks.

3

glue on numbers

Cut out six pieces of white paper and glue one to the bottom of each cork. Paint numbers from one to six on the corks, like this.

4

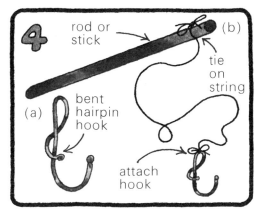

rod or stick

(b)

tie on string

bent hairpin hook

(a)

attach hook

Tie string, about 58 cm long, to one end of a stick or rod. Bend a hairpin or some wire into a hook, like this (a) and tie it on to the end of the string (b).

5 KnowHow Timer

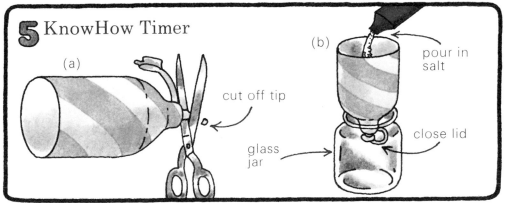

(a)

cut off tip

glass jar

(b)

pour in salt

close lid

Cut a squeezy bottle in half. Cut off the very tip of the bottle, like this (a). Paint the bottle with brightly coloured paint. Leave it to dry.

Close the lid and balance the squeezy bottle, upside down, in a glass jar. Fill the bottle with salt or fine sand (b), making sure there are no lumps in it.

Cannonboard
(for 2 or more players)

The further you pull the pencil out of the cannon, the faster the marbles will go. Pull it very gently to get marbles into the goals nearest the cannon.

You will need
a strong cardboard box (about 34 cm wide and 46 cm long)
a sheet of thin cardboard
a strong cardboard tube (about 14 cm long)
4 rubber bands
6 marbles
sticky tape and strong glue
a pencil, a ruler and scissors

How to Play

Fire the marbles out of the cannon and try to get them into the goals with the high numbers. Each player fires six marbles in a turn. At the end of each turn add up the plus scores and take away the minus scores. The first player to score 100 points wins.

To fire, put one marble at a time into the top of the cannon. Pull back the pencil and then let it go.

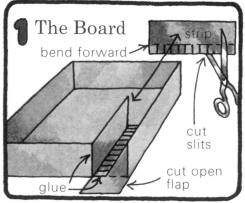

1 The Board

bend forward
strip
cut slits
cut open flap
glue

Cut a flap, about 6 cm wide, at one corner of the box. Cut a strip of cardboard half the length of the box and as high. Cut slits on one side. Glue the strip to the box.

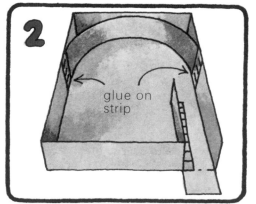

2

glue on strip

Cut a strip of carboard about 1½ times the width of the box and as high. Cut slits at both ends. Bend the strip into a half-circle and glue it to the sides of the box.

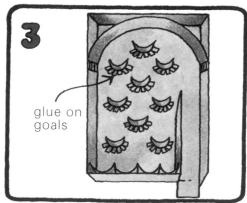

3

glue on goals

To make the goals, cut 13 pieces of cardboard, about 8 cm long and 3 cm wide. Cut slits at one edge of each piece. Bend them into half-circles. Glue them on to the box.

4

Cut out eight strips of cardboard, about 4 cm x 3 cm. Cut slits along the edge of each strip, like this (a). Roll them into small posts and glue them, as shown (b).

Now glue the posts on to the box, like this. They are hazards and make the game a bit harder to play. Draw or paint the plus and minus numbers inside each goal.

5

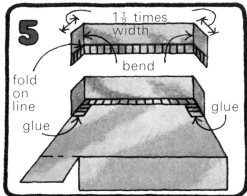

Cut some cardboard about 1½ times the width of the box and about 6 cm high. Cut slits along the edge. Bend the cardboard on the red lines. Glue it to the back of the box.

6 The Cannon

Draw two circles on cardboard, using the end of the cardboard tube. Cut them out, ½ cm smaller all the way round. Glue together. Make a hole in the middle.

7

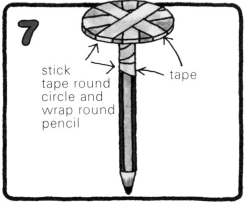

Push the end of a pencil through the hole in the cardboard circle. Tape the circle on to the pencil very firmly, like this.

8

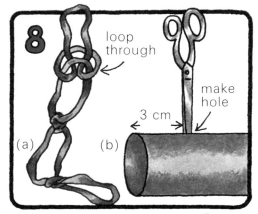

Link four strong rubber bands together, like this (a). Make a hole on either side of the tube, about 3 cm from one end (b).

9

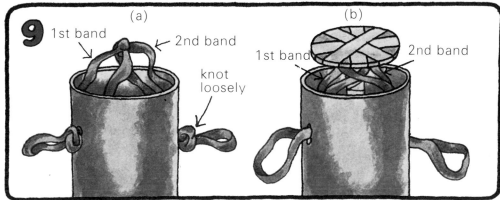

Thread the rubber bands through the holes in the cardboard tube, like this. Knot both ends very loosely (a).

Push the cardboard circle and pencil up the tube. First pull one rubber band over the circle and then the other, like this. Untie the loose knots (b).

10 Cannon Mounting

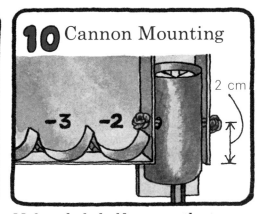

Make a hole half-way up the two bits of cardboard, about 2 cm from the open flap. Push the rubber band ends through the holes, like this. Double-knot each end.

Flick Billiards

(for 2 players or 2 teams)

To play this game, one player or team needs ten counters of one colour. The other player or team needs ten counters of a different colour. Glue a circle of paper to the top of an extra counter. We have used black and red counters.

You will need

a cardboard box with low sides
   (about 72 cm × 50 cm)
4 old nylon stockings
21 draught counters
a small yoghurt pot
thin cardboard
sticky tape and strong glue
scissors and a pencil

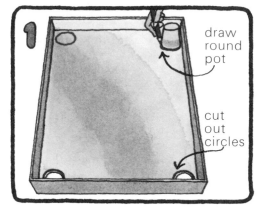

Draw a circle in each corner on the inside of the box, using a small yoghurt pot as a guide. Cut out the four circles.

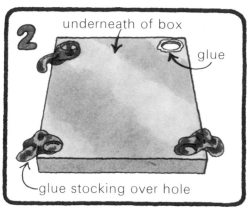

To make the corner nets, cut the feet off four old stockings. Glue one foot over each hole on the underneath of the box, like this.

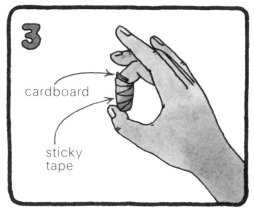

To make the finger guard, cut a strip of thin cardboard. Put it over the nail of your third finger. Wrap sticky tape round it, like this. The picture shows you how to flick.

How to Play

The player with the black counters starts. He flicks a black counter against a red one, trying to get the red one into a corner net. If he does, he has another turn. If not, the player with the red counters tries to flick a black one into a net. If either player flicks the extra counter into a net, he picks one of his counters and the extra one out of the net and puts them back on the board. The first one to flick all the other side's counters into the nets wins.

This picture shows how to set out the counters at the start of the game.

12

Tiddly Pong

(for 2 players)

This is just like ordinary ping pong except that you can play on a small table. Both players need a bat to hit the ball over the net to each other.

You will need
a sheet of thick cardboard
thin cardboard
a sheet of sponge
a saucer
an old nylon stocking
a ping pong ball
strong glue and sticky tape
scissors and string
a safety pin and 4 pencils

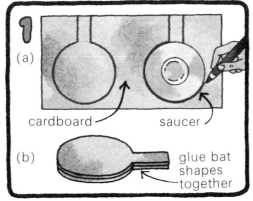

1
(a) cardboard   saucer
(b) glue bat shapes together

Rule two lines, 4 cm apart and 10 cm long, on thick cardboard. Draw a circle at the bottom of the lines, using a saucer. Cut out the shapes. Glue them together. Do this again.

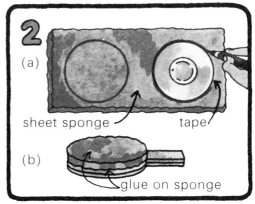

2
(a) sheet sponge   tape
(b) glue on sponge

Using the same saucer, draw four circles on a sheet of sponge (a). Cut them out. Glue a sponge circle to both sides of a cardboard bat, like this (b).

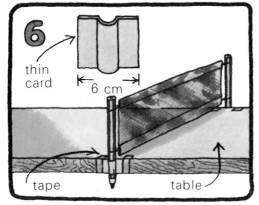

3
tape
string
push pencil up

Wrap string tightly round the handle of each bat. Glue the ends and wrap sticky tape round them. Push a pencil up the handles, between the two bits of cardboard.

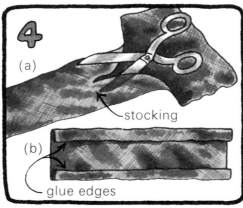

4
(a) stocking
(b) glue edges

To make the net, cut the foot off an old stocking. Cut open the stocking, like this (a). Fold over and glue about 2 cm at both edges, as shown (b).

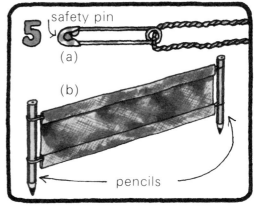

5
safety pin
(a)
(b)
pencils

Cut two bits of string 80 cm long. Loop them, one at a time, through a closed safety pin (a). Thread them through the folded stocking (b). Tie the ends to two pencils.

6
thin card
6 cm
tape   table

Cut two pieces of thin cardboard as long as the lip on the table you use and about 6 cm wide. Tape one to the middle of each side of the table. Push the pencils into them.

How to Play

The aim is to be the first to score 21 points. You score a point when the other player cannot return your shot. Take it in turn to serve.

Each player has 5 serves in a turn. The ball must bounce on both sides of the table when you serve. It must not bounce your side when you return a shot.

13

Sticks and Kicks

(for 2 players)

You will need
a strong cardboard box (about
   48 cm long, 25 cm wide and
   8 cm deep)
thick cardboard
a cardboard egg box
a strong cardboard tube (from a
   kitchen roll)
2 small string bags or a
   stocking
4 garden canes or 4 thin sticks
   (each about 60 cm long)
plasticine and 4 corks
4 big rubber bands
a pencil and paint
a small ball or large marble

How to Play

Put the box on a table. Put the
ball or marble inside the circle
on the centre line. Players stand
on different sides of the table
and hold a rod in each hand.
Both start together.

The idea is to twist, push and
pull the canes and try to get
your footballers to kick the ball
into the other team's goal. The
first team to score three goals
is the winner.

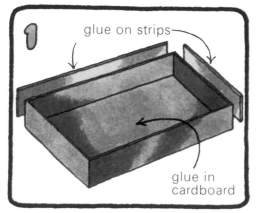

Cut some **cardboard** the size of the
bottom of the box. Glue it inside
the box, like this. Glue strips of
cardboard to the sides and ends of
the box, too.

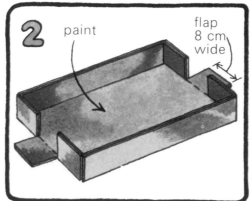

Cut a **flap**, about 8 cm wide, at both
ends of the box, like this. Then
paint the cardboard glued inside
the box. Leave it to dry.

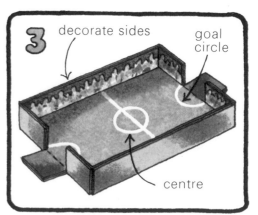

Draw a line across the middle of
the inside of the box. Draw a circle
on the line, like this, using a cup
as a guide. Draw half-circles round
the goal flaps.

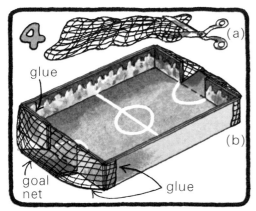

To make a goal net, cut open a string bag (a). Put one edge under the goal flap. Glue it underneath the box. Glue the other edge to the sides and top of the box (b).

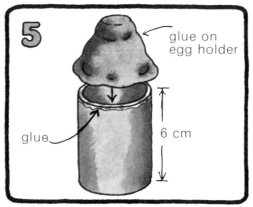

To make the footballers, cut the kitchen roll into six tubes, each 6 cm long. Cut the six egg holders out of the egg box. Glue one holder to the top of each tube.

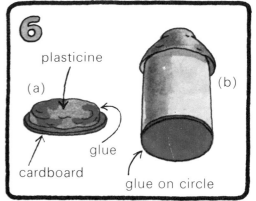

Draw round the bottom of each tube on cardboard. Cut out the circles. Glue plasticine to each one (a). Glue a circle, plasticine inside, to the bottom of each tube.

Paint faces on all the cardboard tubes. Paint three footballers one team colour and the other three a different team colour.

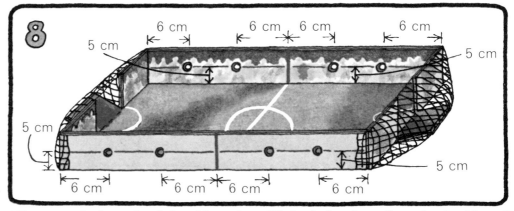

Measure the length of the sides of the box. Divide it in half to find the centre. Rule lines at the centre on both sides of the box, like this.

Make holes 6 cm from both sides of the centre lines and 5 cm from the bottom of the box. Make holes 6 cm from both ends and 5 cm from the bottom of the box, as shown.

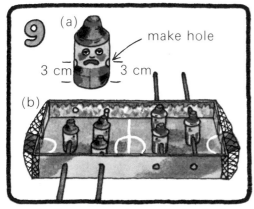

Push the canes through the holes in the box. Make holes in each tube (a). Push one team on to the canes at one end and the other team on to the canes at the other end (b).

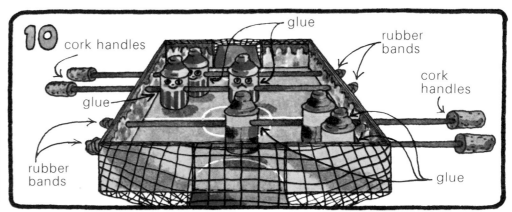

Push each cane through the second hole. Wrap a rubber band round the end of each cane, like this, to stop them from getting pulled back through the holes.

Push corks on to the other ends to make handles. Pull the rods so that the rubber bands are against the box sides. Then glue the footballers to the canes in position, like this.

Grand Derby

(for 2 or more players)

This is a horse race which you can play on any big table. Each player needs a horse and a jockey, and a piece of string long enough to loop round the table.

You will need
thin cardboard
tracing paper
a pencil and paint
string and scissors
strong glue
plasticine
wire bag ties, pipe cleaners or
    thin wire

1

platform pattern

saddle pattern

horse pattern

To make a horse, draw the horse pattern, saddle pattern and platform pattern on tracing paper. Then trace the patterns on to some thin cardboard.

Cut the horse, saddle and platform shapes out of the cardboard. Cut along the red lines on the horse's feet. Paint the shapes and leave them to dry.

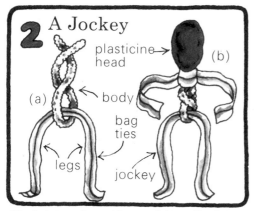

2 A Jockey

plasticine head

(b)

(a)

body

bag ties

legs

jockey

Twist two bag ties or bits of wire together for the legs and body (a). Twist another one round the body to make arms. Push a plasticine head on the body (b).

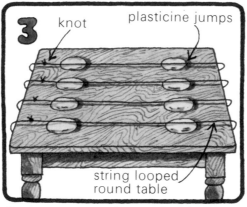

3

knot

plasticine jumps

string looped round table

Loop as many pieces of string as there are players round a table. Knot the ends. Press bits of plasticine down on the table under the strings, to make jumps.

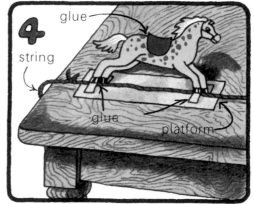

4

glue

string

glue

platform

Glue a saddle on to the back of each horse. Put a horse over each string. Pull the string up the slits on the horses' feet. Bend the slits, like this. Glue them to a platform.

How to Play

The game is to race your horse from one end of the table to the other without letting the jockey fall off. The horses must go over the jumps on the way. Anybody whose jockey falls off goes back to the beginning.

To start, put jockeys on the saddles. Line the horses at the start. Stand at that end of the table and pull the string under the table towards you. The first player to get his horse and jockey to the other end wins.

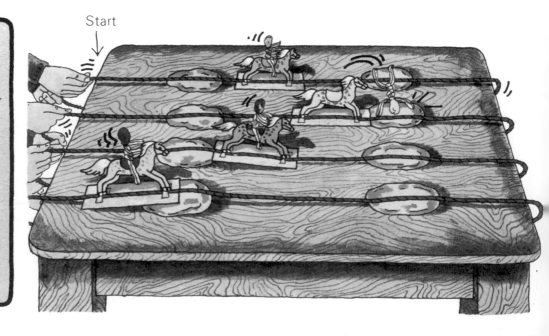

Start

Crossing the Line

(for 2 players)

Practise pushing the coin on to the board. Put it on the edge of the board and hit it with the palm of your hand so that it slides on to a coloured strip.

You will need
thick cardboard (about 30 cm wide and 32 cm long)
thin cardboard
a ruler and a pencil
cellophane and strong glue
paint and a paint brush
2 coins

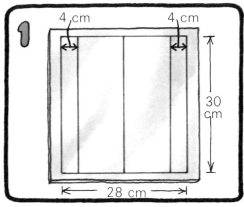

Draw a rectangle, 28 cm wide and 30 cm long, on a piece of thick cardboard. Rule lines down the middle of the rectangle and 4 cm from either side, like this.

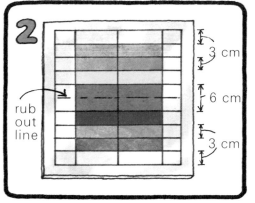

Rule nine lines, 3 cm apart, across the rectangle. Rub out the fifth line so that you have one 6 cm strip. Paint the seven middle strips different colours, like this.

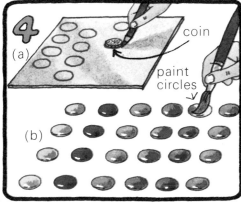

Draw two circles each side of the coloured strips, except the middle strip, using a small coin. Paint the circles the same colours as the strips. Cover with cellophane.

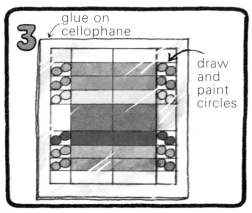

Using the same coin, draw 24 circles on thin cardboard (a). Cut them out. Paint four circles the same colour as each of the strips, except the middle strip (b).

How to Play

Put the board on the edge of a table which is not too high. Lie a heavy book behind the board, as shown in the picture above, to keep it steady while you play.

Both players have a coin of the same size and 12 cardboard circles (2 of each colour). One person plays on the left half of the board, the other player on the right half.

Start with the coins on the white strip closest to you. Take it in turn to push them on to the board. Each time the coin lands inside a coloured strip, cover one of the circles beside it with the same coloured cardboard circle. If it lands on a line, wait for your next turn. If the coin lands on the middle strip, miss your next turn. The first one to cover all 12 circles on his side wins.

2-In-1 Board

1. Matchmake

(for 2 or 3 players)

You will need

red, blue and green plasticine
used matches and drawing pins
a dice

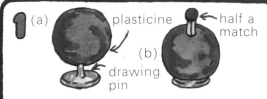

1 (a) plasticine (b) half a match, drawing pin

For the matchmen, push a small
ball of plasticine on to a drawing pin
(a). Push half a match into the
plasticine **(b)**. Make 14 red men, 14
blue men and 14 green men.

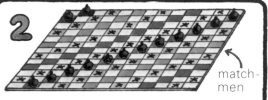

2 match-men

To set up the board, put the
blue men on the dark blue squares,
like this. Put the red men on the
dark red squares and the green men
on the dark green squares.

How to Play Matchmake

The game is to get your matchmen
from the dark squares to the lighter
squares of the same colour with
stars. Each player has 14 men of one
colour. Men can be moved in any
direction except diagonally. Throw
the dice to start. Then take turns.

Each turn move one man the number
on the dice. You can capture an enemy
man by landing on its square if it
is not on its own colour. Take any
captured men off the board and keep
them. You cannot jump over men.

The game ends when one player has
moved all his men still on the board
on to his star squares. To score, each
player counts his men on the star
squares, adds the number of men he
has captured and takes away his
men not on star squares. The player
with the highest score wins.

2. Hop Over (for 2 players)

You will need
12 green matchmen and 12 red matchmen (see Matchmake)
1 dice

How to Play Hop Over

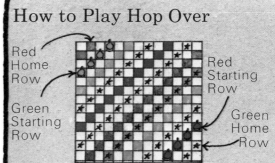

To start, put 4 green matchmen on the pink star squares in the corner of the board, like this. Put 4 red matchmen on the red squares in the opposite corner. One player moves the green men, the other the red men.

The game is to get your 12 matchmen from their Starting Row to their Home Row. Throw the dice in turn. Move one man each turn according to the number you throw. You must move a man if possible. Each time a man is moved out of a Starting Row square put on a new man. Take off any man who reaches its Home Row.

Men can move sideways along the row they are on but only in one direction each turn. If they cannot go the full distance, they cannot move. Men can jump over their own men. Up to 3 men can be on the same square.

A 6 on the dice can be used to move any one man forward to its next row, like this. This is a Hop Over.

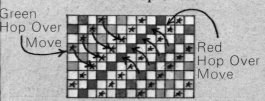

A 5 may be used for a Hop Over from a square with 2 or 3 men on it. A 4 may be used for a Hop Over from a square with 3 men on it.

A man can only Hop Over one enemy man if there are 2 or 3 men on the square it is hopping from. A man can Hop Over 2 enemy men if there are 3 men on the square it is hopping from. The first player to get all 12 of its matchmen Home wins. Or end the game when 6 men reach Home.

Push and Shove

(for 2 players or 2 teams)

For this board game, one player or team needs ten counters of one colour, the other needs ten of a different colour. The bigger you make the board, the more fun it is to play. Flick enemy counters off high scoring circles.

You will need

a big, square sheet of thick cardboard (about 64 cm long and 64 cm wide)

thin cardboard

a KnowHow circle maker (see page 3)

strong glue and scissors

paint and a paint brush

20 draught counters

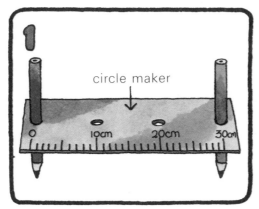

Make a KnowHow circle maker (see page 3). Punch a hole above the 0 cm mark, 10 cm mark, 20 cm mark and the 30 cm mark, like this.

Find the middle (see page 3) of the square sheet of cardboard. Draw three circles, like this, using the 10 cm, 20 cm and 30 cm holes of the circle maker.

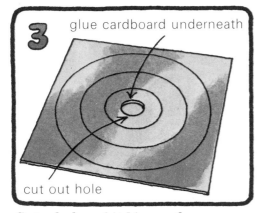

Cut a hole, a bit bigger than a draught counter, out of the centre of the board. Glue a square of card underneath the hole. Then paint the circles different colours.

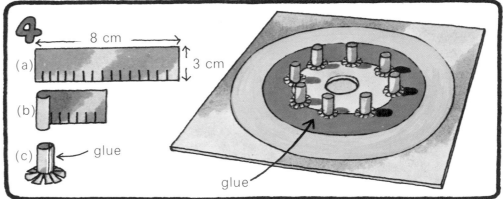

Cut out eight bits of cardboard, each about 8 cm × 3 cm. Make cuts along one edge of each bit (a). Roll them into posts (b). Glue the ends and bend out the cuts (c).

Glue the posts, at equal distances, round the edge of the inside circle, like this. The space between two posts should be big enough for a draught counter to go through.

How to Play

When two people play, each has 10 counters. If four play, in teams of two, each has 5. Partners use the same colour and sit opposite each other.

Take turns to flick the counters, one by one. Try to get them on to the high scoring circles. If a counter lands on a line, count the lower score. Try to flick them behind posts to stop being hit. The player or team with the highest score after all 20 counters have been flicked wins.

= 5 (outer circle)

= 10 (middle circle)

= 15 (inner circle)

= 25 (hole)

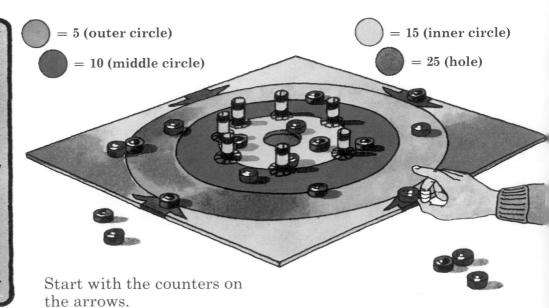

Start with the counters on the arrows.

Jumpers

(for 2 or more players)

This is a different sort of tiddly winks. Try using small, very flat buttons instead of tiddly wink counters

You will need

a cardboard box (about 28 cm long, 22 cm wide and 2 cm deep)
a KnowHow circle maker (see page 3)
a cardboard yoghurt pot
a ruler, a pencil and paint
strong glue and scissors
one big, flat button and 5 tiddly wink counters or small, flat buttons for each player

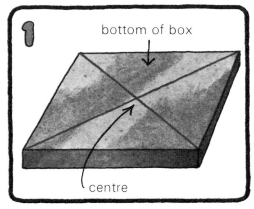

Find the centre of the box by ruling lines across it from the four corners, like this. The centre is where the lines cross.

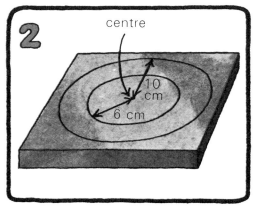

Draw a circle on the box, using the 10 cm hole of the circle maker. Draw a smaller circle, using a hole punched above the 6 cm mark on the circle maker, like this.

Cut the top off a yoghurt pot so it is as deep as the box (a). Put the bottom of the pot in the centre of the box. Draw round it. Cut out the circle. Glue pot inside the hole (b).

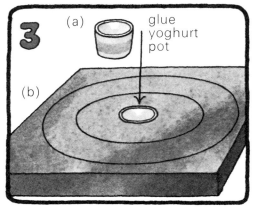

Draw ten lines across the outside and inside circles to make ten sections, like this. Paint the sections different colours.

How to Play

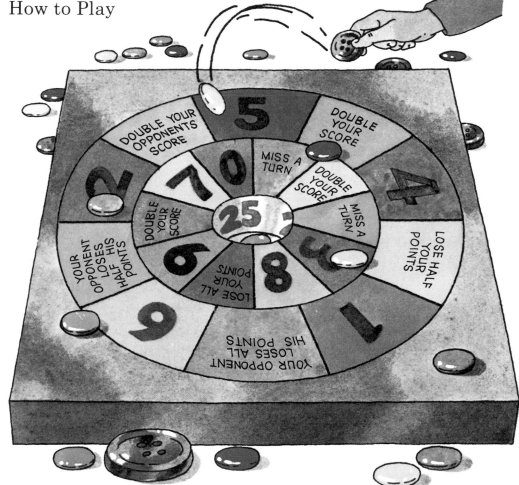

Draw the numbers and words inside the sections. Each player has a big, flat button and five small tiddly winks. Players sit opposite each other, about 1 metre from the board.

Taking it in turns, use the button to make the tiddly winks jump on to the board. The player with the highest score after all the tiddly winks have been jumped is the winner.

Cops and Robbers
(for 2 or 4 players)

This is a hunt through a maze. One player or team has six cops, the other has six robbers.

You will need
cardboard (about 45 cm long and 45 cm wide)
thin cardboard and tracing paper
plasticine
2 yoghurt pots
2 big buttons
thin elastic or thin rubber bands
white paper and strong glue
a pencil and a ruler
a red crayon and paint

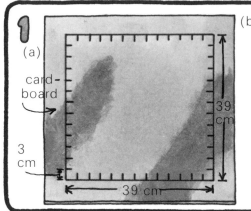

Draw a square, 39 cm long and 39 cm wide, on the thick cardboard. Draw marks every 3 cm along the four sides of the square, like this (a).

Rule lines from the top marks to the bottom marks and from side to side to make small squares. Draw in the red lines as shown (b).

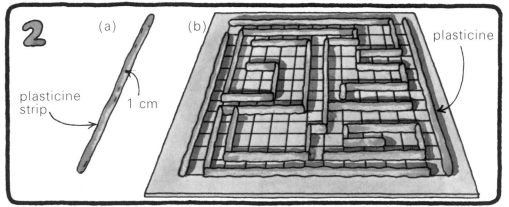

To make the hedges, roll bits of plasticine into long strips, each about 1 cm wide (a). Put the strips along the red lines drawn on the cardboard.

Push the plasticine strips down gently so that they stick to the cardboard. Then pinch the plasticine until the strips are about 2 cm high, like this (b).

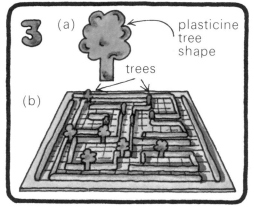

Make eleven plasticine tree shapes (a). Put them on top of the hedges, like this (b). Look at the big picture opposite to make sure you put the trees in the right places.

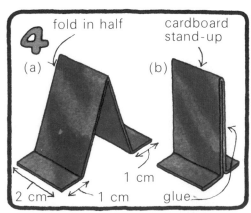

Cut out twelve strips of thin cardboard, each 2 cm wide and 7 cm long. Fold them in half and bend out the ends (a). Glue the two halves together, like this (b).

Draw the cop pattern and the robber pattern (a) on to some tracing paper. Trace the cop pattern on to one side of six of the cardboard stand-ups.

Trace the robber pattern on to one side of the other six cardboard stand-ups. Then paint all the cops and robbers (b).

Cop
Entrance

Robber
Entrance

Robber
Entrance

Cop
Entrance

How to Play

The idea is to shoot all the other player's men. One player moves the cops and has the cop gun. The other moves the robbers and has the robber gun. If you play in teams of two, each player then moves three men.

To start, put three cops at each of the cop entrances and three robbers at each of the robber entrances. Each player moves one man 5 squares in a turn. They can move in any direction, except diagonally. To shoot an enemy, a player's man must land on the square next to one occupied by an enemy. He then pulls the button on his gun and shouts, 'you are dead'. He takes the man off the board.

Men can only jump over a hedge where there is a tree. They cannot shoot through a hedge except where there is a tree. The first player or team to shoot all enemy men wins.

6

knot

button

1 cm

bottom of pot

hole

(a)

(b)

cop gun

robber gun

Make a hole, 1 cm from the base, on either side of the yoghurt pots. Thread thin elastic through the holes and thread a big button on to the elastic. Knot the ends (a).

Cover the yoghurt pots with white paper. Paint a picture of a cop on one of the pots and a picture of a robber on the other pot (b). These are the guns.

23

Floor War

(for 2 players or 2 teams)

You will need

an old sheet or cheap material
   (about 2 metres × 2 metres)
4 drawing pins
tracing paper and white paper
thin cardboard and thin twigs
4 cotton reels, 4 plastic cartons
   and 4 cardboard egg boxes
4 empty matchboxes, 4 short
   pencils and thick cardboard
strong rubber bands and lots of
   strips of paper
a ruler, a felt pen and a pencil
scissors and paint
(You can also mark out the
squares of the battlefield with
chalk on any hard floor.)

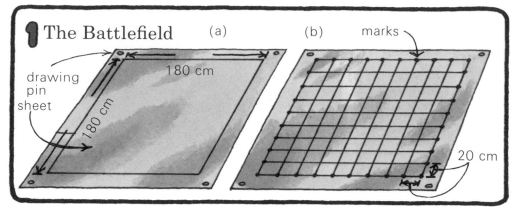

1 The Battlefield

Pin the sheet or material to the
floor or carpet with drawing pins,
like this. Draw a square, 180 cm
long and 180 cm wide, on the sheet
or material using a felt pen (a).

Draw marks every 20 cm along the
sides of the square. Rule lines
from the top marks to the bottom
marks and from side to side, like
this (b).

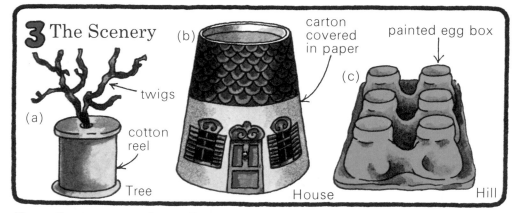

3 The Scenery

To make a tree, push small twigs
into the hole in a cotton reel (a).
Wrap and glue paper round a tall
carton and paint it, like this, to
make a house (b).

Cut an egg box in half. Paint the
half with egg holders, like this,
to make hills (c). Make four trees,
four houses and four sets of hills.

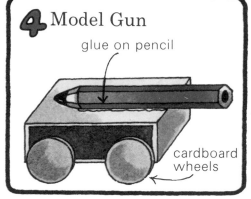

4 Model Gun

To make a model gun, glue a small
pencil or stick to the top of a
matchbox, like this. Glue two
small cardboard circles to each
side. Both teams need two guns.

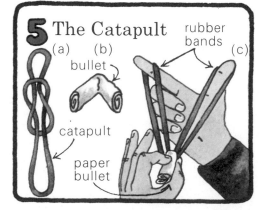

5 The Catapult

Link two rubber bands (a) to make
a catapult. Make paper bullets, as
shown (b). To fire, put a bullet
round the bands (c). Aim, pull
back the bullet and then let it go.

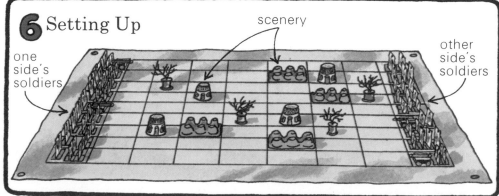

6 Setting Up

One side first lays out the scenery
in any way they like in the squares
on the battlefield. The other side
then chooses which edge they will
enter the field from.

The first side then enters from
the opposite edge. Each team sets
up its soldiers and guns in the
first row of squares at their edge
of the battlefield, like this.

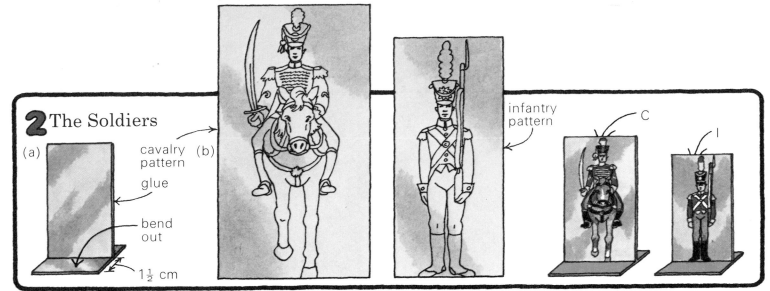

2 The Soldiers

(a) cavalry pattern

glue

bend out

$1\frac{1}{2}$ cm

(b)

infantry pattern

C

I

Cut out 20 strips of thin cardboard, each about 18 cm long and 4 cm wide. Then cut out 40 smaller strips, each about 16 cm long and 3 cm wide. Fold the strips in half.

Bend out the ends, like this. Glue the two halves together (a). Trace the cavalry pattern on the 20 big stand-ups and the infantry pattern on the 40 smaller ones (b).

Draw a C on the back of the cavalry stand-ups and an I on the back of the infantry ones. Each team has 10 cavalry and 20 infantry. Paint each team's soldiers a different colour (c).

PLAYERS MUST BE ON THE EDGE OF BATTLEFIELD WHEN FIRING

CATAPULT

EXTRA BULLETS

DEAD SOLDIERS

GUN HIDDEN BEHIND TREE

CAVALRY GUARDING GUN

PAPER BULLET

DEAD CAVALRY

SOLDIERS HIDING BEHIND HILL

DEAD TREE

SOLDIERS KILLING EACH OTHER

KILLING OFF GUN ESCORT TO PREVENT GUN FROM FIRING

How to Play

The game is to kill all enemy soldiers. Each side has a catapult. Toss a coin to see which side starts. Both sides may move all their soldiers in a turn. Infantry, cavalry and guns can move in any direction except diagonally. Cavalry can move up to 3 squares in a turn. Infantry and guns only 1. Cavalry and guns cannot go into squares with scenery.

You must have 4 infantry in the same square as a gun for it to be allowed to move or fire. A gun can either move or fire once in a turn. When a gun is within 6 squares of any enemy soldiers, use your catapult and paper bullets to knock them over. Fire from your side of the field over the model gun you are pretending to fire.

Take any soldiers knocked over by catapult fire off the field. As many soldiers as you like can occupy the same square, but the more there are the easier they will be to hit. Any soldiers put into the same square as enemy soldiers, kill the same number of enemy soldiers, but also are killed themselves. The first side to kill all the enemy soldiers wins.

Space Mission

(for 2 or 3 players)

Play the game on this space board. There are twelve Galaxies, each with five stars.

You will need
3 red, 3 blue, 3 green spaceships
  (made as shown below)
1 white, 1 blue, 1 red dice

How to Play

A player has three spaceships of one colour, each with a white, blue or red flag. He moves his ships from Start to Finish, going from 1 Galaxy to 12 Galaxy in order. Each turn a player throws the three dice. He moves his ship with the white flag the number on the white dice, the blue one for the blue dice and the red one for the red dice. Ships go in any direction along the lines, moving one red dot or star for each point on a dice. A player must have one ship on a Galaxy star before his other two can move to the next Galaxy. If a player throws the same number on all three dice, he has another turn. No ship can land twice on a dot or star in a turn. No ship can land on the same dot as another ship, or jump over a ship.

How to Score

Mark down your score after each turn. When a player's ship lands on a Galaxy star, it scores 1 point. If his second ship lands on a star while the first ship is on the same Galaxy, it scores 3 points. If his third ship lands on the same Galaxy, it scores 5 points.
The game ends when one player gets his three ships to Finish. Each ship scores 3 points when it reaches Finish. The player with the most points at the end of the game wins.

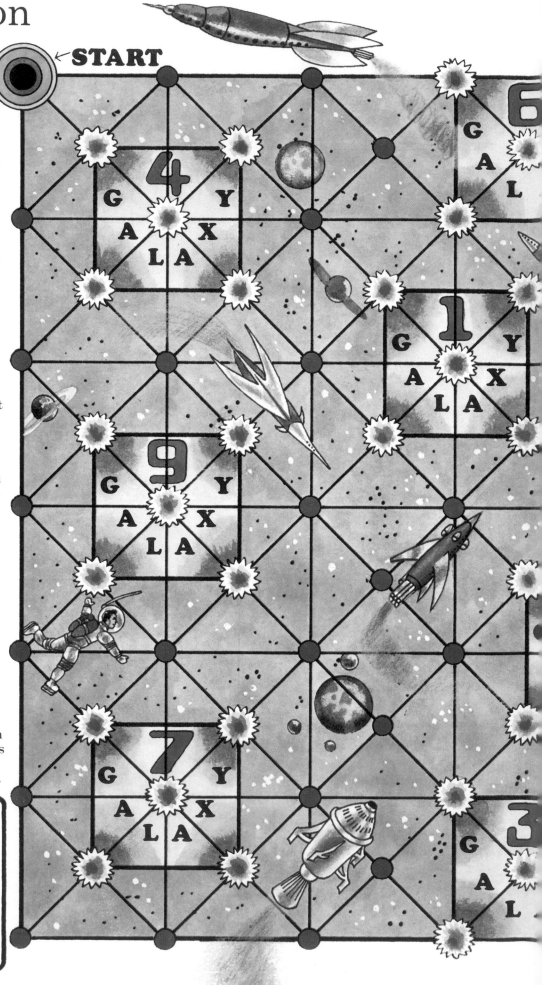

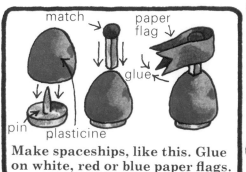

Make spaceships, like this. Glue on white, red or blue paper flags.

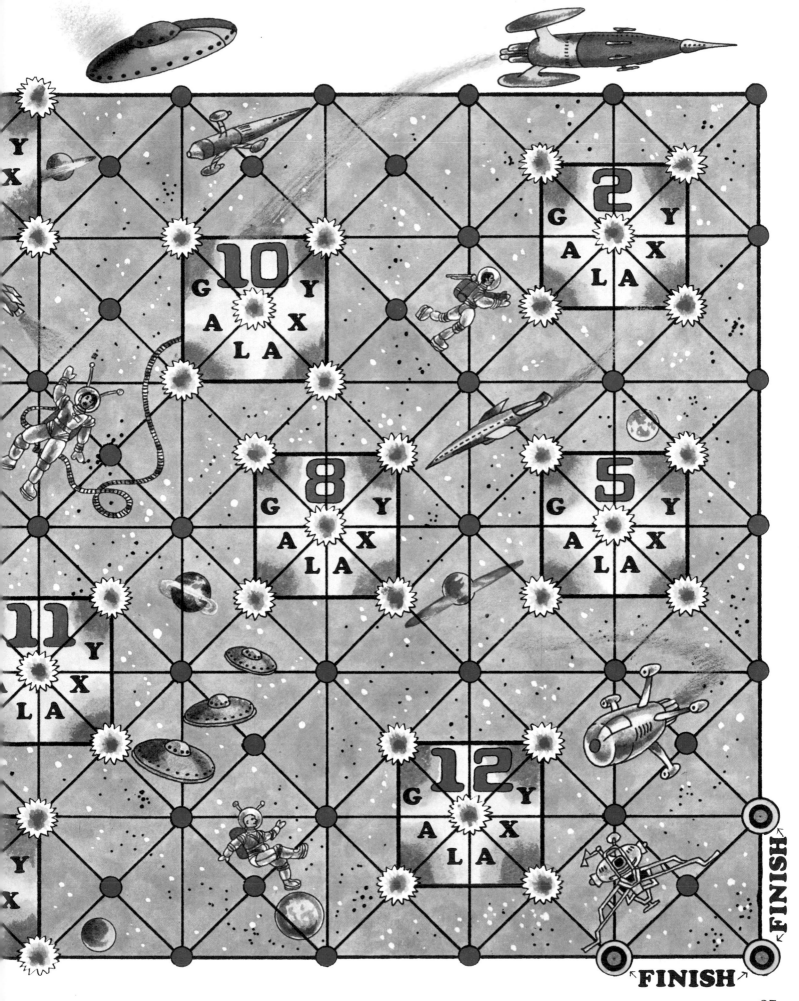

FINISH

FINISH

Party Games

(for lots of players)

Cotton Balls

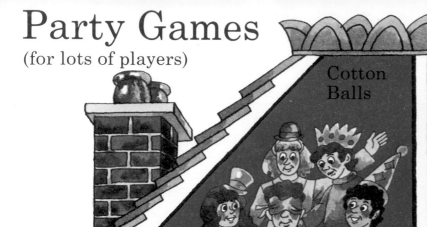

Put two bowls beside each other on the floor. Fill one with cotton wool balls. Each player is blindfolded in turn and given a big spoon.

The idea is to scoop up the balls with the spoon and drop them into the empty bowl. Each player has three tries and scores 2 points for each ball he gets into the second bowl. The player with the most points at the end wins.

Murder in the Dark

Cut out as many slips of paper as there are players. Mark an X on one and a D on another. Leave the rest blank. Fold them in half and give one to each player. The player with the slip marked X is the murderer. He keeps it secret. D is the detective. He tells everyone.

The lights are put out and everybody hides except the detective. The murderer creeps up on a hidden player, whispers 'you are dead' and runs off. The victim screams, the lights go on and everyone gathers round him. The detective asks questions to find out who the murderer is. Only the murderer can lie. The detective has 3 guesses to find the murderer.

Parcel Dressing Up

Wrap a bar of chocolate in layers of paper tied in string. Players sit in a circle with a hat, a scarf, gloves, glasses, a knife and a fork in the middle. They take turns to throw a dice. When someone throws a 6, he takes the clothes from the middle, puts them on and tries to open the parcel with the knife and fork.

The others go on throwing the dice. When one throws a 6, he pulls the clothes off the first person, puts them on and opens the parcel with the knife and fork. This goes on until the parcel has been opened and all the chocolate squares have been eaten.

The Posting Game

Hide ten tins, each with the name of a city written on it, round the house. Each player gets a box with ten slips of folded paper in it. On each slip is written the name of one of the cities. All the boxes are put in one room.

Each player takes one slip at a time, writes his name on the back and rushes round the house to find the tin with the same name as his slip. When he finds it, he posts the slip in the tin and goes back for his next slip. The first player to post all ten slips in the right tins is the winner.

Whisper Story

Everyone sits in a line. The player at one end makes up a long story and whispers it to the person beside him. The second player then whispers the story to the next person. This goes on down the line until the last person has heard the story. He tells it out loud. Then the first person tells the real story.

Sardines

One player hides somewhere in the house. He must hide in a place big enough to hold more people. The other players count to 50 and then go off to look for him. Anyone who finds him quietly joins him in the hiding place. The last person to find him has to pay a forfeit.

Eaties

Everybody is blindfolded. A plate with ten different bits of food on it is put in front of each player. They taste the food. The plates are taken away and the blindfolds taken off. The players write down what they think they have eaten. Put things like cold peas and cold porridge on each plate.

Stop Game

Play this game while everyone is eating. First choose a 'stop' caller. Everybody starts eating. Suddenly the caller shouts 'stop' and everyone has to freeze. No one can eat or move, except the 'stop' caller until he calls 'move on'. Everyone has a go at being the 'stop' caller.

Spin the Bottle

Put a bottle on a table and all sit round the table. One player spins the bottle. Whoever it points to when it stops spinning has to pay a forfeit. Think up lots of forfeits before you begin, such as eating an apple without bending your elbows or chewing half a lemon.

Treasure Hunts

(for lots of players)

Arrange the treasure hunts before the party begins. Try not to hide any clues in dangerous places and make sure that even the smallest player can reach them. Tell everyone which rooms are not being used in the hunt.

Players can either hunt by themselves, in pairs or teams.

In a clue-by-clue hunt, try not to let anyone else know that you have found a clue. When you have read it make sure you put it back where you found it.

Camouflage Hunts

Hide 20 small, coloured things, like a red pencil, a yellow button or a green toothbrush, round the house. Hide each thing in or on something of the same colour, perhaps the yellow button on a yellow book or the green toothbrush on a green plate.

Each player gets a list of the hidden things and a pencil and starts looking. When he finds one he writes down its hiding place. The first player to write down the hiding places of all 20 things wins.

Clue-by-Clue Hunts

Write the clues on bits of paper. Hide them round the house, say in a shoe or tap. Each clue tells the players where to find the next clue until they reach the treasure.

Read out the first clue to all the players. In this hunt, the first clue is: 'You'll find clue no. 2 if you put your foot in me'. Now follow the clues to find the treasure.

Hidden Letters

Hide the treasure, say in the bathroom. Write the letters that spell 'bathroom' on different bits of paper. Hide them. Tell everyone how many letters are hidden.

As they find one, the players write down each letter. When a player thinks he knows which room the letters spell, he runs to that room to find the treasure.

Hidden Pictures

Cut some magazine pictures or old Christmas cards in half. Give one half of each picture to a player and hide the other halves round the house.

The first player to find the hidden half of his picture gets a prize. You can make it more difficult by cutting the pictures into quarters and hiding three pieces.

Scavenger Hunts

Each player gets a list of the same ten things to find, perhaps a shoe, a nail, a potato or a hairpin. All the things are somewhere in the house. A player has to collect one of each thing on his list in a certain time, perhaps 15 minutes.

The player who has collected the most things on his list at the end of the time limit is the winner.

Left Standing

Players are shown a small object. They go out of the room. The object is hidden so only a bit of it shows. Everyone comes back into the room and starts looking for it.

When a player sees it he sits down. He does not tell anyone he has seen it or where it is. The last person to see it is left wandering round the room on his own.

Party Races

(for lots of players)

Stepping Stone Tins

Each player has two tins. They race each other from one end of the room to the other using their tins as stepping stones.

To start, stand on one foot on one tin. Then bend down and, without touching the floor, put the second tin in front of the first. Step on it with your other foot. Then bend down and put the first tin in front. Do this again and again until you get to the other end of the room

Flower Pot Stilts

To make a flower pot stilt, make a hole on each side of a plastic flower pot, near the base. Pull string through the holes and knot the ends.

Players split into two teams. Each team has two stilts. They stand at one end of the room with two chairs at the other. The first player in each team stands on the stilts, holds the string, walks round the chair and back and gives the stilts to the next player. The first team to get round the chair and back wins.

Orange Under the Chin

Two teams stand in two lines. The first player in each team puts an orange under his chin.

The game is to pass the orange from chin to chin down your line without touching it with your hands. If a player drops or touches it, the orange must go back to the beginning of his line. The first team to get its orange to the end of the line wins.

Peas and Straws

Each player has a straw, 30 dried peas in a cup and an empty cup. He puts the cups next to each other on the floor. He has to suck the peas on to the end of his straw and drop them into the empty cup. The first player to get all his peas into the second cup is the winner.

Peas and Pull-Boxes

To make a pull-box, make two holes, about 15 cm apart, in one end of a box. Pull string through the holes and knot the ends.

Players split into two teams and stand at one end of the room with a line of string at the other. Each team has a pull-box with 40 dried peas lined up in front of it. Each member of the team has to pull the box, without losing the peas, to the line and back. The team with the most peas left in front of its box after all the players have pulled it wins.